Notre Dame Review

NOTRE DAME REVIEW

NUMBER 28

The *Notre Dame Review* is published semi-annually. Subscriptions: $15 (individuals) or $20 (institutions) per year or $250 (sustainers). Single Copy price: $8. Distributed by Ubiquity Distributors, Brooklyn, NY, and Media Solutions, Huntsville, Alabama. We welcome manuscripts, which are accepted from September through March. Please include a SASE for reply. Please send all subscription and editorial correspondence to: *Notre Dame Review*, 840 Flanner Hall, University of Notre Dame, Notre Dame, IN 46556. *The Notre Dame Review* is indexed in *Humanities International Complete*.

ISSN: 1082-1864
Ascensions and Recessions ISBN 978-1-892492-27-2
Cover art: (Front cover) *Wake*, 60" x 60", Oil on Panel, 2008. (Back cover) *Shattered*, (Triptych, 1 of 3 panels), 60" x 60", Oil on Panel, 2008 by Adam Fung.

CONTENTS

FROM SONETTI DI NEW YORK

John Peck

Anfiteatro Flaviano

Riots in Latvia, Lithuania,
Greece, Bulgaria, Hungary, Iceland awash,
from Lehman Brothers, the two-handed headless engine
by the doors, windows, cracks in the walls, false paper.
A swipe of my finger along the pink granite
of this bank yields the same grime that settled
on the gilded giallo antico parapet
back of the cheap seats in Rome, where roars entered space.
Decibel dream, stone gleam, the dream dreamed by many.
Four stories down in the Colosseum one gallery
parks a horse-drawn fire rig with rawhide buckets.
A photo from 1900 shows a boy
hunkered over his spinning top at arena
zero, above him the ranks of void arches.

The Web in Central Park

Sangay Choden, twenty-some, sits in harness
to a frame loom from Bhutan in the entry passage
of the Rubin Museum, her hips the yoke for that silk.
At breaks she anchors it like a horse to its post.
The monstrous gods here are meant to scare you quick-time
into reality. Thus, six, astray in the Park,
I faced three toughs converging down a rise
carved by Olmsted from his love for England. And Dickens
was their weaver: mute cut-outs against the light,
they would have done for me in that first chapter.
But I reached the street—an untested C.O., let off
by the motorcyclist who chased me down a Rome alley,
and clear of the clubs at the napalm shipping point:
to tense the weave while walking away, that too is a calling.

Philosophia, East 65th Street

Heidegger's Greeks over against Cassirer
and Jung's memoir, Jaspers, Arendt, and Weil—
a teenager breaking into the seas of
philosophy, or the gleam of philosophy,
I was my village: twenty-five hundred with Poles
and Polish exiles, Hungarians from the failed rising
sponsored in three homes, and the hemlock forest
behind the immigrant college infusing all this
with speckled shade and plausibility,
like the pines in the country fair hung here in varnish
among spurred panoramas—an engineer
stiffing the Russias, ribbons through the mazurkas
advancing in ranks through gloom past a winding stair.
Kosciuszko! metaphysics, the defeat tradition.

The Project

Manhattan Project: Dad smelted sheaths for the thing.
His part in all that has not yet settled in me—
straightforward in the living of professional
momentum and its unknowns, over against
the fact and fate of first use. His gift to me,
however, from near the piers one June night
at a cut-out along the West Side after the war,
met simplest need with his mute fellowship—
going down from the car to the mile-wide river, unzipping,
and letting fly together, grinning at vastness,
we framed a simple stand-off, shielded by
the eternal barrier, toward his open hearths:
alchemical pre-gold streaming from us into
wave-chop set alight by Jersey burning.

The Chrysler Building, Met Life, the Trump Tower

This skyline staggers the gapped teeth of Saturn
chawing his own children: we put him there
and them here, vapor and blood streaming through
his cranium at sunset, the same fading dream
perpetually reenacted. Sunrise, though, that
rude bud of flux unsoldering itself
from the cold rim, bulging through lower heaven
unfiltered—for mere mesh it atomizes—
raw—for no oven cooks primordial fire—
and crashing the levees of social bond and story
terribilis et fascinans it insists,
as illness the herald leaving a man kicked open
to illumination shatters the wall of one being:
acetylene, access, ardor. Killing, and kind.

Still Hanging on Clinton's Second Visit

Andrea Brady

Hope for running out on the flats, under
the overpass that chutes this abstract
into bread home delivery, buckled up
from your front porch to my front seat.

The hyphenated bridge lane where motor
boards a dream of expansive happiness,
dinosaurs trapped in oil pits, a future
to run into red and green eyes

and out till no man's land. Past the refinery
into outlaw verde, unowned hydrotropic
life unclinched by regularity, ownership,
by a loss that has never happened: one of the

kinds of possible losses. You sang this
national anthem, your life parenthesized
by flight into cinema and depiction:
the sun sets orangely, tempers cool

the boss goes nowhere and the land,
lived from, bossily patriotic. Your name
retrieved from the web, the collocation
with the smash given to know

the unknown, blood furls gradually
from the heads and is never less
parenthetical. Texts still bundled
in your pocket switch to discreet mode, rings

engage the natural world in decoration.
Above the concrete marshes, the stars
can't make their empty lines believable.
Stars to shadow by, chase out of manhattan

where that marsh is brown and the old worlds
creep around on stilts with eeling baskets.
Banality will never be obsolete, like the internal
combustion engine: even the tracks

of unbroken yellow too fleet for
the escape artist, a mimic pile-up loops
in place of persons, in a question of sovereignty.
No place unmandated, no stretch without

the service stations marked in bold on the route planner.
These four lanes a horn of plenty blow out at night
the endless hunting lament, a fictional
surplus for continents learning to recognise their bounds.

In the outlaw west the wedding party tips
their guns into starlight glasses, fill space
with pellets to celebrate the belly's axle; fire
falling down burns a noose free, ash and sand

to put fires out and secure a slipless exit. Was this
really what you wanted, to splurge on a rider
the whole real an advert break? Do go on so,
then breath undeterred in the breakbeat meter,

singing for freedom to misuse national space:
the free ride which is no freedom
when at the edge of disaster
you find yourself in the back seat of the patrol car,

the reel catapults into pitch black, and over all of us
who still live the stars
crash down from their heroic outlines
into vacancy

End of Days

Andrea Brady

All radical signs by which on   These radical brackets all around
the component times, by which   We select   Good luck
beauty hard and shining like   Pearls, and   Lozenges
phrasing all these renegade times into the divine message. Choose
Choose to bless. Choose to bless the day falling
into brass jack pot. *I remember all*
the days, they play before my eyes sometimes
I go to watch the ovens rich in natural vitamins
feeding off myself, my dreamed-for.

For too long, sorting tickets in the shade of the thorn
that penny drops affixed to   Find
the opening palm these aces allude
to this life, the desired, and even when dark
fills its haunches with ice and fire I have been on it,
on full voice coarse or passionated, a bundle of nerves
And each with their own head. As I go on I go
west idiotic, free to shout like nothing saffron.
I'll go to that country, the beautiful one

in the cockpit if I learn my trig. The sign says   No
equivalence between those who take pride in dying
and those who vow   When speech is the real action
The sign is an impress blowing down and east out,
treadmills backwards to an origin where that time
split into component sprockets   Two incisors
splitting each other by their petty alignment. *If it's like this*
at the beginning what will it be like in the end   The infant learns
to recognise his box by infinite difference   How
he discovers his father in the line up a testament
to his faith that he is made
for recurring   These times are familiar we
pluck our joys choosily from the sky before it
burns out the last branches.

—in honour of Mohammed Haithem and Suleiman Mahmoud

This Cup

—for Charles Newman

Michael Anania

I placed a coffee cup
on Jhumpa Lahiri's
sweater set (NY Times
Book Review, 4/6/08)
and round it was, the stain

of it, that is, and dark,
and despite her bright eyes,
her modest, round earring
and stern but endearing
refusal to smile, thought

of William Gass' *Willie
Masters' Lonesome Wife*,
the first edition where
coffee cup rings mark
the text and margins

(*Tri-Quarterly*, 1968),
at random, as though some
careless reader had put
his cup down here or there
willy-nilly, though the text

begins to gather itself into
the rings and eventually
comments on them, so it's
the writer not the reader
or the writer as reader

who was careless or perhaps
deliberate and careless
or deliberately careless
with his cup; "this is
the moon of daylight"

one says; another speaks
in fragments of coffee,
in fact—"in early morning coffee
down the little sterling ide of"—
as calculated as such things

inevitably are in fiction,
even, or especially, when
their beginnings seem simple
and more or less accidental—
"the muddy ring you see

just before you and below
you represents the ring
left on a leaf of the manuscript
by my coffee cup," a reminder
(sometimes we need one) that there

was a time of composition
that preceded the book,
its duration different
in so many ways from the duration
of reading, though each, reading

and writing, can be put aside,
each ringed by its own
neglected cup, the circles
left there imposing an order
of their own, ungrammatical

and asyntactic, something
the text seems to rise up toward,
the urgent way that messages
rise through the inky black of
an eight ball to tell us the future,

advise the love-sick, heart-
weary and lonely, letters, words
pressed against the ball's small,
dark window so briefly
it is often hard to be sure

what you read there—"Outlook
good," "Signs point to yes,"
"Most Likely," "As I see it,
yes," "It is decidedly so,"
"Reply hazy, try again."

The book's last coffee stain
encircles the navel of the nude
who has been posing (hard
to imagine these days) or as
the author might say, representing,

page after page, the title's,
if not his own, lonesome wife.
And the stained sweater set,
not the sweater set itself
or Jhumpa Lahiri, the alluring

author with the sideways glance,
but the artifact in black and white
on newsprint wicking coffee
along its random strands of fiber,
occurs as fiction might occur

amid a tangle of causes at once
intended and accidental.
The coffee's damp expands
its ring of paper, which in turn
rises like a blister of cashmere

at once fictive and tangible,
two mother of pearl or plastic
replica mother of pearl buttons
catch the ambient light, twin
crescent moons in their own daylight.

THE HOUSE I LIVE IN; OR THE HUMAN BODY

Jill McDonough

For you formed my inward parts; you knitted me together in my mother's womb. I praise you, for I am fearfully and wonderfully made.
—Psalm 139:13-14

"I am fearfully and wonderfully made" says
the skeleton, exclaims
the skeleton in ink, line
drawing, engraving of his
smooth shaded skull, awkward
pelvic arch, turned toward the arched
door. The *Ossa Innominata* of the pelvis is
unnamable, unlike
any other object
in the world. Our skeleton's arm
is raised, he's ready to knock. Hello! Who should fear
me? I am fearful, and wonderfully made. Forgotten
in the basement, in the shelves that slide
to press against each other. Health and Sciences,
from 1836: foxed
Health. Obsolete Science. Illustrated
with engravings of the body, all
its parts*: The Skull, Cupola
of the House. One
of the Vertebrae. The Kneeling
Skeleton. Hand and the Foot; showing
the beautiful mechanism of both.*

The American Museum of Natural History's Charles Darwin Exhibit

—For Jake, Thea, and Joey

Jill McDonough

We walk in to bones: perfect,
delicate ribs of slow
loris, spiral of Gaboon viper. Some bulldog's cruel
fanged underbite. Darwin
hated Latin, school; he collected eggs and shells;

he spent hours watching birds and lying under the dining-room table.

Now he's carved in marble, bearded
as Santa Claus. Thick eyebrows raised and kind before
his specimens, their jars of yellowed liquid, red
leather notebooks, pill boxes of crystals and bones. Jake,
the eight year old beside me, covets
this, wants it all. In the film, crimson crabs sidle up
to maroon ones, and komodo dragons embrace
one another in a komodo dragon pile.

When Darwin saw Angraecum Sesquipedale's
foot-long nectary—graceful, attenuated beyond
belief, he wrote, *Astounding. What insect
could suck it?* He predicted we'd find a moth
that could. The museum lays out the long
snout of Xanthopan Morganii Praedicta—
whip-like—next to the orchid's whip-like spur:

endless forms most beautiful and wonderful have been, and are being, evolved.

Touch the megatherium skull. See
the heavy-lidded green
iguana struggle up his borrowed boughs, his snakeskin-skin
sloughing from his forelegs. His masseteric
scales as big as quarters. Feel the glyptodont's armored shell.

The reticulated python spine curves to and fro
like a river; toward the east, *tiny hind legs*
sprout, useless. To the python.

Poem About the Body

Jill McDonough

After the winter indoors watching the same
planes, same buildings, repetitive puffs
of smoke, I was afraid to fly without her, afraid to fly,
trying to decide if I'd rather die or live with her dead.
We are young enough to joke about this, old enough
to have our own doctors, who tell us after 9/11,
they should just pass Xanax out
like candy, bowls in the waiting room.

The poem about the body
is a love poem, poem about wonders, misery,
being relieved you found someone to grow old with,
being terrified that she will die. Both, relief
and terror, symptoms of love. Her body:
stretch marks shiny as scars, indefinite spots
on the backs of her hands. Broken blood vessels branch
like fractal coral on her cheekbones. On her right thigh, a scar
shaped like the end of a handlebar, shiny
as a stretch mark.

The poem about the body, the beloved, is David Ferry's
from the Bannatyne manuscript, the one
I copied out by hand for Josey that first year, the one that goes
Of love and truth with long continuance and ends *God grant*
I go to the grave before she goes. Comforting
someone thought those things a thousand years ago,
and wrote them down.

You are fearfully and wonderfully made. All of us—you,
me, her, David Ferry, the doctors, the anonymous poet
a thousand years dead—wonderful, capable
of wonders, of wonderful fear.

CLASSMATES

Mark Brazaitis

You suspect the lawn hasn't been mowed since sometime in the summer; it is full of weeds and intrudes onto the concrete walkway from both sides. The house is in a similar state. Its gray vinyl siding was doubtless once white, and a section of gutter dangles from the roof like an arm over the side of a bed. You drop the knocker, shaped like a dragon or snarling dog, on the wooden door. A moment later, you knock again, three quick strikes. In your free hand, you hold six yellow roses.

Presently you hear a whine, the door's complaint as it swings inward. Standing in front of you is a woman with shoulder-length hair, its black conceding to gray. Her eyebrows, entirely black, are so thin they seem inked on. She is shorter than you imagined, the top of her head no higher than your shoulders.

After you introduce yourself, there is a silence, so you remind her of your phone call. She stands fixed in place, staring at you with neither irritation nor curiosity. Time passes, and you feel, as you sometimes have in the last year, like a phantom or dream figure, a shade shy of invisible. You are about to speak again when she says, "Come in."

She accepts your roses without comment and leads you into the living room, painted baby blue. Against the near wall is a white couch, like a cloud, with matching armchairs on either side. Against the far wall is a stand-up piano, the dust on its keys exposed in the yellow-gray afternoon light.

You expect to see pictures on the wall or on the mantel above the fireplace or on top of the piano. In their absence, you recall the only picture of your classmate you have ever seen—the photo at the back of his lone book, in which he appears to have gained thirty pounds since your graduation. But you didn't know him in college; he might have been overweight all of his life. In the same fifteen years, you have gained twenty-two pounds. The weight hasn't altered your face, which preserves its hard angles; instead, it has settled around your belly, a beer gut on someone who drinks wine.

Your classmate's wife has yet to invite you to sit down. You wonder if she is hoping you will leave. But you've driven five hundred miles to be here.

At last: "Sit down." In a softer voice: "Please."

You sit in one of the armchairs. After placing the roses on the coffee table in front of the couch, she sits in the other. "I'm sorry," she says, "I didn't ask if you wanted anything to drink."

"I'm fine," you say. "Thank you."

"Oh," she says. She has pulled herself to the front of her armchair. "Are you sure? All right." She slides back.

You wonder if she has friends or family to help her. She must. But it has been two months since her husband's death, and they probably have stopped calling and visiting as frequently. She is moving in a couple of weeks—she told you this on the phone—and doubtless she will feel better when she does.

"I've come because…" What you said to her during your brief phone conversation and repeated at her front door was: *I'd like to write a story about your husband for the alumni magazine.*

"You told me why you're here," she says. She adds, "Does anyone ever read the alumni magazine? Don and I used to stack them in a closet, saying we'd get to them when Hell sold ice cream."

You smile at her joke; she doesn't. "I'm sorry never to have known either of you when we were in college," you say.

"Big school," she says.

"Did you meet in a class?"

"We met in a bathroom. In his sophomore year, he had a job cleaning dorm rooms. He was cleaning the bathroom in mine when I walked in." Her smile, though slight, is genuine. "I don't think he cleaned another bathroom in his life."

"It was love at first sight," you say, although you are thinking of the first time you saw your wife.

"I don't know," she says. "I can talk to anyone for hours." She looks at you. "It's probably hard for you to imagine, me being talkative. But it's true, I am." Her smile softens her. "Or was."

You offer her a smile as her smile fades. You wonder if she would have found you attractive in college. Your wife, during the early, easier days of your relationship, told you you looked like a movie star "in the age before the leading men grew goatees, before their skin glowed like tropical sunsets, before they depleted their mystique by thinking they could sing or save the world."

In the lingering silence, you imagine you are here to play the part of your classmate resurrected, to seduce his wife from her sadness. Yet all you see when you conjure her bed is a pair of pillows lined against the headboard like tombstones.

"Maybe it was love at first sight," she amends. "I've deleted the emotion from my memories of him. It's like watching someone else's home movies."

You wonder if your wife would have done the same. Or would she have grieved briefly, intensely, purging you in order to free herself to feel again? *Is this why I've come here? To spy on the world I would have left behind?*

"He was a piano player," you say.

"We both played. But six months ago, he stopped playing. I should have distrusted the silence."

You remember your own estrangement from what you loved, how everything you enjoyed became torture, and how the gulf between the pleasure you once felt in such activities and the burden they became made your pain all the more acute. "I imagine this wasn't all he stopped doing," you say.

She frowns. "To go from being someone who lifts weights four days a week, who writes five hours a day—most of the time with the computer keys clicking ecstatically—who fucks like a freshman on spring break—to go from being this joyful person to being someone who has to be prodded into shaving and brushing his teeth..." She sighs or huffs, a sound of exasperation and something darker.

"This summer he was supposed to be working on his novel," she says. "I was teaching a couple of classes at State, which is an hour-and-fifteen-minute drive from here, so I couldn't keep a constant vigil over him. But he didn't look sick. It was like he was only under a spell and if I snapped my fingers, I could break it."

"How long had he been depressed?"

"It's hard to know. Maybe two-and-a-half, three months."

"The same," you say.

Confusion crosses her face. "The same what?"

You hesitate. "The same with me."

"Oh," she says. "So you…"

You suppose you had always meant to tell her: "After three months with severe depression, I tried to kill myself. This was last year, ten months or so before your husband…before he…"

"Succeeded?"

"Succeeded." The word rings oddly triumphant in the small living room.

She sits up in her chair. "Why didn't you succeed?" Her tone is skeptical.

You tell her the story: At one-thirty on a warm September night, you left the living-room couch, where you would often retreat when your restlessness threatened to disturb your wife's sleep, and stepped into your garage. After getting into your Mercury, you turned on the engine, rolled down the windows, and waited to die. You were unconscious when a neighbor, a bartender returning from work, pulled you free of the fumes. *Five more minutes and you would have been dead*, the emergency room doctor said. *Five minutes, no more.*

"You left yourself a chance to be saved," she says, her voice cool, almost accusatory.

"That wasn't my plan."

"But some part of you wanted to live. Otherwise you would have jumped off a bridge or blown your brains out."

You don't think this is true, but you don't want to argue with her.

She sighs, and her expression softens. "Don's psychiatrist was asking him to consider shock therapy. He shouldn't have been able to buy laundry detergent or Drano, much less a gun. But he drove half a mile down the road to a pawnshop and, a minute later, held his passport to eternity. Great fucking country. I'm glad the right to kill yourself with a semiautomatic pistol when you're so depressed you can't fix yourself a sandwich or read the sports page is constitutionally guaranteed." Her eyes meet yours. "He shot himself in the mouth, in the shed under the crabapple tree in our backyard." She pauses. "I found him, of course."

She looks at the piano again, as if expecting to see her husband seated on the bench. Your classmate had a widow's peak and an aquiline nose—like you do. You don't know why you are seeking these similarities. You look at the flowers in front of you, laid as if on a grave. *Only one of us is alive.* The thought feels selfish and boastful, but it lingers.

"If I had been well enough to buy a gun, I would have," you tell her. "It was all I could do to leave the couch and stumble into the garage. If I had let another day pass, I was sure I wouldn't have been able to move. I was sure I would have been an invalid—paralyzed—with everyone thinking I was weak or lazy." You feel again what you felt the moment before you raced to your garage: dueling currents, hot and cold—extremes of discomfort—swirling inside you. The feeling passes, and you lean back in the armchair. "I was convinced my wife was going to leave me."

Her eyes catch yours. "Was she?"

You shake your head. "But frustration was an understandable part of her response," you say.

"I'm sure she didn't think you would try to kill yourself."

"Even *I* didn't think I would try to kill myself—most of the time, anyway. And even in the worst of my depression, I had moments when I understood exactly what was happening to me, when I knew my suicide lust was death's seduction and not the right prescription to end my pain. But before long, I would return to thinking—to *knowing*—that suicide was the only way to stop my pain and end the humiliation I was causing myself and my wife and everyone who knew us."

You want to say more; there is so much more to tell. But you aren't here to unburden yourself of your story, although at the moment you can't remember why you've come.

"When you were depressed, did your wife have help—people to look in on you or take up the work around the house?" she asks.

Your memory of this period is imprecise; sometimes the months seem like a single, agonizing day. "Her sister lived in the area. She was around." You lean forward. "And you?"

"Don's mother came once, for a week. She fixed him chicken soup and told him if he'd only bother to bathe every so often, he'd feel better. After going home, she'd call him, and he'd tell her he was doing all right. It wasn't close to the truth."

"We lied to protect our egos," you say, "to spare ourselves from having people think we were weak and helpless and unmanly. We spared ourselves from having them think we couldn't overcome our sadness or the blues or whatever mild affliction they thought was troubling us. In the meantime, knives were being driven into our foreheads. Fires were raging in our brains."

She holds her gaze on you before putting her palms over her eyes. Time passes. You hear sounds outside: a dog bark, a siren. The house itself is silent. "I saw the receipt," she says.

"The receipt?"

She removes her palms and looks at you. "For the gun."

"When?" You try to sound unimpressed.

Her voice has a hollow quality, as if she were speaking over the mouth of an empty bottle. "The day he bought it? The day after the day?" She draws in a shallow breath, releases it. "I could probably figure out exactly when, but I'm afraid it would only…" She closes her eyes, holds them closed a moment, opens them. "I'm afraid it would only incriminate me more. If I saw it four days before he killed himself instead of three, I would be all the more guilty of aiding and abetting his murder."

"You didn't aid and abet."

She shakes her head. "When I found the receipt—a cash receipt, with the name of the pawn shop—I asked Don what it was for. And there was a moment, maybe half a second, when his face filled with worry. It happened so fast I couldn't swear I'd seen anything suspicious. The next moment, he said, 'It's for a fishing rod.' And I said, 'A fishing rod? You don't fish.' 'I'm trying everything,' he said. 'Maybe I just need to sit in a boat and listen to the mosquitoes and wait for a miracle to pull on my line.'"

She closes her eyes again. A few seconds pass before she opens them. "An hour later, he showed me a fishing rod. It wasn't much more than a stick and a string. The people who rented the house before us probably left it in the shed or in the storage space in the attic."

"He deceived you, the way I would have," you say, "the way I deceived my wife." You tell her: When your wife wasn't home, you listened obsessively to requiems—Brahms', Dvorak's, Mozart's, music you hadn't played in years—but before your wife returned, you hid the CDs under the couch, as if they might announce your intention.

If to be depressed was to show weakness, to consider committing suicide was weakness itself, you thought. So as you became obsessed with oblivion, you held your obsession private, like a secret you'd promised to guard with your life.

"I knew where the pawnshop was," she says. "I could have driven over and asked if they'd sold my husband a gun."

"You didn't want to believe he was so ill."

"Maybe. Or maybe I was so tired and frustrated I didn't care to know for sure." She bites her bottom lip. "Three months. He was sick for only three months. But each day was like walking a mile in quicksand."

She begins to cry. "I knew what the neon sign in the pawn shop window said: 'We sell guns'! What more did I need—a telegram? A message written across the sky?"

You leave the armchair and move to the end of the couch closest to her. Her face is a patchwork of white, pink, and red, and you notice the imperfect growth of skin over the piercing on her left ear. You smell cigarettes and wonder if she has resumed an old habit. "You didn't want him to die," you say. "You only wanted the pain to be over—for everyone."

"Isn't it the same thing?" she asks.

"No—because you're still in pain. In worse pain."

Presently, her crying ceases, and she stares past you. "Right," she says softly. "And for the rest of my life—the downhill, wrinkled, wretched second half of my life—I get to live with memories no one will be here to validate. I get to suffer the consequences of decisions two of us made—like the decision not to have children so we could pursue our fucking artistic dreams. I might as well be a nun married to the Holy fucking Ghost."

When her crying resumes, you reach across the arm of the couch for her hands, which are ringless, dry, and warm. She looks at you, and you are surprised to find her eyes hard and suspicious. "You've come back from the dead to tell me something," she says. "Well, what is it?"

When you can't think of anything to say, she continues, "Or did you come here to survey what the aftermath of your suicide would have been like? Did you come here to interview your wife's grieving double?" Her voice rises: "Did you come here to gloat?"

You release her hands and, using the arm of the couch as support, stand. For a moment, you feel dizzy, and you think you might fall. Slowly, the world reorders itself, although your stomach remains unsettled. "If I've come here to gloat, or even if it seems I have, I'm sorry," you say, your voice uncertain, quivering. "And I am deeply sorry for your loss." This you say without equivocation. You turn toward the door.

"Wait," she says, standing. When you turn back to her, she steps into your arms. Her embrace surprises you with its fierceness. "I think you wanted to explain him so I would feel better," she says, her cheek against your thundering chest. "This is why you came—came without so much as a notebook and pen." She looks up at you. "Isn't it?"

Sobs threaten to rise from your throat. Meekly, you nod, although you aren't sure of anything.

She gives you a last hug and lets you go.

‡ ‡ ‡

You call your wife, but she isn't in. You leave a message saying you will be spending the night at a hotel and will be home sometime after noon the following day. Two hundred miles or so down the road, you pull into a Days Inn, where you rent a room. You eat dinner at a Cracker Barrel, thinking about your last exchange with your classmate's wife, as you stood outside her front door in the vanishing light. "I don't suppose you cured your depression by trying to kill yourself," she said from within her house.

You shook your head.

"What did make you better?" There was something hopeful in her voice, as if she might yet discover a remedy for her husband's pain.

You told her about your stay in a psychiatric hospital, the antidepressants you were prescribed, your twice-a-week talk therapy. "And time," you said, although she no longer seemed to be listening. "And luck."

You vow to call your classmate's wife, Jennifer—Jen—tomorrow, to thank her for seeing you, to see how she's doing.

You return to your hotel and watch television until midnight, but even then you aren't tired. You read articles in the four alumni magazines you have brought with you. It is nearly two in the morning when you turn off the light, but after fifteen minutes, you know you won't be able to sleep. So you check out of the hotel and drive home.

You pull into your driveway at dawn. You don't have the garage opener, so you leave your car in the drive. You have crossed over from tiredness into numbness, a dreamlike sensation, what you might experience in the first few seconds after receiving anesthesia. It is like existing between two worlds, neither of them quite accessible through your five senses.

You walk around to the back of the house and stand outside the kitchen, in front of a window whose yellow curtains have been drawn back. As you anticipated, the kitchen light is on and your wife, her black hair in a ponytail, is at the table, the newspaper and a cup of coffee in front of her. Your eyes have trouble focusing, and the scene seems as much memory, or wish, as reality.

She reads for a few minutes before taking a sip. When she puts down her cup, she looks out the window. You want to acknowledge her, but you find yourself frozen in place. She continues to stare directly at you, her expression, if it holds any emotion, downcast. You remember the fume-filled garage and the blackness overwhelming your consciousness. *Five minutes, no more.*

You step forward and press your lips against the window, kissing its coolness. Your wife smiles and kisses you back.

HALF CENTS

Kevin Ducey

How did literal translations start? Borges asks. I suppose it couldn't be helped. Pontiac, Zapata had their translators and they were immediately suspect. We stopped to watch a gray bat illuminated against the evening sky like an x-ray vision: Tiny fingers of bone stretching the membrane so that we don't fall. In Wisconsin, translation has the taint of s.thing theological. A tongue of flame is the preferred method. This bat has no tail. What do the swallows think?

***

You have to hate the Romans. I mean those elephants ain't gonna cross the Alps unless s.thing's driving them & that ain't love. I suppose you can leave out the elephants if you love Rome. If it's the Hollywood version, you'll need a helicopter. Simon Bolivar always required a fast frigate to be standing by, just in case things went awry. Turns out, he never needed it. Do not miss blockbuster image of helicopter cloud rising above the occupied capital. Here comes my elephant.

***

Toward an aesthetic of the ugly. After going on for some pages about the power of the poet as image-maker (and getting in the bit about 'legislators of mankind'), Shelley talks about the need to destroy the images, the turns of phrase, those constructs that have done so much to legislate the now. This iconoclasm is usually overlooked—and how much more do we need it now that the images overwhelm our ability to shove them out of the way and the planet groans under the tyranny of commodity.

***

With a white cream filling. Who'd've thought, looking at the persons and style of the American 1950s that they were gazing upon the dawn of Empire? Did Alexander's Macedonians, did the Romans, the Carthaginians, the Aztecs, ever look such dorks? Okay, I grant you the English, but who'd've thought? Like looking into a nest of hairless mewling raptors. If the period were a building it'd be a Mies Van der Rohe concrete slab bank/missile silo with gingerbread vermiculation around to bring in the children.

***

The god of frustration. A cloud of snow blows along in front of the street sweeper: a small green car—like a golf cart with a rotating brush on the front. When it brakes and reverses, it does so suddenly, with a loud, piercing beeping; as if it were in pain, or frustrated, "why must I stop? This was just getting good." In Sumer, archeaologists have found no histories, though all kinds of things were written down. Why make a chronicle? Everything is as God willed it. Why note our follies? It's not as though the Nachfolgen will read.

From Zoofismas

Raúl Fernando Linares

La Tarántula

Era la tarántula imposible
con su nombre hermoso de clepsidra
como un acurrucar en terciopelo negro,
musgo y entresueño púbico,
esdrújula y advenimiento.

The Tarantula

It was an impossible tarantula
with its beautiful name of waterclock
like a curling up in black velvet,
mossy and between pubic dreams,
when the syllable antepenultimate arrives.

La Serpiente

Era la serpiente buscando el origen de su extremadura:
recurrió al rasero extremo de ritmarse a empellones
la sonaja cauda
(previo cisma maxilar);

terminó emblemática y especular,
convertida en juego de palabras,
pobrecita,
hecha un palindrama.

The Serpent

It was the serpent whose origen began at her ending:
She turned upon the extreme measure of her shuffling rhythm
the rattling tail
(prior to the maxillary schism);

she finished emblematic and spectacular,
converted in a play of words,
poor thing,
into a palindrome.

El Cuervo

Era el cuervo y su pico nublado
la poesía que trasnoche y argumento:
esos armatostes de polifonía
disfrazados de aforismo
dispuestos,
moraleja y ceniza,
al graznido – queso de sus chapoteos.

The Crow

It was the crow and its beak of clouds
poetry that stays up all night and argues:
those hulking great polyphonies
dressed up as aphorism
disposed,
moral and ash,
to the cawing – squelching of cheese.

—*Translated by Kevin Ducey*

5 Days In

(in memoriam Keith Douglas, 1920-1944)

Robert Estep

How to find his way in
was not the thing he was afraid of
nor the quandary now of getting back out.

Dust drifted like a layer
of Parisian café foam
from the third story windows to the roof.

Glancing up from the alleymouth
gave him no compass, no sense
whether staying put or hurrying along

was his better-or-best
next pawn's move.
The three bodies he had passed on his way

into darkness were strewn
the rise of the Norman stairs,
fallen ragdolls in nevertheless tidy order.

He had stalked past the
chronology of that quick triple-
kill, taking from it those details he could use.

The first to fall bore no marks
at all, though turning the body over
might show ruin's realm clear enough.

The others were torn wide open
and continued to leak out
what little was left onto the slippery stairs.

The sound around him and
behind him was the same No-Sound
that had swallowed the outskirts two hours before first light.

A cat's tinkle through bottle
glass, his own breathing, a sheet
flapping somewhere up in all that dust.

And the sea breaking in his head
as though it belonged there.
He braced himself for the noise of another something

human, counting down the
languages to expect, flexing, tensing,
shifting from eyes-wide sleep to skin on fire,

strung to hear and relax
at a Home Counties' regimental curse,
hear and strike if the voice sang east-of-Rhine.

Queen Of Night

(in memoriam W.S. Graham, 1918-1986)

Robert Estep

A black rectangle catches starshine and blunts
to a fold of fish, skimming the wet side of the surface,
tapering to the left in veer and flight.
Look back and see whether terror or beauty
has emerged as Queen of the Night, or merged,
a Medusa dancing on a rim of cold air.
The wake, the escaping fish, and now
the crescent moon to make a fleur-de-lis of light on black.
Transparent as a dream of death.
The shape that gobbles darkness and moves
forward into greater darkness,
shadowing the boat that speeds on,
under the threat of burnout.
Holiday lights strung upon the skeletal platform,
the sounds of sacrifice so raucous, so merry
that only in a dream will one steer that way,
control going and going as sleep deepens.
I have been there and I have seen her.
Queen of the Night, Queen of Failure,
boxing the ears of the bickering words
whose loyalty to language she despises.
Subversive as a night-fisher, drunk with
compass on his knees, bellowing orders
to the boatswain drowned in Norway's
gleaming shallows. Mutiny, like suicide,
nominates itself as best of friends,
idling time and whispery with dream's
unbearable jargon, showing what could have
been seen, if eyes had only stayed open.
The sleeping princess, prised wide as delta,
the fish mobs nibbling their undead cousins,
an electric torch, swung from the steps of a lighthouse,
the sudden loom of hope across the pitchblack sea,
hope as terrifying as what swims beneath one's legs,
measuring a man's moonlit shape,
measuring the desperate distance back to shore.

BARGING ABOUT

(in memoriam Lynette Roberts, 1909-1995)

Robert Estep

Found rough and polished pell
mell on the skirt of wreckage,
any action slow as blunder
in the wee hours' ice, the wind
impairing the channel so that

watching it was watching velvet
darkening, theater-wide and riding
the quail as if touched, pummeled
from the other side. High tide
arrived, departed, carried back out

what was slow to catch the eye.
First dibs and losers weepers
and a fist trumped by a blade,
the mere threat of it pricking
shadows to their back-down,

switching interest like hyenas fresh
to the collision and its radius.
Convoy caught bobbing the fly-
swatter's lane, the passing shark
away and iris-addled when the

sea went up in flames, luxury
of tracers planeing the prayer-
wall. Mist danced the radio waves,
the static accountant out of
inky digits, rounding the tally up.

The pub news is cod and ersatz
buttery peas, the Andrews Sisters
triple-teaming a wah-wah reed-
washed buckaroo, and what's this
about Leningrad open at last?

Oh to be a child, oh to be
a scooter-siphoning son of the
black market, swarthy happy homegrown.
Dank with drowned tawdry,
banned from the hammering mint.

The holidays were but a whimper
of their former selves, with
fairy-lights and cream cakes
locked away as dream.
The doctrine of the evening

laid its frail cheat along
the shining tap-watered street.
A redhead stood watch for
con and law and the kiosk
empty, postered with acronyms

and gentle reminders not to
be a fool when all the sea
was listening in. A handkerchief,
a rose, a cartridge case.
Best of three for a cherry's song.

The Fertile Land

Mary Gilliland

He doesn't say, but my growing thistle
does not capture the castle. One each year
to thrive where its seed set. This one

in the shade is higher than my husband's head
still branching and still growing. I promise
not to let it go to seed when he flies to

a place far far away. Then I wait.
Lying quiet, head bent, the pair of hills
rising from flat white expanse. Stroking them

myself. Thistle's down is silkier and stickier
than any other, striking on the stalk, hard
to see when fallen. Like the water bug in

the cleavers ointment, the web at dusk
across the threshold, the snake that speaks,
the water of life. Like Susanna Clarke's

Man with the Thistle-down Hair, who bewitches
English ladies in the wake of the Napoleonic wars
with a severed little finger or a log of

moss oak in a casket. Can Jonathan Strange
magically retrieve them for his wife and her
best friend and place them where they properly

belong? His way is eerie as the drift
of one strand floating from the mound,
his task to pluck before the down is down.

HOME OF THE WINDS

Mary Gilliland

When her hair's life nearly severed scalp from skull
as a scattered sneakered toe lipped the pressure

treated stair over the dune, when slanted
breakers leveled brown, their spent foam shored

then the pattern of her musings wheeled away
fabricked like shorebirds escaping beachcombers.

When she wished for calm, a canvas hat, a call to

someone she imagined walking past her down the beach
as stinging sand turned her face into a shield

then a laughing gull swept its shoulders below hers
stretched over the rail with a custard, companions

in the bell-ringing bonus of pinball, the flashed arcs
of red, drop of the silvered marble filling the empty goal.

Taken

Mary Gilliland

Seven years it took me to untangle
the vow I made before I ever met you
to not slip to a bedroom down the hall
from the way I felt beside you at the Mahler
after knowing you five days, and then two nights away.

Early at the track. I'd missed the train,
clocks sprung by summertime. I had to take in
Exultate Jubilate standing at the foyer video.

Across the wynds that night snow fell, melted
the next day. The next month, home, freeze-
framed in my marriage bed, out on the street
twa corbies beaked a flattened squirrel.

The years have rinsed my straitened cells, developed
our art's aim: to reveal the life we live as it effaces
your shutter capturing my shadow on a lawn.

INTERSECTIONS

Amina Gautier

Jack waits in his car parked in front of a Kennedy Fried Chicken, a conspicuously inconspicuous white man in the Bedford-Stuyvesant section of Brooklyn, looking for all the world like an easy target. The Kennedy Fried Chicken has no Formica tables bolted to the floor and no chairs. Evidently, patrons are not meant to linger. Jack watches them crowd into the chicken joint, bustling in the small rectangle of space. They press against barriers of bulletproof plastic and have to shout their orders. They slide their money through and remove their biscuits and sweet potato pies from a revolving cube. Three boys loiter outside by a metal dumpster and pass a forty in a brown paper bag. Across the street, women clad in suits and shod in sneakers emerge from the underground subway on Fulton and walk briskly, the straps of their shoulder bags slung across torsos to deter snatchers. Gripped between index and middle fingers, innocuous house keys become weapons, ready to jab any offender in the eye, eager to maim. He cannot watch the women. Though he knows they are being smart, proactive even, about protecting themselves, it somehow seems to him that they are the aggressors, that they court violence simply by preparing for it, that they are egging on would be purse snatchers and rapists. They unnerve him. When they pass in front of his white '91 Volvo SE Station Wagon they seem to him a potential threat. Because his car does not have power locks, Jack has to check each door individually to double check that it is locked and he does. It is an old car, bought fifteen years earlier when he and his wife were trying for children. He cannot believe Jasmine lives here.

He never meant to begin seeing her.

On leave to finish a non-existent monograph on an obscure Civil War poet for the past academic year, Jack had not even met her or any one else in her cohort until this fall's Colloquium for the Medieval/Renaissance candidate. By then, she was already a second year doctoral student. Jack first saw her sitting there in the Rare Books section of the library in those uncomfortable metal folding chairs arranged in 10 by 10 rows before the podium. That is to say, he saw the back of her head and, when she turned slightly in her chair to allow a fellow student to exit the row, he saw the angle of her face, the curve of her brown cheek, the fall of braids hanging like a sheet between the two sharp points of her shoulders jutting through her gray hoodie.

She was seated in the second row, allowing him to look his fill as he pretended to give his attention to the speaker at the podium. The candidate, a petite brunette, was easily categorized and dismissed. She wore a basic black pants suit, the academic uniform that women in the humanities had long since adopted to give them a unisex look and deemphasize their femininity. Every time he went to MLA, he saw these ugly nondescript women. He was not interested in the candidate or her analysis of Margery Kempe. He was a scholar of Early American Literature. Medievalists held no interest for him anyway—he'd come merely as a show of departmental support—what interested him most was the black girl in the second row with the hair he could not fathom.

Some of the braids followed a pattern like a chain-linked belt he'd seen his wife wear slung low on her hips. Other braids snaked under, over, and between the links, as impossibly complicated as King Minos's labyrinth. Writ on her scalp was the map of his life and all the winding paths it had taken. Laid out like a blueprint, Jack saw his years in graduate school, his first failed job and his subsequent tenure and promotion at his second appointment. Her hair showed him where he was going and where he had been.

Thirty minutes and still no Jasmine.

If he headed for home right now, he'd only be slightly late for dinner. There would be time to pacify Margaret with tales of traffic. Right now, his wife was preparing two separate dinners—a normal one for him and a low-carb, sugar free equivalent for herself.

‡ ‡ ‡

Jack stood in their vestibule, sorting through their mail.

"Are you home?" his wife called out from the kitchen.

"Yes, I'm home," Jack said, answering the unnecessary question.

So far, none of the mail was for him. He lifted a small yellow envelope. His wife's name showed through the plastic window. He carried ten similar pieces of mail in with him, dropping them onto a pile on the kitchen table. "You have admirers," he said.

"What's that?" Margaret was spooning sugar substitute into a cup of herbal tea.

"The American Vets want you," Jack said. "So do the Hospitalized Vets."

Margaret turned and looked at the growing pile of envelopes. "Oh, that."

All of the surfaces in their kitchen and living room were covered with envelopes addressed to his wife. The coffee table, the end tables, the kitchen table, the top of the television, and two TV trays were covered with pleas from the less fortunate of the world, thanking his wife for her unswerving generosity and beseeching her to bestow it yet again, just one more time, for a cause that really needed it. The American Diabetes Association and the American Heart Association wrote to his wife along with The National Cancer Research Center, the National Association for the Terminally Ill, Feed the Children, the Christian Children's Mission Fund, the North Shore Animal League, a foundation for children with crooked smiles, and a tribe of Hopi Indians. They all asked money from his wife and Margaret gave it freely, her way of mothering the world.

"What kept you?" Margaret asked. Her red hair was fading into strawberry blonde. Her face was pale without makeup; she looked as if she had no eyelashes.

"Traffic."

"Hungry?" she asked. "It's ready."

"I'm sure I could eat," Jack said. He had not thought about food in quite some time, distracted by not having seen Jasmine in two weeks, preoccupied by the suspicion that she was purposely avoiding him. He reviewed a mental outline of his day and realized that he had not eaten in eight hours. Suddenly, he was famished.

He was wrong about the two separate meals. Margaret had made only one, a healthy lasagna made from low-carb noodles, sugar free spaghetti sauce, extra lean ground turkey and low fat mozzarella. They ate in the living room, balancing their plates on their knees since there were no tables upon which they could set their food.

"How is it?"

"Good," Jack said, tunneling through the tasteless meal as quickly as possible. It was like no lasagna he'd ever eaten; the noodles were thin as air, buckling under the weight of cheese and sauce.

"It's good for you, too," she said.

"Is it?"

"Yes. It is."

"Good."

The last time he'd had Italian had been with Jasmine.

He'd arrived at her place early. Jasmine opened the door in a short white terry robe that belted around her waist, her hair wrapped turban style in a fluffy blue towel. Water trickled from her hair down her cheeks. "You're early," Jasmine said. "Dinner's not ready yet."

He followed her into the kitchen. Her nimble fingers broke a stack of brittle spaghetti noodles in half and dumped them into a pot of garlic-scented boiling water. "Is spaghetti all right with you?"

He wanted to grab her by her shoulders and kiss away the damp spots at the back of her neck where the water trailed. "Fine with me," he said, watching her add a drop of olive oil and stir. "I was once a poor grad student myself."

"Back when dinosaurs roamed the earth?"

"Not that long ago."

"Awww." She kissed his cheek. "Just a joke."

He was a full hour early and he'd caught her just as she finished washing her hair. When she pulled the towel off, a soft damp bush of hair stood out all over her head. Her hair carried the fruity scent of her shampoo and conditioner. She tilted her head to the side and roughly dried it.

She disappeared down the hallway and into the bathroom. "You're just in time to help me," she called back to him.

"Help you what?"

"Tell you in a minute. Why don't you pour us some wine and light the incense?"

Jack poured out cheap wine for them. He filled the paper cups and placed them on the edge of the coffee table in front of the couch. He lit the small brown cones, releasing the scent of patchouli.

"Here," she said when she came back out. "Make yourself useful." She held a jar of hair grease. Jack took the jar, looking askance at the label with the face of a woman with long silky hair embossed upon it. He scanned the capitalized and bolded letters that boasted jojoba, rosemary, nettle, chamomile, coconut oil, and Indian hemp as well as secret African herbs. He'd never seen anything like it. "What should I do?"

"You can oil my scalp," she said. "Sit there."

Jack sat on the edge of the couch and Jasmine sat down on the floor in front of him, between his knees. She ran the end of a rattail comb through her hair to divide it into sections. It was his job to make sure that the parts were straight. She sectioned off portions of her thick hair into squares, tiny little boxes of black hair surrounded by pale scalp.

As she braided each section, the top of her head began to look like an orderly maze. He sat behind her and helped her part the back where she couldn't see. That day he'd been her mirror. He had to hold the portions of hair that she was not working on to keep them from falling into her eyes. He had fistfuls of her hair at his disposal and he didn't know what to do with himself.

They were still early in the relationship and he reminded himself why it was wrong, why he would end it soon.

He was much too much older than her.

She was black.

He was married.

She was a grad student.

It didn't matter. All the parts in her hair converged like a map, pointing to her and—against that— none of the reasons would hold.

Jack took the comb from her and sank one hand into the portion of her hair that was still damp and unbraided. With the other hand, he reached for his wine. He drizzled it over her neck, drank it from the hollow of brown flesh where her neck and collarbone met.

‡ ‡ ‡

"Something on your mind?" Margaret asked.

He wondered where Jasmine was, why she had not gone home, why she was not returning his phone calls. "No."

"Something is on mine," Margaret said.

"Oh?"

Margaret toyed with her food, twining mozzarella around her fork. Her plate was still half full while his was nearly empty. Jack wondered how it was that he never saw his wife eat, yet she constantly struggled with her weight. "I think we should have a baby."

"We're too old," Jack said.

"You haven't even heard me out," she said. "I didn't mean one of our own." She had been hinting for some time about wanting to raise a Third World baby, to adopt one of the children she'd seen on the feed-the-children commercials. He'd heard it all before. If she couldn't have her own child, she wanted the responsibility of knowing that by helping a child she was helping an entire village. "I'm serious," Margaret said. "I would like to adopt a baby of color."

"There are plenty of those right here in our own country," he reminded her. "You can simply take your pick. Cheaper that way." He took his plate to the kitchen, rinsed it and set it in the dishwasher.

"You are sooo white," Margaret said, twisting her upper lip in such a way that drew attention to the soft downy blonde hair above it, drawing out the word "so" the way his undergrads did. She said it with a sneer in her voice, as if it were an insult, as if she weren't just as white as he. "Don't make fun. This is important to me."

He tried to escape her in the den where he had one stack of abstracts for an upcoming conference and two stacks of dissertation chapters spread over the couch, but she followed him. Since she could not sit next to him because of the papers, she stalked to the TV and turned it on, pleading her case to the background of *Kojak*.

The children were African, Asian, and South American. Single-handedly his wife wanted to rescue three continents of hungry children. She sounded like the late night programming she'd watched. It was just the price of a cup of coffee and he drank three cups a day. She had a child already picked out. She'd called one of those 800 numbers and they'd sent her three profiles from which to choose. She wanted the little boy, Manolo.

"Would you just look at him?" She held an envelope in her hand and extracted a glossy eight-by-ten photo of the boy and dropped it onto the third chapter of a dissertation on Walt Whitman's novel, *Franklin Evans*. "Here, take a look." Eyes as big as saucers in a brown face peeked out from under long black hair, shaggy as a mop, and stared up at Jack. He couldn't tell if the boy was Indian or South American or Filipino and he was scared to get his wife excited by asking.

She stood by his side, watching him watch Manolo. She rested her hand on his arm, assured. Her touch did nothing for him, though he remembered a time when it could have moved him to tenderness. He tried to hand Manolo back. "Why?" he asked, tired of the whole thing. She wouldn't take the photo, so Jack set it on top of his papers. She knew he hated those begging commercials where overweight has-been actors coddled half-naked bone-thin children. Looking at those children with their big heads and bellies, skeletal limbs and gaunt expressions disturbed him. Why did they always have flies buzzing near them?

"Why?" She repeated his question slowly as if it had been in another language and she'd had to translate. He used to not deny her anything; she used to not have to explain. The envelope dropped from her hand and fell on top of the glossy photo, covering little Manolo's face. Margaret's eyes were bright with unshed tears. "I just want to save something. Honey, can't you see what's happening to us?" she asked, searching his face.

"Nothing's happening," he said. The way he saw it, Margaret had her life and now he had his. He had never complained when she begged out of department functions, or was too tired to proofread one of his conference papers, yet had energy enough for Phil Donahue, Oprah, and telephone conversations that never seemed to end. He no longer reminded her that when they were first married, she would bring him coffee and stay up half the night with him, listening as he rehearsed conference presentations.

There had been a time when his wife had been just as excited about his career as he. A time when she dressed carefully for department colloquiums and holiday parties and laughed at ease on his arm.

"Do you think I can't see it?" she asked. "You're leaving me," Margaret said. "And you don't even notice."

‡ ‡ ‡

Two nights later and Jack was parked once again in front of the Kennedy Fried Chicken, waiting to catch Jasmine. He'd called her from his office and she'd not answered. He'd called her from a payphone and she'd not picked up, either. Two weeks without a word from her and he had no idea of what he'd done wrong. He no longer saw her in the copy room or anywhere in the department. He could not imagine why she would not want to see him. They had words between them. Together, they could talk of hegemony, representation, dichotomy, elision and slippage, terms that Margaret would not understand.

Seemed to him it was just yesterday that Jasmine had pulled him out of his office hours and dragged him to Union Square even though it was snowing. They lined a bench with newspaper for warmth, sat and huddled, the only idiots seated in the park while a stream of people rushed into and out of 14th Street station.

She blew on her mocha, rippling its surface. "I taught the Calamus poems today."

"Ah," Jack said. "Homoeroticism."

She made a face. "Please, I don't want to hear that word for the rest of the semester. No one paid any attention once I said it. Half of the class snickered through the entire lecture."

"At the risk of sounding facetious, I must say that I did advise you to leave it off your syllabus."

"I know, I know," she said looking into her mocha and not at him. "I had to include those poems. They made me think of us."

"Two men in love?" he sputtered. "Us?"

"A secret love that must go unnamed," she said. "Us." Beneath her direct and assessing gaze, Jack felt revered and important, a way he never felt at home. She set her drink down. "Give me your hand."

He did.

"Take off your glove."

"You are aware that it's freezing?"

"Just do it," she said. Jack re-wrapped his hot dog in its aluminum foil.

Then he took off his glove and gave her his hand again. That's the way it was. Though he was the one with tenure, and she a mere slip of a second year grad student with a weakness in theory and rhetoric, and a fondness for overwriting, Jasmine had all the power. She could make him laugh, could make him come, could touch him in a way Margaret never could.

"Now what?" he asked.

She pulled off her own wool gloves and brought their bare hands together. Like a soothsayer of old, she held his palm and explored it with the tips of her fingers. He didn't know if she was actually reading his palm or merely pretending. He didn't know what she saw in his hand or what she saw in him at all and it frightened him. He wanted to pull his hand back, in case there was something in it that might condemn. He didn't want to lose her. His hand shook in hers and she grasped it with both hands to steady it. Her bare head was lowered over his hand. Her hat rested in her lap. As she bent forward, her braids fell forward and then resettled, hanging in layers, their ends overlapping at her shoulders. Their ends brushed his palm and burned him.

"'Not heat flames up and consumes.'"

"What did you say?"

"'Not these, O none of these more than the flames of me, consuming, burning for his love whom I love.' It's Whitman," she said. "You should know that, *professor*." She said professor like it was a dirty word and they were in bed with the lights out.

She unzipped her down jacket and unbuttoned her shirt, revealing her skin inch by inch, naked above the waist save for a lacy burgundy bra. "'My soul is borne through the open air, wafted in all directions.'"

She stopped one button shy of her navel. She pulled his naked hand to her throat and collarbone, guiding it downwards until it skimmed the skin above her heart and breasts. The flesh above her heart was warm as his hands explored her. The cold wind stung his cheeks. Gingerly, he reached out and touched the ends of her braids where they hung just above her breasts. They were damp with melting snow; the ends curled under and began to unravel. He grabbed a handful of her braids and pulled lightly, using them to bring her mouth to his, feeling nothing that resembled cold.

When they separated, Jasmine asked, "Will you leave her?"

"Sure," Jack said. Then, because he thought it sounded glib, he said, "Yes. If you want me to, I will." He knew that it was what married men always said to the woman on the side in the hopes of appeasing them and continuing the affair, but he actually meant it. There was nothing keeping him with Margaret; he stayed because—until Jasmine—he didn't have anywhere else to go, nothing else to do with his life. In his mind, Jasmine was not the woman on the side; Margaret was.

"I don't want you to," Jasmine said.

To his surprise, he was standing. He sat back down on the bench. "Then I won't," Jack said, hoping it was the right response. "Okay?"

"Okay," she said. "I just wanted to know."

‡ ‡ ‡

Over an hour now and still no Jasmine. While he waited across the street from her apartment, Margaret was likely wondering where he was. He could see her now, diligently covering the night's uneaten dinner in plastic wrap for him, eating standing by the kitchen sink, looking longingly at the picture of little Manolo while she ate dry cereal in a bowl over the kitchen sink. The bowl, he thought, was unnecessary. Why bother to pour the cereal into a bowl if you weren't going to add milk? It would be just as convenient to tilt the box directly into one's waiting mouth and bypass the middleman. The cereal, he knew, would be low calorie, sugar-free, and fiber-filled. She tried to make him eat that stuff in place of his toasted bagel and cream cheese, but, after he'd seen all the parts in Jasmine's hair, Margaret no longer held sway.

Leaning half across his seat to double check the lock on the rear right door, he spied Jasmine through the back window, hurrying from the train station. He waited until she made it to her block and he saw her go up her stoop and disappear into her building before he began timing himself. Five minutes should do it. That way, it wouldn't seem as if he'd been sitting out here waiting. That way it wouldn't seem so desperate.

‡ ‡ ‡

She opened the door, unsurprised to see him."In the neighborhood?"

"Just to see you," Jack said. She motioned him in.

"Is something wrong?"

"You tell me," Jack said. "I haven't seen you in two weeks. I've called, left messages. Didn't you get them?"

"I got them." He sat down on the couch.

"Well?" he said, hating the way he sounded.

"I'm sorry. It's just that I've been busy," she said. "You know, grad school and all. Grading midterms. Trying to get my proposal written before spring break."

"That's all?" he asked.
"That's all."
"So, are we fine?"
"We're fine."

‡ ‡ ‡

Two hours later, Jack awoke, feeling as if he'd been tricked. Instead of answering his questions, Jasmine had silenced him with sex. He raised himself on his elbow and tried to take a clue from her hair while she slept. With her back to him, he couldn't see her face, couldn't see the small mole above her left eyebrow, or her lips, the upper one brown and the lower one pink. He could only see her hair. It was braided in a simple pattern, one he could tell she had done herself. Cornrows followed the contours of her head and the ends of her braids, hanging down past her shoulders, disappeared into small wooden beads. He didn't know what they might signify, but he didn't trust them.

He nudged her awake.

She turned to face him. "What is it? Do you have to go?"

"Not yet," he said. "You changed your hair."

"What?"

"What happened to all of your fancy braids?" he asked, slipping his arm around her.

"Those take hours," she said.

"Do you think I could be a good father?"

"In what sense?"

"My wife wants to have a baby."

She edged out from under the crook of his arm. "How?"

"With me."

Jasmine sat up and propped her back against the headboard. The beads clacked against it, discordant. "I meant, fertility treatments? Surrogacy? Isn't she somewhat old? There might be health concerns and possible complications."

He was expecting something different from her. A little more jealousy, a lot less curiosity. "I'm only three years older than her," he reminded her, feeling old by association. "She wants to adopt."

"You know all those people who bomb abortion clinics? They should all adopt at least one baby. They try to save the ones who aren't even here yet, but they balk at spending tax dollars on the ones already born. Why don't they revamp the foster care system?"

"I'm pro-choice," he reminded her.

"Sorry, I just got a little carried away," Jasmine said. "Adoption is good. I'm going to adopt when I get married."

"It's not a real adoption," he said. "Just one of those programs where you send money." How blithely she spoke of a future without him.

"I don't see what the big deal is if it's just on paper."

It would never be that easy with Margaret. She would want get to know Manolo. To write and send care packages. She would want to visit, to see his village firsthand. He thought the paper responsibility would not bother him. It was something else. Once—just once—he wanted to be able to tell his wife no and stick to it. He wanted not to give in to her.

"Plenty of things on paper are a big deal," he said, thinking aloud. "Birth certificates. Marriage licenses. The fact that it's on paper doesn't lessen its significance. If anything, it solidifies it." The adoption would be just one more thing to bind he and Margaret, which is what she wanted, hoped for. Young couples did it when their marriage was on the rocks, using babies as glue to mend that which could not be mended. Older couples used pets, adopting dogs and other animals known for their longevity, pretending the pet was a child. Jack's allergies made pets impossible, so she was trying to save their marriage with a monthly donation and a paper adoption. She thought she could finally give him the child they had wanted, give him the family they had desired so long ago, when now all he wanted from her was to be left alone to go his own way, undeterred.

"I just can't do this," Jasmine said. She flicked on the tall halogen lamp by her bed and the sudden light after hours of darkness blinded him, making him blink just to see.

"Did I say something?" he asked.

"No, Jack, it's not what you said. It's who you are." Her eyes made him flinch. There was nothing in them when she looked at him. Just as she had looked at his palm and gone to the heart of him, she now fixed a look on him that went right through him. She had finally seen whatever it was in him that destroyed love.

She picked her tee shirt up from the floor and pulled it on. "You're married; you promised to love somebody else. Somebody not me."

"You told me not to leave her."

"It wasn't real to me yet when I said that. I mean, I knew you had a wife. I just hadn't thought about what that really meant. But then I saw her and I thought—"

"You saw Margaret? Where?"

"I saw a picture of her. Of you both, actually. You know those pictures posted all over Fennimore Lounge, all the old pictures of the Fall Colloquium and the annual holiday party? We were having our monthly American Literature meeting in there and I noticed them for the first time. All these old pictures of faculty and former grad students at department gatherings and I see one of you with your wife. You're holding a small plate with brie and crackers and she's holding your arm and I see her and I think she seems kind, like a woman I could meet in a grocery store and befriend. What right do I have to undermine her? She is a real woman living a real life and she's done no harm to me." He watched her reach for her socks, knowing that each piece of clothing she put on took her farther away from him. Jasmine lifted one knee, balancing on her other foot to pull on her sock. She scooped her boxers up from the floor and stepped into them, as indifferent as if she were dressing in front of a roommate or a mirror. "We're so trite, Jack. The professor and the grad student, what a cliché. I guess what I'm trying to say is, please don't come here any more."

Except for a quick nod, he didn't respond. He leaned over her side of the bed and turned the light back out. In a minute, he would get dressed and go, but before he did he wanted a moment. From the beginning he had known that sooner than later, it would end. That they would drift, only running into each other occasionally in the hallways between office hours, mingling during department events, pretending to know each other only distantly. Now and again they would meet by accident at different conferences. Perhaps they would sit on a panel together. Over and over again, their lives would run into each other's, quietly intersecting. Yet he had not seen this coming. Her hair had lied. It seemed just the other day he'd had his hands buried in that crackling bush of hair and her thick and kinky hair had wrapped around his fingers, gnarling them, as impenetrable as the woman herself. It seemed but a minute ago that he was sitting in the Rare Books room, staring at her inscrutable hair and hoping for a chance to get to know her. He reached over the side of the bed and fumbled for his socks, blindly.

‡ ‡ ‡

He let himself into the house. All the lights were off, Margaret already in bed. Jack took off his shoes and padded in his socks to the bedroom. When he slipped into bed beside her, Margaret rolled to him, her face slack with sleep. He wanted to hate her for what had just happened to him. For marrying him. For not being Jasmine. For busying herself in paper causes, behaving as if her world was real and his was not. He wanted to hate her, but it was not her fault. In life, they all had choices to make. He had made his. Was it a mere two days ago that he'd sat in his car and locked the doors to protect himself from a group of harmless women? He had chosen to see them as a threat, chosen not to expose their lie. Instead of waiting for Jasmine, he could have chosen to get out of his car and follow one of those key toting women. He could have followed her up the steps to her brownstone and taken her purse despite her precautions, upending it in front of her to show her as she scrambled for her wallet, breath mints, tampons, hand sanitizer and old receipts how uninspired and unimportant were their lives, how—when you came down to it—nothing really mattered.

Jack climbed out of the bed and went down to the den. There he turned on the lights and searched through his stack of papers for that brown envelope and photo. His hand slid over smooth gloss and he picked up the photo of little Manolo. How smug Margaret had been that day, he thought. Inside the envelope he found two more photos. A Venezuelan girl named Isabella smiled at him. He smiled back. The second picture was of a six-year-old Kenyan girl with her hair in cornrows. Rows of braids traveled from her high, wide forehead and convened at the top of her head to form a small braided bun. Her eyes were eyes he'd seen before. The profile said her name was Tzipporah. Tzipporah stared at the camera, unwilling to smile, her face as serious as any adult's. The profile said she lived in the Kwa Vonza village and was a member of the Kamba tribe. Had Jasmine not discarded him, they could have had a little girl just like her.

Jack dug his hand deeper into the envelope, removing an unsigned check, the forms and a pen. Margaret had filled in all of the spaces. He had only to add his signature to hers to make it legitimate. He amended the form before he signed it, substituting Tzipporah for Manolo, making his choice. He signed both documents. He held the paper and check up to the light to examine his scrawl, barely able to recognize his name.

To Build a Quiet City in My Mind

Kathleen Rooney

Your absence breeds/A longer silence through the rooms. We haunt ourselves.
—Weldon Kees, "Return of the Ghost"

I am in love with another man, but my husband doesn't mind.

I have come to the city to find this man's apartments. Over the course of the week, I will seek out all nine—one in Brooklyn, eight in Manhattan—but I will never find the man himself.

I am in love with a dead man.

I love his poems, his writings, his looks, his life and the way the Library of Congress Cataloging in Publication Data at the front of his handful of books reads: "Kees, Weldon, 1914-1955?"

I am in love with Weldon Kees—poet, painter, and jazz musician—creator of Robinson and mysterious suicide.

Or I am in love with Weldon Kees—photographer, film-maker, and cultural critic—creator of Robinson and mysterious disappearee.

This morning, I wake up with an aching head and a fading black stamp inked on the back of my right hand that says *dead*. I'm not of course, but the fading stamp haunts my skin like a ghost. It faces away, toward my fingers, upside down to me, but upright to others.

Last night, Beth and I, along with Elise and a bunch of our friends who live in the city had gone to a bar in Brooklyn. The black-clad man checking IDs at the door stamped our hands with the word "dead" to signify we were of age to drink. "Enjoy the afterlife," he said as we slipped through the black velvet curtains, beneath a box fan facing out the transom, blowing silver Mylar streamers, like rainclouds.

Today, as wet gray light slides through the blinds on the windows of Elise's illegal loft where Beth and I are laying atop an air mattress, I know I am alive and will feel even more so after a shower and some coffee. My dead-yet-not-dead status makes me think of the disappearance of Weldon Kees, how he is one or the other, obviously—either you're dead or you're not—but he is not clearly either, or at least he wasn't for a long time. He was neither or both.

He had been talking for years about committing suicide or starting over in Mexico when he vanished. That was almost 52 years ago, in San Francisco, July, 1955.

My sister Beth and I have both come to New York in January 2007 for a visit, her to meet with photo editors at agencies and magazines, me for Kees and a launch party in Boston at the end of the week. But first and foremost we've come to feel more alive.

Weldon Kees makes me feel more alive every time I read him—every time I read his biography, even. He makes me write "yes, yes, yes" in the margins of his poems, at the ends of his letters. I feel like I get him so well, that he would surely get me—that is, if circumstances had been such that he ever could have met me. His wife called him Weld, but I've decided that I'd have called him Kees, as though we were working toward the same goals for some fabulous team.

Beth and I are in the middle of a long slow season. I am a college professor and my small, religious university is on J-term, which means I still get paid, but I don't have to teach, leaving me nothing but time to kill in Tacoma. Beth is a freelance photographer. Her bread and butter is shooting for the business school of a Chicago university, but everyone's on winter holiday so there's no one to photograph.

We are both succeeding, but feeling success-less. We are feeling that maybe we are getting somewhere, but not fast enough, and whenever we arrive, "the room is cold, the words in the books are cold;/And the question of whether we get what we ask for/Is absurd." "What we have learned," we are finding "is not what we were/told." Delays and frustrations were bringing us down, so we decided to quit our bitching and take a break, and now here we are and already we are having the best time.

"Are you guys hungry?" Elise calls from the base of the stairs leading to our sleeping space. "Are you guys awake?"

Elise is from Ohio. She is talented and beautiful. Our sleeping space is set up behind a cloud of what looks like hand-made curtains, but which is actually part of her latest installation, a tribute to her dead grandmother—childhood and memory. The last time I saw her before this visit, she was rocking a femme-hawk, but she's grown it out. Now her dull brown hair is elegantly ratty, forming a shabby bird's nest of epic proportions.

"Starving," Beth answers.

"Great. I'll have Tom start breakfast."

Elise's boyfriend, Tom, is a dead ringer for the young Bob Dylan; the resemblance is uncanny.

Elise and Tom live with approximately eight other people in a commercial-industrial space they have illegally turned residential. Their flatmates include a transgendered New Zealander, a female drag queen, a composer with a deal on Nonesuch Records, a small-press editor and a woman from France, who seems to wear only a red bathrobe for the duration of our visit, and who shuffles in and out of the kitchen gruffly, but never speaks. Every couple or set of roommates has their own loft, and shares the single kitchen and bathroom built into the center of the compound—like living in a hostel—but it has to be this way, or else they might get caught. All the rooms have heavy blinds to keep the light inside at night so they don't get found out and evicted.

The place used to be a mortuary with a coffin factory in the basement and a funeral parlor on the main floor, where they all live now. When they first moved in, they had to clean out jars and vials of sharp-smelling liquids, caustic cleansers, and embalming fluids. The basement beneath them has been taken over by welders, metal sculptors who like to work on their heavy projects late into the night. We can hear them clanging, sometimes, and imagine the heat below our feet.

When I peek out the curtain on my way to the shower, the streets are still slick with listless rain, just as they were when I arrived on my redeye yesterday, "Seattle weather: it has rained for weeks in this town…" Elise says it's been this way for what feels like forever, an unseasonably warm winter, and I feel as though the Pacific Northwestern climate I was trying to escape has followed me.

Quick and wiry, Tom's an excellent cook. He and Elise feed Beth and me brunch—eggs and coffee, bananas and grapes, pears and pancakes—then they roll us a joint and we all four get high. Kees smoked up with Khalil Gibran Jr., a painter and the son of the poet, on the beach in Provincetown, a place I used to live, and liked. A place I miss. I picture this and smile after a deep inhale.

Tom, employed as a decorative painter during the week, decides to stay in and work on his own paintings, while Elise and Beth and I take the subway to visit the galleries in Chelsea: airy, brightly lit, warm and dry spaces in the middle of the dim and rainy Saturday.

Weldon Kees wrote often about interior spaces—room after room after room after room—though his rooms were typically austere and empty at best, severe and disquieting at worst. "The room was monstrous, overgrown," he writes in "First Anniversary." "Love," he writes, "is a sickroom with the roof half gone/Where nights go down in a continual rain." But if it's bad in the rooms, it's worse outside, where "The ragged trees in lightning, blacker than before,/Moved nearer to the room."

It is important to me to try to see these rooms, places where he invented his own still scenes, ghostly vignettes with the air sucked out. I want to see the places where he felt so trapped, where he lived when he wrote, "The crack is moving down the wall./Defective plaster isn't all the cause./We must remain until the roof falls in."

I want to see the places where he fought with his wife and received rejection letters, the places where he wrote, "Held in the rouged and marketable glow/Beyond Third Avenue, the city hums/Like muffled bees./Sheeted, we lie/Above the streets, where headlights/Search the mirrors through the heat/And move on, reverential over the cement," and the rooms in which he couldn't sleep, "Sleep. But there is no sleep. A drunk is sobbing/In the hall./Upstairs, an organ record/Of a Baptist hymn comes on. Past one o'clock."

In the early evening, after the galleries, I have my first chance. Hungry and wet, Beth, Elise and I are in the mood for Indian food. We take the subway to Union Square and walk quickly to where Elise, with her outsized umbrella and beige thrift store trenchcoat, has suggested we go: Curry Row. This whole visit, I have a folder of notes and maps in tow, keeping track of the Kees sites I need to see, and I realize we are about to walk by one now.

"Hey, Elise, hold up," I say as we're heading down a numbered avenue, about to cross East 10th Street. Beth and Elise agree to check it out with me; they know about the project. Elise thinks it's "neat," and Beth's offered to photograph all the buildings, and then there we are, Kees Site #1, not the first apartment he lived in in the city (actually, it's the fourth), but it's the first place I see: 129 East 10th Street on the block between Third and Second Avenues, well in range of the bells of St. Mark's, ringing as we approach.

Kees landed the place thanks to a connection through Ann, his wife, who was working for *Antiques* magazine. It was 1943 and one of the correspondents had to remain in the UK thanks to the war; an Atlantic crossing would have been too dangerous. The Keeses got to sublet her furnished apartment, in a neighborhood their friend Janet Richards said had the aura of a "decayingly elegant cul de sac [...] with mossy homes from the Eighties." The windows were filigreed with vines and ferns and faced St. Mark's. "There was an alcove," Richards said, "just big enough for a little Jacobean dining table. There was a kitchen that was only a short hallway between the alcove and the bathroom and [...] Ann washed the dishes in the bathroom sink. In the living room there were two single beds, covered with faded brocades, one against the wall, the other in the middle of the room, since there was no other place for it [...] and all of the furniture, the chairs, bookcases, little chests and tiny tables were relics of the eighteenth century, inconspicuously maintaining their unalterable perfection of design. On the floor was an ancient Oriental rug." The writer James Agee visited them there often, and they moved in just in time to impress Kees' parents when they came to town for an October visit.

Of course, I can't tell any of this from looking at the place, from the brick sidewalk on which I am standing outside the building's doorway. I jot in my notebook as Beth snaps away with her Nikon. Elise has wandered up the block to watch the tourists flock around St. Mark's; it is a long weekend—Martin Luther King, Jr. Day is Monday—so there are a lot of them. Everything I know about this building and what may or may not have transpired in it, I know from my research. From the outside, the building looks more or less like all the rest on the block, a gentrified residence in the East Village of the 21st century. It has six floors, iron lattices on the windows, and black iron balustrades. I don't even know what floor he lived on, and that the odds are good I never will. I want it to be the third floor, though, because that is the one that is amber and lamplit with off-white curtains, curtains like the one Kees wrote that Ann made. A car with huge woofers drives by, playing slow bass, and an impatient guy honks for someone in the building next door.

"Are you done yet?" Beth asks, having waited patiently for fifteen minutes. "Let's go get some curry."

And I guess that I am done, for now, with this one. We walk on. This first stop wasn't a disappointment, but it wasn't totally satisfying. *But,* I tell myself, as we walk down a narrow street lined with Indian restaurants, their owners standing in front, wheedling for patrons, *I've only just begun.*

I've heard the voice of Weldon Kees, smooth and deep, on a recording he made of his original songs. I imagine him using it to recite: "This is the castle then, Fmy dear,/ With its justly famous view./There are other historic sights in store—/ Battlegrounds, parks we might explore,/The hundreds of monuments to war;/Now that you've seen the castle, my dear,/We'll see them before we're through."

That is what I intend to do: see his castles, see their views. I think I still think that if I map out his reckless trajectory, it might spell out some kind of message, like Hawksmoor's churches in London or the Nazca Lines of Peru.

After our massive dinner—Beth haggled with the owner to throw in dessert with our vegetarian special, which already came with appetizers and a free bottle of wine—we strike off to a bar. The rest of our visit will be the non-stop pastiche of subway rides, walks, drinks, restaurants, restrooms, museums, and friends we came here for, and will make me feel like a raw nerve in a wonderful way. But the major points of interest, the parts that will stand out the most, are the subsequent Kees sites. Weldon and Ann lived in the city from 1943 to 1950, but I will not visit the spots in chronological order; rather I will see them in the order I come upon them, hitting them when I come close anyway to visit living people and do living people things. But each one will fill me with a little thrill, like I'm collecting items for a scavenger hunt, like I'm catching ghosts out the corners of my eyes.

Sunday is an idle Kees-spotting day; I see none of his rooms, rooms that he might call "dwarfed, immutable, and bare." But Monday morning, the chase is back on. The next point in the dartboard—Kees Site #2—is the Hotel Albert, a place where Kees didn't live, technically, but where he and Ann stayed when they came to visit with his Nebraskan parents in 1939 for the New York World's Fair. Kees chose the hotel—23 E. 10th at the corner of University Place—for a reason that makes perfect sense to me: Hart Crane had a furnished room, from 1919-1920. The building—five sumptuous stories with bright green awnings—is not a hotel anymore. It contains luxury apartments and a Dean and Delucca's on the ground floor.

I'm not sure where to picture him here, among the old brick structures with molded windows and potted shrubs. I try to imagine whether the same smells, fetid and sour, would have been on the breeze, if that's what he was thinking when he wrote, "this rank wind/Blows through your rooms, untenanted." The trees stick up as spare as rakes—they have no leaves—and the sidewalks are littered with orange peels and receipts. There is probably way more plastic on the ground now than when Kees was here with his parents. I know he loved being here from way out in the middle of nowhere, from Denver, where he was stuck in the Rockies, working in a library.

Born in 1914, Kees made it to New York for real before he turned 30. I'm 26. I resist the way this city acts as though if something doesn't happen here, then it doesn't happen, but I can't convince myself that Tacoma is really where I'm meant to be.

Kees' biographer, James Reidel, writes of how Kees could, if he wanted to, have taken a professorial position at a university since his first book of poetry, *The Fall of the Magicians,* came out with a major press when he was just 33, but Kees was determined to reject that career path. Instead, he wrote in his satiric novel, *Fall Quarter*, of "the bad dream [he] imagined his life would be had he become a young college professor." To my dismay, it seems that I am living that dream, locked away in a back-biting backwater while the action happens elsewhere.

Beth snaps away with her Nikon.

I have no idea which way to look at Kees Site #3, lower Fifth Avenue and 10th Street. The directions are vague. "We have a remarkably cool apartment on lower Fifth Avenue and 10th Street"—a letter from Kees in July of 1943—is all I have to go on. It's the same street, at any rate, that Emma Lazarus lived on, where she was a "Poet, Essayist, and Humanitarian" as the helpful blue plaque with white letters tells us, as well as the same street that Dawn Powell lived on, another literary Midwesterner come to the big city, now all but forgotten. "The past goes down and disappears," Kees writes, "The present stumbles home to bed,/The future stretches out in years/That no one knows, and you'll be dead." You'll be dead, but someone you never knew might still love you in spite—or because—of it.

It is Martin Luther King Jr. Day today. Tom was looking at a book of photo essays about him this morning at the kitchen table, and now, a black man in a minivan with faux wood paneling is listening to "I Have a Dream" turned up so high, you can hear it through the closed windows.

Picture Kees here if you want, I tell myself. *He doesn't care. Picture him anywhere in the city—he got around. Picture him, if you want, in Mexico.*

Then off we go again to the sound of construction drills. I wonder if the city sounded this way in his day, too, if a city is always in the process of becoming?

Kees Site #4 is much the same, the directions nebulous. "In June, the Keeses moved back to East 10th Street, subletting from Dwight and Nancy MacDonald, who were at the Cape for the summer," says the Reidel biography. But this lack of specificity is probably all right, because precision isn't exactly what's significant anyway. These buildings are in some ways like people, like strangers; their interiorities are not available to me so I have to use my eyes and my imagination, to size them up the way people keep sizing up Beth and me, the women scanning: shoes, coat, purse; the men scanning: legs, ass, face.

I know from letters Kees wrote about the place, whichever one it is, that it had "wonderful quiet," tropical fish, and bookshelves "topheavy on Marxism," as well as a Steinway grand that he liked to play. I know I could, if I chose, infuse every window and doorway in my line of sight with meaning—maybe he touched that railing, sat on those stairs, or smoked on that fire escape. Because now that he must be dead, regardless of what happened to him that day in July of 1955, and because of the way he vanished, nothing in his life or work can ever be strictly as it seems. Everything becomes a symbol, a coded message. Donald Justice, an early Kees revivalist, himself now dead, writes in the introduction to *The Collected Poems*, "If the whole of poetry can be read as a denial of the values of the present civilization, as I believe it can, then the disappearance of Kees becomes as symbolic an act as Rimbaud's flight or Crane's suicide." Little facts and details become seemingly fraught, "These bilious things, fracturing/the night's surface, swerve/into graphs, hanging like crags in jagged lines:/—profound, perfect, and/not without meaning."

In spite of the rain and in spite of the stink, we are happy to be here, Beth and me, because the city is such an eyewash, such a visual change. On our way to meet a friend for lunch at a Thai place, we come within striking distance of another Kees bonus site, not unlike the former Hotel Albert, although he and Ann visited this one while they were actually living here: Saint Vincent's Hospital at 144 West 12th Street, a part of the structure that became the Jacob L. Reiss Pavilion in 1955, the year Kees vanished, six floors high and with a delicate view of the ornate white building across the street.

I jot in my notebook and Beth snaps away with her Nikon. She has begun a series, abandoned Christmas trees, since everyone appears to be throwing theirs away this week, dry and brittle at the curbside next to the NY RECYCLES bins. Saint Vincent's is the site where, when he and Ann were returning from a 1947 trip to the Cape, their car, an ancient Plymouth they named Tiresias, caught fire. "You should have seen Weld's blistered thumb," wrote Ann. It is the same place Dylan Thomas would die in 1953.

We have time, before lunch, for one more stop, Kees Site #5: 152 South 7th Street, at the corner of Charles Street near Sheridan Square. Kees had been writing for *Time* magazine, but in September of 1943, he returned from a week's vacation to learn that he—and several other men who seemed on the brink of being drafted—had been "suddenly canned." A pacifist, skeptical of the use of war of any kind, Kees had long been wary of what he saw as a patriotism that was frequently blind and mindless. "The men who were haters of war are mounting the platforms," he writes in "June 1940." "An idiot wind is blowing and the conscience dies."

There are still "United We Stand" signs and American flags all over the city, over five years after 9/11, and headlines call out from the newspaper bins about the deaths today—soldier and civilian—in Iraq, in Afghanistan. Donald Justice writes that Kees is "one of the bitterest poets in history," and that "the bitterness may be traced to a profound hatred for a botched civilization, Whitman's America come to a dead end on the shores of the Pacific."

Ann and Kees lived on 7th for only a month before they found a more "'commodious and quieter' place that would not shock Weldon's parents when they arrived from Beatrice for a visit in early October." In the meantime, Kees was "lovingly placed in classification 4F" by the selective service office, perhaps for "defects above the neck" or perhaps just because he was "a man with a slight build who said he wrote poetry."

Something about this place looks especially sad, romantic, and dilapidated, even in a neighborhood that today seems upscale, even though there is a Sawa Sushi on the ground floor and a store called Khazam, and jingling dogtags on purebred dogs, mammoth Escalades, and streamlined strollers with lattes in the cupholders pushed by skinny women clad all in black. There is a sex shop up the block called the Pleasure Chest. A bus pulls up and tourists throng, bundled up and doughy in their puffy jackets. Beth snaps away with her Nikon. "What the hell?" she says. "It's just a sex shop—it's not like there isn't a porn barn and a gentlemen's club by every truckstop in the U.S."

I wonder about the grim and dingy interior of the apartment when Kees lived here: "This is your familiar room,/With your familiar odor lingering and real,/The known disturbance in the hall,/Worn rug, the broken chandelier,/The flowered paper peeling from the walls." I wonder what he smelled like. Soap? Cigarette smoke? Brillantine? Despair and hope and tailored fabrics? There is a Charles Food across the street. I know Kees liked to drink, but what did he eat?

After we eat, Beth and I (sort of) locate the last Kees site—#6—that we'll see today. We head to Union Square to hunt for the "flophouse" where he flopped after another move in 1948, a furnished room where he and Ann stayed until they could fix up another, more permanent place, an old factory that they and another couple would renovate and share.

I lack an exact address, but regardless, this area, out of all the rest so far, must look the most changed, with its DSW, its Filene's, its Forever 21 and its Strawberry—with all its teenybopper clothing shops, shoe stores, and fast cafés. Beth doesn't know what building to photograph for me, so she stands in the center of the square at the base of a statue of a man on horseback and shoots 360 degrees, a circular panorama, just in case. There's nothing else to do, but stop at a Starbucks to pee before we hop the subway to a dive bar in the Financial District to meet more old friends, some from the city, some in from Jersey. As we do, I can't help but think of Kees doing that, not in a Starbucks obviously, but just peeing in general, just being alive. I like to think of him that way: alive.

At the same time, I wonder if I would love him the same if he hadn't vanished. All I know about him now is all I will ever know. I haven't learned anything about him that can make me stop loving him, and I am never going to. He can do no wrong. He is perfect in my mind, frozen in time, "one of the last great romantics," as a novelist friend, Anton Myrer described him, "who he genuinely believed that sensibility and talent would receive due recognition with time."

The death of a poet, I think—not just in a Lit Crit, death-of-the-author way, but literally, the fact of a poet's no longer being alive in the world—does not merely make that author's work *seem* better; rather it actually *makes* their work better. These details of the author's life and death are, like language itself, the material and the medium of which the work is comprised.

Well-respected dead poets, it seems, almost always enjoy a higher status than well-respected living ones. For instance, if you know that a particular poet is dead, you know, too, that he or she is probably not going to do something later that will embarrass you for liking them. Nor will he or she keep writing the same poem over and over so the impact is dulled. Nor will he or she produce work that is so obviously bad it causes you to question—and actually reduces—the value of earlier work.

By making all utterances more significant because of their finality, death—particularly death at one's own hand in the bloom of relative youth—gives poets the voice of authority, permitting them to say whatever they want. Ultimately, this power has to do with separateness, since separateness is part of the condition to which much of what we consider art aspires. If you as an artist intend to comment authoritatively on something—anything—you have the best chance of doing so from outside, free of all earthly entanglements. So you see, Weldon Kees is perfectly free, trapped though he often felt in what I know of his life.

The next two Kees sites, numbers 7 and 8, I locate alone on Tuesday. Beth has her appointments with photo editors today, so I take my own crappy digital camera with me after I help her find her first meeting and strike out solo. The rain has finally stopped and the weather's snapped cold, though it still doesn't feel quite cold enough. This is not the January Kees wrote of in a poem of that name, this is not a "Morning: blue, cold, and still" with "the wedge of light/At the end of the frozen room/Where snow on a windowsill,/Packed and cold as a life/Winters the sense of wrong/ And emptiness and loss." Hesitant snow falls from the low gray sky, the flakes like mistakes not confidently made.

I take the subway to the seventh apartment, 227 East 25th Street, the place Ann and Kees had to move when the correspondent from *Antiques* made it back across the sea in November 1943. Howard Nemerov tipped them off to the place, as he was apartment-hunting too with his new English bride. Working class and noisy at the time Kees arrived, this place was nearby the Third Avenue El when it still existed. Kees called it a "noisebox" and said it "combined the poorer features of Grand Central Station, Ebbetts Field, Bellevue and the Chatauqua Bell Ringers."

Today, the apartment—five stories, cream-colored, with enormous fire escapes—seems bustling yet tucked away, next door to the Ninth Church of Christ, Scientist. Trucks go by, lumbering and encumbered, impatient cabs behind them. A tattered wreath with a red bow still hangs above the entryway. Depressions in the sidewalk, wet with yesterday's rain, have begun to freeze around the edges. I love Kees and I love his poems for their revelations and incisive satire, and for the precision of his imagery and for the turns of phrase seem to me, cold and sharp: "Like spines of air, frozen in an ice cube."

I stand across the street and watch people come and go. Even if I could get inside, I still wouldn't know which apartment to look in. And I know that even if I did, I'd be as likely to see Kees as I would his character Robinson, his poetic alter ego. A dead man is just as absent—seems just as invented—as the man who never existed in the first place. "The mirror from Mexico, stuck to the wall,/Reflects nothing at all," writes Kees in "Robinson. "The glass is black./Robinson alone provides the image Robinsonian.// Which is all of the room—walls, curtains,/Shelves, bed, the tinted photograph of Robinson's first wife,/Rugs, vases, panatelas in a humidor./ They would fill the room if Robinson came in.//The pages in the books are blank,/The books that Robinson has read. That is his favorite chair,/Or where the chair would be if Robinson were here."

I walk down the street, past the American Academy of Pet Grooming, a psychic's, and a clutch of low colorful buildings with laundry hanging out the windows—red blue, yellow. I meet a friend for lunch in Koreatown, then head to Kees site #8, 31 East 30th Street, where Kees first lived, alone, in 1943, moving in from a room at the Chelsea Hotel. Separated from Ann at the time, he chose the spot because it was furnished, convenient, close to the Fifth Avenue offices of Russell and Volkening, his literary agency, where they let him use a typewriter. Now that I've seen this place, another shortish brick building, much like the others, there will be only two more spots left to locate.

Ultimately, my haphazard yearning to be where Kees used to be, to see what he saw, is unsatisfiable. None of these spots are the same as they were, or maybe they simultaneously are even as they are not. It's like that philosophical paradox, the Ship of Theseus: when Theseus returned to Athens having saved the Athenian youth and slain the Minotaur, the Athenians were so grateful, they kept his ship as a monument in the harbor. As the ship decayed, they replaced its planks, until none of the original timber remained. Was it still the Ship of Theseus? The whole city is this way. It *is* New York and yet it's *not*. I think of a fragment by Kees: "The ruined structures cluttering the past,/a little at a time and slow is best..."

Snowflakes fall like ash from a cigarette. I am blocking the sidewalk. I am in the way. I miss Beth and I want to tell somebody about what I've just thought, but none of these pedestrians gives a fuck about Theseus or Kees. Why should they? I take the subway uptown. I go to the Frick.

While I am there, looking at art alone, listening to the commentary on my audio-guide, I notice: one of the guards looks like Weldon Kees. Thin, slight, not much taller than me, his dark hair swept back, he wears tailored slacks and a uniform jacket. I keep looking at him in a way I think is discreet, but evidently isn't. He catches me staring so often, he comes over and asks if I need anything. I smile and say no, then he smiles back and asks if I have plans that evening because he gets off at five, and I say thanks, but no and extricate myself politely.

The next morning, Wednesday, we wake up early, the same time as Elise who has to be at work in the shipping department at Christie's by nine. When I peek out the curtain on the way to the shower, the sky is as clear and blue as a very blue sky. It is cold again, and finally feels like January. Beth and I have been and gone and done and seen until all that's left of our visit are two packed suitcases and one unmade bed, and a little trail of Kees site pushpins in my mental map of the city. There are only two left to stick in: one in Brooklyn and one kind of near Chinatown, which is where we are and where we're headed anyway, to catch the Fung Wah bus from lower Manhattan to the South End of Boston.

These last two stops will turn out to be the most arduous. We hug Tom and Elise goodbye, luggage in tow, as they lock the door behind us. According to my research, the apartment in Brooklyn was the place Kees moved after the East 10th Street sublet from the MacDonalds ran out. "This time they looked in Brooklyn Heights, since they had heard that the neighborhood, with its handsome brownstones, was quiet and affordable." Hart Crane had lived in the area "with a rooftop view of the span that inspired his long poem 'The Bridge'," a piece of Brooklyn trivia which Kees had liked.

Brooklyn Heights, though, we discover, is not especially easy to get to from Greenpoint. We take three trains, hike up and down a ridiculous number of stairs, go against the flow in the middle of rush hour, and have to ask a sweet old lady for directions, but eventually we get there. The neighborhood *is* handsome, full of brownstones and quiet, though as for affordable, we guess not anymore. Elise told us they used to film *The Cosby Show* here, and that looks about right: homey houses with prominent stoops. She said that movies were shot here too, that you'd walk by in the summer and see signs with various film companies' names and the message "Rain Machines Operating from ___ to ___" containing the dates.

Kees site #9—144 Willow Street, a beautiful structure on a street lined with Federal-style buildings—is now a residence hall for students of the Brooklyn Law School. Again, I don't know which apartment used to belong to him, but I do know that whichever one it is, it "was on a floor high enough for them to have a view of the harbor if they went out on the balcony," and that it had a living room big enough for the Knoll furniture they took out of storage, as well as for Kees' paintings and a small art studio.

It is so bright and so cold and so clear today that it is hard for me to believe that they—Kees and Ann, and even Hart Crane—were sad all the time. *Because they were not,* I remind myself. *Sometimes, they were happy.* Looking at this place makes me happy, too, and I wonder if these were the rooms about which he wrote "Late Evening Song": "For a while/Let it be enough:/The responsive smile,/Though effort goes into it.//Across the warm room/Shared in candlelight,/This look beyond shame,/Possible now, at night//Goes out to yours."

"Can we go yet?" says Beth, Nikon around her neck, rubbing her fingers in her fingerless gloves. "It's freezing out here."

She has a point, and we are running out of time to catch the bus we want, so we turn and head back the way we came.

We emerge one last time from the subway into the light of Canal Street in Chinatown, as close as we'll get to the one Kees site I wasn't able to find, the converted factory at 179 Stanton Street. Kees Site #10—the last place on my list and, fittingly, the last place in the city he and Ann lived before leaving in 1950—was, according to the biography, "in the 'lox and bagel section' of the Lower East Side, running just north of and parallel to Canal Street." But based on Mapquest and Googlemaps, I couldn't figure out how to get to the street easily that day—it was not parallel to Canal at all, it turns out, but further north and east, parallel to Delancey.

If the place were still standing, which I have reason to doubt, I might have seen that it was fifty feet long, with thirteen windows. The tenant prior to Kees and Ann and their friends the Myrers had been a designer who left nasty adhesives and modeling clay behind her. It took the two couples forever to get her junk down four flights of steep stairs. Even post-restoration, Ann called it "a 'barn' with 'practically none of the comforts of home except hot water and a toilet, but lots of windows which I count whenever I'm feeling depressed about the gallons of paint we slapped on this place." There was no phone, so Kees got his messages at the Peridot, his art gallery. That winter, from 1949-1950, seemed to both of them the worst of their lives.

As we walk along Canal, I picture the old factory as a place Kees felt, "Nailed up in a box,/Nailed up in a pen, nailed up in a room/That once enclosed you amiably, you write, 'Finished. No more. The end,' signing your name./Frantic, but proud of penmanship," where he felt "These rooms of ours are those that rock the worst./Cold in the heart and colder in the brain,/We blink in darkened rooms toward exits that are gone."

Kees and Ann made their exit from the city in such a hurry that when Ann remembered she'd left cookbooks in the kitchen of a friend, Kees refused to turn back.

Walking up Canal Street, wheeling my luggage behind me, I am not in a hurry, though I am excited about Boston. I am sorry to be leaving New York already, sorry too that this means I'm that much closer to having to go back to Tacoma. Beth and I stop at a crosswalk. There are two man-sized footprints, full of ice, in the cement at my feet: shoes, not boots, stylish and belonging to a smallish man. They cannot have been made by Kees, but I wish they could have, and I wonder if he ever stood here. I've seen so much, and yet I wonder if I've seen anything.

A woman pushes me from behind, gentle but annoyed, muttering something in Chinese, and I have to walk again. The light has changed. Beth is looking at me quizzically, saying "C'mon, you said it was this way, right?" I nod and say yes and we make our way to the spot where the Fung Wah buses stop, the ticket counter camouflaged in a row of Asian sandwich shops and stores with misspelled signs hawking cheap electronics.

As the bus lurches north, through Queens, towards Connecticut, we pass the distant site of the New York World's Fair of 1939, of which there is essentially nothing left: no more Trylon, no more Perisphere. Nothing but maps and souvenirs. After Boston, I'll fly back to my husband whom I love, in a town that I like, and a job at a place that I have come to hate. I have found some things here, but none of them holdable; "I have come back/As empty-handed as I went."

Note: The Weldon Kees poetry quoted in this essay is from T*he Collected Poems of Weldon Kees* edited by Donald Justice. The biographical information in both this essay and the following two poems is drawn from *Vanished Act: the Life and Art of Weldon Kees* by James Reidel and Weldon *Kees and the Midcentury Generation: Letters, 1935-1955* edited by Robert E. Knoll. The author is grateful to Justice, Reidel and Kroll, and to the University of Nebraska Press for publishing all three books.

Robinson Walks Museum Mile

Kathleen Rooney

the ideal city building itself in his brain.
Is this mile magnificent? He's lived here

a while, but the mile feels unreal. Robinson's
training himself to act blasé. Do museums

amuse him? Yes, but not today. Would he
like to be in one? Of course. Why not?

An object of value with canvas wings,
an unchanging face in a gilt frame, arranged—

thoughtless, guilt-free, & preserved
for eternity. Robinson doesn't want to *be*

exceptional. He knows he is. He wants to be
perceived exceptional. Trains plunge by, steam

rising from the grates. Sing, muse! of a man
ill-met at the Met. A man on his lunch break,

heading for a heartbreak, a break-up with *Time*.
A break-up with time? Feeling filled with ice,

the way you chill a glass, Robinson passes
the Guggenheim. He craves a sense

of belonging, not to always be longing. To be
standing in a doorway, incredibly kissable,

not waiting at the four-way, eminently missable.
Is this mile magnanimous? He wants it

unanimous: that this is his kind of town—
up & down & including Brooklyn. The sky

is clearing, but the isolation sticks.
Robinson's not sure what a camera obscura

is for, but he thinks he should have
his portrait done with one. Faces

blur by as he heads toward the Frick.
Something used to photograph the obscure.

After the Holiday

Kathleen Rooney

Dead tree after dead tree,
white curb after curb curbs

the vigor of the season,
Robinson reasons. January,

emissary of the year to come,
shines dull & dumb so far.

Who do others think you are?
Robinson wheedles, kicking

the needles of the pine re-
pining at his feet, reminding

him of the "Tree Menagerie"
on the grounds surrounding

his first college in Crete,
Nebraska, branches & leaves

replete with shapes: animal
& abstract. How to react

to the gothic middle west? To
the middle west grotesque?

The trees were not evergreen.
What did they mean & to whom

did they speak? Best to forget.
It hurts to think of them, hurts

to think of sly sex perverts—
bachelor professors, sweaty text-

book reps—who stepped up
to him then. Was it his communism,

frilly & pink? Was it his eyes,
sad & deep? The whys & where-

fores interest him less now, but
the roots tap at his soul, sole

proprietor of his parents' love.
Darling of their hearts, land-

locked in the heartland, posed
for Baby's First Christmas

in a tiny sailor suit. The halls:
decked. The walls: flecked

with light. An ornament falling
from the Scotch pine behind

him: out of focus, a cute
Icarus arcing through a life

of sub-normal calm. What
has changed since then?

Here, he is hailed, hailed,
hailed again—Hello, sailor!

Why this appeal? It doesn't
feel like it belongs to him.

Still, he'd like to keep it, lock
it up in a locket like a lock

of hair where it won't cause
worry. Sometimes he thinks

of himself, dark as a pocket,
scattered to the wind.

He should hurry home.
Yet even when hidden,

Robinson stands out. Gold
flashing at the back of a mouth.

Ancient History

Beverley Bie Brahic

1.

60 years after D-Day, over two weeks
washed with sunlight and occasional rain,
my father died quietly:
a small, civilian hospital.
Nurses and doctors deployed
their arsenals—ice chips, morphine—
swab, void. He must have felt fortunate,
though he never spoke of it, he survived
that war, much of it spent, the citation
tucked in his handkerchief drawer says,
"well forward," evacuating "casualties"
(from Latin *casus*—meaning chance,
meaning the less fortunate).
I sat at his bedside reading
long thin columns of crime, heartbreak
dropped on my doorstep each morning,
and some handfuls of sweet peas mother
culled each day in the garden
and set in a glass on the sill
alongside a plate of ripe apricots
we brought in—which day?—just in case.

2.

Waging war is safer now
"leaner faster surgical teams"
accompany the troops, "vehicles
fitted with sterile instruments,
operating tables," anesthesia
    and the
Deployable Rapid Assembly
Shelters—acronym DRASH—

nowadays, this writer says, “only”
1 wounded soldier in 10 will die.

I peep at the centerfold: spine
mashed by “a roadside device”—
nails, bolts and the “bones
of his assailant”—with “injuries
unsurvivable in previous wars”
this soldier won’t be “numbered
among the fallen” (I wince
at the sound bite of sanctity):

cobbled together like an old script
airlifted to mother—

maybe what Pericles meant
when he told the Athenians

heroes don’t need monuments
heroes have the whole earth for their tombs.

3.

I am reading at the kitchen table.
Now I lay the book on its spine.
I stir the apricots I bought for jam,
five kilos on the market this morning.

After the first season of the Peloponnesian War
wheat threshed, grain stored in silos,
grapes pressed to dark wine

the Athenians bury their dead.

Thucydides records their rituals

The bones of the dead laid in chests
of cypress wood
still smelling of trees

are borne to a monument in the finest part
of the city. A citizen—that first winter
they asked Pericles—delivers an oration

mourners bring offerings
the women come to lament...

How solid the world of the Athenians—I think—

I sample the thickening fruit
I skim the cane-sugary froth

as if it had all happened yesterday.

Hortus Conclusus

Beverley Bie Brahic

In the mosaic of the Last Judgement,
whose ochre flames and comic strip
perspectives light the dank cathedral
on Torcello, when the damned souls
gasp to the surface of their underworld
a crew of angels stands by with poles
to push them down. They bob
on ochre flames, like boat people. Demons
sting the jetsam heads.
Some purgatorial
levels higher up, Christ looks bleak.
His arms fly back as if to say
"Now what can I do?" Beside him Mary
holds out her hands beseechingly—
but mourning is her default mode.

I stand, one of the tourists fascinated
by the grotesque bodies of the damned. Hands
shield their private parts.

High up, the Blessed, with here and there
a finger raised, a bunch of keys.
Behind Adam, waiting to be judged
Eve cowers, tip to toe in scarlet—
elder daughter slapped for disobeying
the parent who said *just because.*
She keeps her plucky hands tucked
into her sleeves; or maybe—I think
fleetingly—maybe—were they lopped?
to teach the girl a lesson for daring
to dream beyond the garden walls.
My eye slips down the brightly glazed
chips of clay or glass—the *tesserae*—
across the blessed and to-be-blessed
(like a game of snakes and ladders)
to the tiny bodies tumbling
into the slick of oily flame.

Drunk in Bed with a Book about the Day the Music Died

Michael Hudson

It was as if God Himself had wadded up Buddy Holly's plane
and spitballed it hard

against the wire fence. For it was one of those *pissed off*

looking wrecks with everything: toothbrushes,
neckties, bodies, a guitar case, curled snapshots, a lone black

pointy cowboy boot, bent aluminum struts and
a punctured landing gear tire spilled out behind the fuselage—

A local farmer thinks he remembers hearing the *brrrraappp*
of it buzzing overhead with iced-over

wings, but probably not. Ice, booze, an almost teenage pilot,
wild rumors about the accidental

discharge of a .22 caliber pistol found a couple months later

in the thawed-out muck and stubble from last season's crop
five miles short of Clear Lake, Iowa—

It doesn't matter. It doesn't matter. It doesn't matter.

Feeling Sorry for Myself After Saying Goodbye to Heather

Michael Hudson

My heart, that old panhandler, shambles into traffic to get
to your side of the street, flashing a greasy

cardboard sign: *Nowhere To Go! Will Sing For Food.*

It's harmless. Off its meds, it thinks it has a cathedral
to limp back to, thinks it'd make a pretty

good hero despite the clubfoot and
crooked back. It believes there are bells to be rung, ropes

to be jerked. Lower the portcullis! Raise the drawbridge!

It whets the blades and fletches the arrows. It shoulders
a tub of scalding pitch to dump

on the Bishop's wicked minions. Doesn't the gypsy girl
need rescuing? She's huddled

in the nave, wet-haired and
fretting about her umbrella's busted rib. She's barefoot

on broken glass! There's hot candle wax *everywhere*...

Jesus. It drags its thick-soled orthopedic shoe off the curb
only to smear its filthy sleeve

across your windshield. Give it a dollar. Make it go away.

TRYING TO EXPLAIN THINGS TO SALLY TWENTY YEARS LATER

Michael Hudson

If you'd take the one-point-two percent of me that is *not*
chimpanzee what would you have? A dab

of something as big as your thumb, a wad of ganglia
too hot, too salty but bean-green, slick

with mucus and talking a mile-a-minute: a stump speech
for another big idea; or an elegy

composed on the spot for the sharks' teeth and broken

shells littering the beaches of Florida. Next, a theory
to cover the tumbled lion-colored plinths of

Asia Minor; something dazzling about the pyramids…

It rubs a hairy knuckle in its eye, this non-chimp part
of me, still trying

to wake itself up. What else? O what possibly else?

HOLY FEET

Renée E. D'Aoust

> "[Shawn] used to say that every American should have to stand naked in Times Square one day a year—then America would be a nation of beautiful bodies."
>
> —Mary Kerner, *Barefoot to Balanchine*

Ted carried a four-by-four foot Marley dance floor around New York City. The floor was made of heavy duty, slip-resistant linoleum. Rolled up, it looked like a yoga mat in a purple pouch, but the dance floor was much thicker and much heavier than a yoga mat. When the spirit moved him, or when someone pissed him off, he'd throw down his floor right in the middle of the sidewalk. People had to walk around him, or stop and watch.

Usually Marley floors were gray or black, especially the ones dance companies used for travel. Ted's floor was light brown. He took to wearing matching brown tights and a bicep-revealing T-shirt. He never put out a black felt Busker hat, or any hat at all, because he believed in donating his services for the general benefit of art.

What he did could be called education or craziness, depending on the movement or the place in the city. If he threw down his floor in Times Square, in the summer, his routine came across as free expression, part of the teeming mass of the city; if in Coney Island, in the fall, he came across as a man who missed his time in the circus.

Ted threw down his floor, and he moved his hips first. Forward, if someone made him angry. Side to side, if someone made him happy. The tights revealed all. Then he started moving his head in free form, a combination of wham-bam-thank-you-ma'am jazz and Isadora Duncan ecstasy, fantastical sideways and circular motions, around and around until it looked like the head—his head—started to fall off.

Isadora Duncan lost her head because she loved wearing long scarves. The red scarf with painted yellow autumn leaves and eighteen inch fringes on either end caught on the wheel spokes of the red convertible, an Amilcar, not a Bugatti, as others have written, her scarf trailing in the wind only momentarily, the brief moment of a life. Isadora's head was pulled back, fantastically wrenched into extension, and the world lost the other thread of modern dance. Ted loved that image. He often used it on the street.

After Isadora died, the focus concentrated on that other woman, Martha, and her ugly, staccato, contractions. Ugly is supposed to generate response—an emotional response in the viewer that makes one feel a wrenching in the gut similar to the wrenching felt in the dancer's gut. Without Isadora to breathe for the wind, dance lost its flow and musicality and ecstatic origins.

Ted had studied the Martha Graham technique. Briefly. He was too much the jester, the wisest one around, to succeed at Graham, but he could have played King Lear's fool. Of course, Martha re-interpreted the Greeks—not Shakespeare—and always from the point of view of the woman, the ugly woman. There was no role for Ted in her ballets, and he knew it.

When he first moved to the city from the Midwest, leaving his Lutheran collar behind, Ted had taken the Corvino ballet classes, religiously, starting his training with the father, who later became a ballet master for Pina Bausch Tanztheater, and continuing with the daughters. Ted still took a Corvino class every Saturday at 580 Broadway when a live pianist played for class. A live pianist is standard fare in NYC dance classes; without one, dancers do not show up. With his living room turned dance studio, Ted easily could have done all his training and rehearsals at home. But he didn't have a piano.

Ted aimed to bring back the ecstatic in modern dance. This was his new ministry. There was an aspect of God in everything he did, even if what he did wasn't successful. Ted throws his floor down on the sidewalk across from the Orpheum Theatre on Second Avenue; even though, he doesn't particularly like the show *Stomp*. He begins.

It doesn't really matter if there is an audience or not because in his former life he was a Lutheran minister. He always dreamed of being a modern dancer, though no one, including himself, is sure how he got the dream. Even his mother doesn't know. After he moved to the city, he didn't go to church again, but he did *pliés* and *grande pliés* every single day thereafter. Ted was taught to preach whether or not anyone showed up. God still hears your words, he was taught. This knowledge carries over into his new profession. Dance whether or not anyone shows up. God still sees your body move. Ted dances on a street corner and wiggles his hips and walks the square of his dance floor and stares out at the traffic on Second Avenue. Taxi horns and pedestrian footsteps become the musical score for Ted's dances.

Ted can't do any of the clown repertoire, so he pretends. He can't really walk a tightrope or a loose rope or down into a trunk or up into the moon. He can't really make us feel his loneliness; although, he tries, and often we do. But when people stop to watch Ted on the street corner, puzzlement masks their faces. They do not know what to think. Nevertheless, Ted is a performer. He notices the faces watching him. From Martha, he has learned how to stand still and command attention, so he does that for a while.

I imagine I saw him once, with his floor, on the sidewalk. I watch, without announcing my presence. It was long past the time that I had danced with Ted and Claire, long past the time that I'd injured my shoulder lifting Claire, long past the time I felt guilty when I didn't take daily class or do *pliés* in my studio apartment.

Ted takes a step forward, to the edge of the Marley dance floor, raises his arms overhead and juts his right hip out of joint. The graceful position of his arms is a distinct contrast to the distorted position of his hips. His aggressive expression, almost a frown, says, "This is my body. What are you going to do about it?"

Gradually an audience forms around him. Ted continues to step and thrust his hip left or right, moving his arms gracefully to Fifth position with each step. It could be an imitation of an ugly duckling learning to walk, out of his natural environment on a New York City street.

I thought there was a charisma about Ted, a poignant charm, and I was always transfixed by his focus. He was a force out of the sixties, out of place in nineties New York, a man out of step with his dreams.

Ted had legs that were well balanced and in proportion to the rest of his body. He had wide feet, with a good arch, because he had worked at it. His hands were as wide as his feet, and as expressive, and had he started dancing earlier there is no question he would have made it into a major company. Ted had forceful, strong movement, and he wasn't afraid to fail or to fall, occasionally throwing his body to the floor (or the street) with such force we would gasp until he broke his fall with his hands, lightly landing on them as if they were feet. He wore his brown hair alternately long, and free, or cut short, and proper. By the time I danced with him, he had a small balding spot on the back of his head.

Other dancers speak of him with awe. They are very impressed that he has taken dancing to the streets. Not through the program "Dancing in the Streets" with grants from the Lila Wallace Readers' Digest Fund, on various stages around New York City, but actually to the street itself, to different neighborhoods. Ted has freed his body. His mind no longer controls what is and isn't art. The other dancers in the company he and Claire formed, the Antipodal Dancers, are impressed. Modern dance is an elite art form, they know, and they applaud Ted's perseverance. They applaud him putting his body in other people's way, as if modern dance could be guerrilla theatre, as if modern dance could change the world, make it stop, make it take notice of the way we move through our lives.

It takes dancers to applaud the art of the street, but the pedestrians watching simply do not get what Ted is about. He isn't like that mime who pretends to be the Statue of Liberty, painted all green, and found at the South Street Seaport or in Times Square, depending on the day or the season. He isn't like the Latin dancer in the 42nd Street Station who dances with a lady puppet. He isn't like the Nude Cowboy in his tightie-whiteys and cowboy boots and cowboy hat. The reverent dancer Ted isn't like GhettoOriginal who moved their break dancing and hip hop from Columbus Circle into P.S. 122 and then on to the Victory Theater.

Ted is just a former minister without a shtick and with a love of moving and putting his body in people's faces. Maybe he should try wearing his collar when he dances.

Ted answers the question of whether dance is a young people's game or not. If we're trained in one approach and one aesthetic, we automatically blind ourselves to any other possibility. Liz Lerman Dance Exchange goes on and on, and her projects involve community, people who love to shake rattle and roll, people who want to express themselves, people whose thighs and tummies wiggle and shake when they dance. Who cares if one man's gesture is another man's death? We can tell when art is bad—when it doesn't fit our aesthetic—but can we tell when it is off-center?

Ted was off-center, some said past his prime, but who knew what his prime was anyway? He was preaching the gospel during his dancing prime. Maybe that was God's plan—to free him through his body. His pecs were strong; he could lift. I like anyone who can lift me.

Before Ted decided to take art to the people, he spent years performing with the Antipodal Dancers in the Antipodal Gallery in SoHo. We spent hours rehearsing in Ted's Park Slope apartment. He'd converted the living room into a dance studio with the same dimensions as the SoHo gallery in which we performed. The fourth wall was covered with a floor to ceiling mirror. The mirror was pretty good. It didn't distort much and even took a few pounds off of the thighs.

Ted had gotten a deal on the mirrors when American Ballet Theatre updated their Broadway studios above where Ted took class with the Corvinos. Ted had hired glass movers to do the job, and he said it was like how he imagined moving art, a delicate process made superstitious by the knowledge that in this case the art was glass.

At the same time, Ted had purchased the Marley floor from ABTII, which he rolled up at the front of the living room when we weren't rehearsing. Most dancers have very little furniture. Their living rooms are bare stage sets. There must be room to move, but even if you are sitting, there must be room to contemplate. If there is too much furniture, it is too hard to think. The body begins to feel crowded. The cells over stimulated. The mini floor Ted rolled up in a bag and carried around Manhattan came from extras of his living room turned studio floor.

‡ ‡ ‡

The whole troupe of Antipodal Dancers spread out on the floor, warming up. Ted didn't mind coffee cups on his Marley dance floor—it was an old one, particularly sticky—and I had a cup from the Two Little Red Hens Bakery. Each birthday, Claire bought a cake from there, and we ended rehearsal early to celebrate or mourn the passage of another year. In a dancer's life, the center cannot hold. Ellen, Ted's partner, and I had already started on barre, but Claire, the group's co-founder with Ted, still lay on the floor. She'd had a lot more Graham training than the rest of us, so it was even harder for her to get off the floor. She'd also studied a lot more ballet than I had, so once she realized she could dance lying down, she never wanted to do anything else. Claire's long brown hair was loose all around her. She had worn it clipped back for so long she said she couldn't trap her hair any longer.

Ted had built the barre Ellen and I now used. He worked as a carpenter for his day job. Ted's barre had the most solid construction of any since the one I'd used as a kid. When I was a kid and started in ballet, my dad had built a barre in the dining room, so I could practice on the weekends.

"Shall we begin?" Ted asked.

Always dancers begin formally with a polite request. It takes the edge off of the hard work. It doesn't lessen the sweat.

Ellen and I lifted the barre and carried it to the corner of the room. Claire put on the music. Ted took a position, and we sat in a semi-circle around him. He was the lead choreographer for this project; we, the women, were the chorus. We'd still develop the movement collaboratively, using Authentic Movement, and Ted would shape it, making the final decisions.

Ted's eyes closed. He began to move. He flexed his foot up and down. He flexed his hand up and down. We'd all agreed Ted needed a three-minute solo as part of the piece. It was a piece based on an oil painting of a red door. The solo would represent Ted walking barefoot through the door. The painting was called *New Red Door.*

"Keep going," Ellen said, encouragingly.

"Don't interrupt me," said Ted.

Claire had recorded Massenet's "Meditation" from *Thais* on loop, so it played over and over and over. The violin adagio relaxed me; I felt my eyes closing. I sat, straight backed, forcing my eyes to stay open, forcing myself to witness art in the making. It's a slow, tedious process, the making of art, but one must bear authentic witness to the movement of the soul. Otherwise, what's the point? Especially if, in the end, the audience doesn't get it. And often, the audience doesn't get it.

The next rehearsal, Ted asked us to sit in a circle before we started improvising.

"Listen," Ted said, "How would you feel if the costume for my solo was nudity?"

Ellen said, "Really, Ted, your mother is coming from Minnesota to see you dance for the first time. Like I said before, I don't think you want her to see you naked."

"As a baby," Ted answered.

"She probably has a good idea what you look like now," Ellen said.

"It's my coming out," said Ted.

"You're not gay," said Ellen. "It's not your coming out."

Occasionally at rehearsal, Ted and Ellen had to work out some aspect of their relationship. If Claire and I realized soon enough that the volley was about to start, we just kept quiet. Dancers are very good at not saying anything. Talk back, speak up, you get fired. Simple. You can only talk back if you're involved with some aspect of production.

"My mom is coming to see me dance for the first time. I want to be completely exposed when I dance for her," Ted said.

"Then dance for her, but keep your clothes on. Nudity isn't part of this piece."

"As I walk through the red door in the painting, I become my real self. Me. Naked."

"Naked isn't a costume," Ellen retorted.

"It's the original costume. God's finest work." Ted pointed to the ceiling. To God.

Ellen uncrossed and opened her legs. She leaned forward. "Look, this isn't the bully pulpit. It's a dance piece for a tiny art gallery in SoHo."

"All the more reason to show myself as I really am. My aesthetic demands loyalty to the principle of the piece. The principle is self revealed."

"You're talking like a dancer now. I have no idea what you mean." Ellen straightened her back, opened her legs on the floor to a wide second. Even for a dancer, she was incredibly flexible. She had trouble with her knees hyper-extending because of her flexibility.

"A naked body is a beautiful body. A naked body reveals the self," said Ted.

"So, we'll put it in the program notes, and you can keep your clothes on," suggested Ellen. She could be very practical.

"My costume is nudity. God's work."

"Your costume is a Lycra unitard. I'll make it a pretty color. Your naked forty-eight-year-old body belongs in the bedroom where your wang can flop around at your whim. Your flopping wang does not belong in your mother's face."

"It does if it's part of the piece."

"And if it's not? What do you lose?" asked Ellen. "Nothing. What do you gain? Your dignity, for Chrissakes."

"Don't take the Lord's name in vain," said Ted.

"Don't be gratuitous in your mother's face," said Ellen.

"Look, you're just saying that I don't have a Pilobolous body, so I shouldn't go naked."

"You don't have a Pilobolous body," said Ellen. "I don't see you dancing for that company. Second of all, last I looked we call ourselves the Antipodal Dancers."

Claire reached over and pressed the pause button on Massenet.

"I'm talking about the integrity of the piece," said Ted, softly.

"I'm talking about your mother sitting and watching your wang flop around, which is exactly what will happen without your dance belt. She'll look away so she doesn't have to look at the flip flopping, which will be completely out of time to the music, and everyone else will look away, too."

Claire and I avoided looking at each other. Dancers are very good at not looking at each other when rehearsal becomes stressful. They are very good at the art of control, at not showing what they are thinking. Tabula rasa—a beautiful blank body.

"David Parsons went nude," Ted said.

"Come on, if you had that body, you'd go nude, too."

"You're such a prude," said Ted.

"No, I'm not," said Ellen. "I have a point. Your member will flop around out of rhythm, and it will be distracting. Your dick won't keep time to the music unless you hold it. And that would be disgusting."

"I'll wear my dance belt. Naked otherwise."

"I'm listed as the Costume Designer on the program. You'll wear your goddamn unitard. It shows everything you've got anyway, for Chrissakes."

"Don't take the Lord's name in vain."

Ellen got up and walked into the kitchen. We could hear the tap running. She came back and stood at the side of the room with a glass of water. Ted turned to Claire and said, "Music. Again. I must dance."

He began to dance, to explore with his eyes closed. Slowly he took off his T-shirt, took off his brown tights, it was hard to keep dancing as he did it, and then he stopped and opened his eyes.

"Oh God," he said. "Naked isn't part of the piece at all."

Ted stood in his dance belt, his legs together, his hands on his thighs, and he began contorting his face, opening and closing his mouth, and started chewing, slowly, then quickly. It's a popular exercise to warm up the instrument, all this face scrunching, especially for actors, but on a dancer it looks odd. Ugly. The continuation of Martha Graham, but a post-modern Martha, one who no longer makes any sense, whose center has not held, whose tide is unleashed upon the world, and whose proprietor is over the hill, but still one with the dance. A soul without the instrument. A body old before its time.

The Antipodal Dancers made movement based on art installations, and like most small modern dance companies, we had a five-year shelf life. Then everyone moved on. Claire had children. Ellen started scuba diving. I went back to college.

But Ted kept dancing. He started carrying his purple pouch around Manhattan, throwing down his dance floor, and standing still or moving his hips, depending on the ministry needed. God continued to speak to him, but through circular, ecstatic motions, through the language of the yogis, through the language of his body.

STARTING UP AGAIN

Michael Patrick O'Connor

1.

There was a day bore no aspect
took no beauty though it yielded.
I stood in the camp. I lay
on the ground. I put the letter
over my chest. Continents drift
around islands to search out straits.

That is not enough for what we mean,
foam on the dirtiest shore
of a homeland. The raids have not
had any effect but neither
then has anything else.
When we say home we mean dirt.

The violence was never so close
before. It is what comes after fit
while reclining in new nerves.
Perhaps the place will change itself
the crime become another place
where you can't get in for love.

Poke around the leaves looking up
old options. Around that corner
what you do will be enough.
Up a street, old movies, gardens,
dirty tricks: you can't see what you're
looking for ever in this weather.

2.

The lights keep the thorns a kind
of company in the bungalow.
The day began with vagueness. This here.
That over there. Not like
reverence for good technique
or snakes but as we used say:

Whatever, wherever it can go
given a lack of limits
and the chat always Why not?
if something so long and quiet
is a chat and not a monologue
whatever speaking stillness.

Nothing more than that happened
until there was too much
for nothing more. More added itself.
Kissing the ground, wrapping yourself
nights considered grand enough
for pastels. That was easy.

More added itself. The thorns make up
the day's new start. The rose
you can have for the time you can
hold it. This here, that over there
is thorn enough to find you out
below where you always seem to be.

3.

There are going to be differences
starting up again here.
We will have held them off
too long. Their commerce will have
sought our nerves, years taking on
turns that the earth offered us.

We revolve under similar stars
islands seeking in the crust
levels that do the slightest harm.
We revolve under similar stars
unities to be observed
in a future mind and recreated.

On a day that falls between
two stools and destroys
flowered lampshades, secular
means the centuries running
across our face to the restoration
of rivers we failed to observe.

But now we say year for tomorrow.
It is the prepositions
will change to fill out all
the unfinished thoughts. Up and down.
In and out of dirty straits.
Far and away and very near.

4.

Why is there never enough
catching ourselves up to see
that the law of lease does not apply
in spring, the perfect antique thorn
bleeds every antique life?
Things get taken apart again.

What comes disassembled comes
to look like things instead of parts.
The romance of suicide and old age:
feeding sparrows with hay for horses.
The power of performance spreads
to sound like will itself did once.

The skin remains intact.
The hour passes soon a way
across the sea, around and up.
Not because it comes with ease.
It will not: soon enough
we will get the arms and legs.

It comes of us as praise in silence
of ambition (enter with speed
the solitude of places
past the pain) and strength and fear
still too loud to pass
the loving fake it's meant for.

5.

So much depends on what we mean
but starting up again here.
The little we know is precious
and who ever claimed revelation
came from blowing flowers
and sucked-off slips of willow?

Absence of doubt, a weighty term
to be heard from at so great
a remove moves the weaver
to thread again out of mind.
No local language uses proof
the strength of investure.

Out of sight in winter sun
we come ahead of one another,
miss having enough to remember.
The murk descends or we do
the sound of fingers set on what
we need to want to wait for.

It is filling higher chambers
rising leftward endlessly
and it leaves us here alone
so utterly so soon in spring
neither love nor a better machine
could cause this cot to pay a way.

6.

There are moves with the day
that air demands and night deserves.
The grass round the tar
has claims to make that want
a nod or the time and go on
wanting as others play.

What is left of old shifts
as if spring were fall, as if
to spring meant he had to fail
in their gaze and so he did
falls itself and the bounce is there
as if the lights could care.

The defense he makes of himself
is less than the circus his nerves
mean to mean for his body
laying up light for moving on.
Without the ball bones bear
marrying flesh wanting instruction.

The pleasure here is the pleasure
of cooking, nothing to bend
or tug at or love. Round and round
and the walls close up where they can.
We know what we saw. It is enough
for the spirits of the dead.

7.

We need to learn what it is
we're supposed to be saved from.
First of al, water, in all
the shapes it has or steals
and like art in the blood it is
liable to take the strange ones.

And art. And unless we oversimplify
and call it water, blood
on the tracks, behind the eyes
under pressure and underground.
The violence is not so close
that art can be told from water:

Snow on the day after spring starts,
incredulous snakes looking for frogs
to render with their venom
teaching aids for hopelessness,
students of use and form and time
in a landscape of withering grass.

They lack the flocks to leave them
alone. That is their problem.
Here the problem is circulation.
The breeze enters hither but yon
is only a wall to restrain
masses and motions we called for.

SUR LA MER

Robert Bense

Still a dark tumult of sky
like the falling arm of
each morning's metronome.
Heavy clouds startled to storm
the bronze marechal's prancing
statue stuck square in a square
—though he died
it's said by some
wizened old in bed—
wind's sideblast of rain washing
him to leaden blue:
I'm here with the summer French
looking for their pagan past. Also
for the Tribune, a cup of coffee.
There are forced smiles on
the yellow, pink facades.
This is not Italy—
the sunny, chatty gulls.
Some summers Proust came to
visit, no one now remembers
after his grandmother's death, after
Combray, the shadow scenes
he wanted grey.

Making Sense of Where

Robert Bense

In December dusk a light
across the water
winking its obscure knowledge
turns up the volume.
A parade stops at the edge.
Backlit silhouettes stepping
out into a single file—
the lives I've helped myself to.
Their secrets I've lifted
like candy. A man
I never saw even once.
The first woman whose
skin I ever touched.
Winter! silence coughs.
Now in overcoats—the lives
return to their vanishing.
It's cold enough to go.
Wind already in the tamarisk.
Powder of snow
on the orchard grass.
Yet who would want to leave—
breathless now, details forgotten?
Arriving somewhere else afraid.
And where everything is known.

FLORENTINE GOLD

Robert Bense

Those freighted visits, the Splendor
Hotel, Florence itself now elegy
the Orto fenced behind tall gates
Diana hunting across the ceiling
putti holding down
corners of the night
when at last we looked up
I at the end of summer
the long drapes sucking in air
you choosing a blue peignoir
after the long visits to love—
like our limbs, our forms
gone shapeless—
like leaves treading water
water pooling, through the fog
a mist remembered, and with it
exorbitant nights, the cost
in summers.

TROUBLED BY THUNDER

Allan Peterson

Crickets are opening their room dividers.
Colorful gasses of morning float in like good-for-nothings,
voices upturned at the end like questions.

It's crazy to think you can confront anything without presumptions,
even this, in which no people, o one or two, remind you,
no, that sort of thing only happens at the lower levels of organization.

Take for instance how the forming of the stove pipe cloud
over Long Island means trouble for something small,
how grumbling has already begun, with lightning the resolution

of differences melted in a sudden explosion. Plain description turns
into substance by continued attention and when prophecies fail
because the oracles grow old and forgetful we fail to notice.

Who are the seers. Who sees for them. Now the cloud is a table
the county can sit around. From here on this is a long story,
and no way of making a long story short.

MESSAGE

Allan Peterson

A sign for what can happen when one is several things at once.
Not mere decoration but a fierce sun in the necklace of bear claws
that shines around his shoulder. Head symbolically on fire.
The rays speak for themselves but uses the face of Walks-Quickly.
Or they are teeth so his head appears in the mouth of a beast about to bite down.
Fearful but not unknown. Nothing can be done about that.
Rather the common around it must be discovered as it must with a stick crack
whether an animal is deciding itself away or a man sneaking up.
If fire among the hearth-stones gives birth to animals dancing on tent walls
or they were there all the time and *they* allow fire to let them be seen.
Each time he raised his arms his head must have roared out or glowed.
The message in the photograph now dead though his eyes yet to be closed:

> *I am living in danger more than ever. I am standing in grass*
> *so new it is practice grass. My knees are believeable*
> *because they don't move in the face of Crawls-like-Shadows.*
> *I think rain tries to speak clearly but its hand is over its mouth*
> *its eyes under water. Listen how wind in trees is a car in your driveway.*
> *What they've told you so far is lies*
> *Live to tell about it.*

At Tlalocan with Yma Sumac

Brian Swann

From my window more windows, more frames,
no blue, just glass, cordoned, confined, and reflections
of blue and sometimes white or gray, and when night comes
it makes everything night, sucking up any color and turning it
splotchy, yellowish, in patches, to go with the black that keeps
building up and slipping off in flakes like skin, and behind
the glass people watch TV's unearthly light and dream. Or not,
or do things, or not, like working out on a treadmill
that doesn't really work and jerks along, and stops, though
why I imagine a treadmill I don't know. Maybe I should have them
doing yoga, except nobody round here does yoga unless maybe it's
Octavio Paz, and he's dead, or unless it's because I write
fast with a pencil that goes where it feels like and treadmill means
something special to it, like this famous Swiss writer I read about
who used "the pencil method," its rhythmic flow, the rhythm
of reverie, the "unique bliss" that calms you down and
cheers you up, slipping over the page's white ice,
cutting figures you had no idea you knew or even knew
were there, and that's how they found him after he'd
gone insane, frozen in a field, cutting his own figure
on his back, sprawled in the snow, all he had to
fall back on, eyes wide open as if still trying to see,
mouth agape, as if still forming a phrase, though the hand
that held the pencil was a claw, like Big Foot's at Wounded Knee,
his world gone with him forever, taken, never to return,
the world where everybody talked, animal, tree, stone, us,
as easily as the way birds slip through air, expand and link the air,
make it thin enough to move through, thick enough to glide on,
where you can see further and further even when you know
so little and can say even less with hands stiff from rheumatism
and a right metatarsal thick from gout, punishment for gluttony,
double comic because I eat little. I wonder: When
you're reborn from this place are the hands healed
and is the big toe and the other parts reborn like a baby's,
cool and placid as the swans that swim like clear ideas on the lake?
"Can anything satisfying be found on earth?" sang the prince

Nezahualcoyotl, which sounds a bit petty for one who had it all.
"Wait it out, señor," said the doctor when I told him I couldn't pay.
"This too will pass." Pretty good advice, I suppose, that fits
about anything, one way or the other, even here in Tlalocan in the rain
where the buses from the springs of Chapultepec and all points beyond,
red, black, white, blue, pull up and let out the various
drowning victims, those with legs and ankles swollen with dropsy,
fellow hobblers with gout and those lightning struck down
on mountainside and golf course. If you photographed this place
in the valley, aside from the willows and waterbirds, the accustomed
and conventional green corn, squash, sprigs of amarynth, green chiles,
tomatoes, string beans, flowers and quetzal plumes, you'd get
a foamy effect, like detergent, a glittering like fishscales, a flickering
like fireflies on water thick and opaque as isinglass. And if the camera
could run backwards to before I even got here it might also show me
planning at least in my mind to train eagles to hunt iguanas
in the Sierra Madre after I'd counted on the draft to be a hook
to snag on, catch me falling, except the board made me 4F, or later
after the one review of my only novel to date, the one that said
my characters (which I'd carefully drawn from life) were like
fairy-tale creatures whose world had ended and who couldn't cope
with "the real world." "Real world"! But it might also catch me
arriving here because I'd heard that the wondrous liquid
Yma Sumac was from these parts and I wanted to get to know her
in her natural habitat. It turned out, however, that she was either
an Incan princess, as she said, or Amy Camus from the Bronx,
as the papers said. And in any case, she wasn't from hereabouts
and I haven't met her, yet.

REFLECTIVE

Brian Swann

To imagine a language is
to imagine a form of life. I imagine
a life of quotes since *there is no new thing*
under the sun so how
does it matter much if dying's only
a quote, a turn with words, part of an order
which is only a
paradigm of thought , of numbers,
a world of ranked earth, water & sky
with all sorts of helpers
in the after-world, androgines
with wings, others with a hand for a tail
& so on, analogies
& recombinations in a world held up
by trees, one to a corner, for words are
the pleasure of what you
imagine so you can then believe,
& then choose to spend your time e.g.
(a) sporting in the
Gardens of the Sun, sipping
flowers, returning when ready or (b) there
are too many (b)s
to count but we know the way to
make everything cohere into coherent
mirrors & better ways
of going into the dark so vivid
it can be thought of as light. So bright it
cancels itself out
the way soul can be thought of as
excess of being & the dark itself excess
of light, a blinding blackness,
vastness moving into vastness,
the dark beat of el oscuro corazon
where stars swim &
the moon reflects & we measure time
with *fictive music* since earth's so much of

the things we are &
the self self-consumed is trapped behind glass
like a *sunflower crazed with light* , when the iridescent
peacock-blue flowers of the magnolia
hang onto euphoria hanging over
the gulf & shining back on us with some heat
for *how can one be warm*
alone, defective & unrhymed?

The phrases in italics are from, in order:
—Ludwig Wittgenstein, *Philosophical Investigations,* 19, p8e.
—*Ecclesiastes, 9.*
—J.M.Coetzee, "On Zeno", *Diary of a Bad Year:* "The order we see in the universe may not reside in the universe at all, but in the paradigm of thought we bring to it. The mathematics we have invented (in some accounts) or discovered (in others) which we believe and hope to be a key to the structure of the universe, may equally be a private language...with which we doodle on the walls of our cave."
—Wallace Stevens, "To the One of Fictive Music".
—Ibid.
—Eugenio Montale, "Portami il Girasole".
—*Ecclesiastes,* 4.

PARIS

David Black

"Guy asks me, can I do a somersault," Paris said. "A somersault? I says. You know, he says, you put your head between your legs… If I could put my head between my legs, I told him, I wouldn't've been married three times."

Paris is a hooker who used to work out of the Belleclaire Hotel on West 77th Street, the 20th Precinct. I'd met the detective she was talking to—Diogenes Nunez—when I'd written a book about a murder at the Metropolitan Opera. Occasionally I'd ride around with him, doing research for *Law & Order* episodes. Sometimes I'd pick up a useful detail—like frying up coffee grounds to kill the stench of a ripe corpse; the following year, cops on three other shows were frying up coffee grounds—or some dialogue. Like what Paris told Nunez, which I've put into half a dozen scripts—which the networks have taken out every time.

When I met her, eight years ago, Paris was in her late-thirties. Claimed to be from upstate. Hudson. Near where I go in the summer, which became a kind of bond between us.

"You ever go to the Sunset Drive-In?" she asked me. "Across the river? Over in Coxsackie? I saw *Waterworld* there."

Six years later, when they found her half-scalped, one of the other detectives from the 20th said, "I didn't even recognize her with her hair pulled back like that. She was good-looking."

"Took the good citizens of this city six hours to call us," Nunez said. "She was lying in the hallway. They were stepping over her to get to their mailboxes. Head wounds… Right in the door, you could smell the blood."

When I first met her, there was something off about her face, like a broken china plate that's been crazy-glued together: A chip missing here, a seam not quite aligned there. But, when she smiled, you smiled, too—as if you were a mirror into which she was looking.

"The worst part about this business," she once told me, "is, outcall, when you ring the buzzer to the guy's apartment and he opens the door and you got like a second to decide whether or not to go inside, whether or not he's a psycho…"

"How often do you pull the plug?" I asked.

She shrugged.

"Never. They're all psychos…" Then she smiled—that wonderful smile: "You want a guarantee, buy a toaster."

The day I met her, we were driving around the Upper West Side, just cruising. Nunez was in a bad mood. He'd been called in on his day off to cover for some co-workers who hadn't shown.

"Bunch of humps," he said. "Seventy-percent of the detectives take the day off for the Sergeant's test. I'm left holding the bag."

When he spotted Paris coming out of H & H bagels, he pulled up beside her, leaned across me, and called out to her through the open window. She came over, leaned down—her hair smelled like cherry soda, some kind of shampoo—and held out the bag, a dozen bagels she just bought.

"Onion," she told Nunez. "I got two onion. I know you like onion."

"You know I'm trying to lose weight," Nunez said.

"That's what happens when you stop walking the beat," she told me. "Detectives… Bunch of humps," she echoed what Nunez had just said.

Nunez asked her about one of the junkies in the Belleclaire—it sounded like *Gedde Mongstab*—an East African.

"In Eretrian," Paris told me, "*Gedde* means *good luck*."

"Yeah," Nunez said. "Good luck to this guy… The first anti-crack ad they put on TV, it said something like: *Crack. Do it once, you'll sell your grandmother to do it again.* And Gedde goes: 'Man, it's *that* good!' He runs out and buys some."

"He's okay," Paris said to me. To Nunez, she said, "This gonna take long. It's cold. And I ain't got my panties on."

"Get in the back," Nunez said. "I'll turn up the heater."

She got in the back. He turned up the heater. I rolled up the window. In the closed car, the cherry shampoo was stronger.

"I don't make you for a cop," she said to me from the back seat. "You some reporter? Gonna put me in the newspaper. Make me famous?"

"He's a writer for that cop show," Nunez said. "You know…" Nunez made the *ta-dum* sound that separates the scenes of *Law & Order*.

"Oh, yeah," Paris said.

"He doing research," Nunez said.

"That young cop, on the show, North—"

"Noth."

"He's hot," she said. "Bring him around, I'll give him all the research he wants."

"So," Nunez said. "Gedde."

"What's he done?" Paris asked.

"It's what he maybe isn't doing," Nunez said.

"Like breathing?" Paris said.

Nunez shrugged.

"You seen him around?" he asked.

Paris shook her head *no.*

"But then I'm not looking," she said.

"I thought you and him..." Nunuz raised two fingers together, indicating they were close.

"Yeah, well," Paris said, "when I was broke and he wasn't..."

"What'd you do?" Nunez asked. "Close your eyes and trust God?"

"God's one thing," Paris said, "hygiene's another."

Nunez shook his head. "I thank God every day He made me an atheist."

We'd been circling the neighborhood, Nunez clocking everything—who was selling books on the sidewalk, who was loitering in doorways, who was sprawled on the bench on the median, face tilted up to the sun.

"What a bunch," he said... "The Homicide Squad used to have caps, baseball caps, that said, *Our day begins when your days ends...*"

"Not *my* day," Paris said.

Nunez reached back. Paris held up the bag of bagels. He fished one out. Poppyseed.

"You want onion?" Paris said.

Nunez shook his head.

"Some days I can't taste the difference," he said. "They're all the same."

"I know what you mean," Paris said.

"It's tough to be a gunslinger," Nunez said.

"Those Clint Eastwood movies?" she said. "*The Man With No Name.* I'm the woman with no name." To me: "Twenty-four, twenty-five years I've been singing for my supper. Not once, not one time, no date ever, *ever* remembered my name."

"What the fuck difference does it make?" Nunez said. "It's not your real name."

"You're going up the stairs, you trip, guy says, *You okay, June-bug?* On the way down, you trip, guy says, *Clumsy whore.*"

"The Theory of Relativity," Nunez said. "Einstein got that one right."

"*They* can be stinky as ground round left out for a week," she said. "But me? I don't floss regular, they're on my case." To me: "Date I had last night—guy has the ninety-proof flu—could barely stand up. But he complains because he thinks I need a haircut."

"You talking south of the border?" Nunez said.

"Bite me," Paris said.

"So what else you got for me?" Nunez asked.

Paris ignored him. Turned to me:

"Girlfriend of mine, she used to say, *When I see a gutter, I see my bed.* Forget it! I'm saving up to buy this house in Nyack."

"Here it comes," Nunez said.

"What? I'm going to hustle a trick in a cop car?" Paris said.

"Don't give her your phone number," Nunez told me.

"I'm just saying," she said, "maybe your friend needs someone like me on his show."

"So now you're an actress?" Nunez said.

"I can be whoever you want me to be," Paris turned to me. "What do you think I do every night."

"On camera?" Nunez asked.

"I got friends do movies," she said.

Nunez nodded at me, said:

"He doesn't do that kind of movie."

"That's why TV sucks," Paris said. To me: "You want a big audience, consider it."

"Gedde," Nunez repeated.

"Screw Gedde," Paris said. "I see him again I'll punch the bitch so hard he'll see birds and stars, Looney-Toon land."

"Yeah," Nunez said. He reached for another bagel. "Onion," he said. Satisfied. "When's the last time you had a real meal?" he asked her. We were passing Happy Burger. "Best hamburgers in the city," Nunez said. "You want me to get you a Happy Burger."

"How long you know me?" Paris said. "You know I don't eat meat."

"Not off hours," Nunez said. And gave a dirty laugh.

"I'm a vegan," she told me.

Nunez wiped bagel crumbs and onions off his jacket and shirt. "This stuff's like puppy shit," he said. "All over the place."

We passed the OTB parlor.

"Know what we should do," he said. "Shoot out to Belmont. Catch the last race. Hey—" To Paris. "You want to take the afternoon off, go watch the ponies?"

"Is that before or after we club the baby seals?" she asked. "I support PETA," she told me.

"Kind to animals," Nunez said. "You got to be in her business."

"You bet," she said. "I kill my father a little bit every day."

"Who's Gedde hanging with?" Nunez asked.

"Who?" she said. "Who?" To me: "The people I know don't have names, only nicknames."

No matter how many times Paris evaded the question, Nunez kept cool.

He's trying to wear her down, I figured. Or maybe it's just their dance.

To Nunez, she said: "I told you, I haven't seen him."

Nunez glanced at her in the rear-view mirror. She scratched her cheek. Scratched her neck. Scratched the top of her head.

"He's probably out with the other poor bastards," she said, "slugging rats for a living."

Nunez shrugged.

"Life is full of broken glass."

"And me with no shoes," she said. "Life's tough for everybody. One of my regulars, he went home one day with his underwear on backwards. So his wife wouldn't be suspicious, he had to wear it backwards for two months."

Again, Nunez shrugged.

"You gotta get your gotta gets," he said.

"Hey, Nunez," Paris said. "All the girls wonder about you. How come you never get your gottas?"

"You never asked me nice," Nunez said.

"I'm not in the resurrection business," she said.

"Some day, when things are slow," Nunez said, "I'll put you on my dance card."

"Don't thrill me," she said.

"Why not?" Nunez asked. "I make you laugh."

"So does Kermit the Frog," she said.

"Well?" Nunez said.

Paris smiled: "I don't do frogs."

Nunez smiled. Like a shark.

"I know, I know," Paris said. "Gedde."

"Yeah," Nunez said, checking her out in the rearview again. "Gedde."

"What if he's dead?" Paris said.

"You asking or telling?" Nunez said.

Paris didn't answer.

"Life is full of *what ifs*," Nunez said.

"Sometimes," Paris said, "I wonder how much longer do I have. Ten? Fifteen? Twenty years? My business, sooner or later, outcall, incall, you go on a date and open your arms to the guy with the scythe. Sometimes I figure why not die just to get over the suspense."

"A tag on the toe?" Nunez said. "Better another nose ring."

A guy at the Korean market on Broadway at 93rd Street was pouring a bucket of fresh ice on the plywood stand holding clear plastic containers of watermelon chunks. Paris watched him raking the ice smooth with his fingers.

"Life is fine," she said to no one in particular. "When you been on your own since fourteen, you make it fine."

"Amen to that," Nunez said.

"You taking me in?" she asked.

Nunez studied her in the rearview.

"You're looking at the body," she told him. "You should be looking at the eyes." To me: "Fourteen, I get this big chest. So from then on, guys talk to me, their gaze drifts down. Someday I'll meet a guy and his gaze won't drift."

"Prince Charming," Nunez said.

"He busts me," Paris told me, "because he knows he'll never get a freebie and he's too cheap to pay."

Nunez glanced at me.

"I hate toll roads," he said. "I go on a trip, I take local roads."

"Back roads," Paris said. To me: "He couldn't handle it." To Nunez: "You'd waste your money." To me: "What I do, he couldn't handle… Full moon sex. *Star Trek* sex: Dare to go where no man's gone before."

"You're too skinny," Nunez said. "Making love to you would be like fucking a bicycle."

"That's the lick that killed Dick," Paris said. "Pull me in or pull over."

Nunez stopped in front of H & H. We'd made a full circuit of the neighborhood.

"You hear anything about Gedde," he told her, "you give me a jingle."

"You'll be the first to know," Paris said, getting out of the back seat.

"What they say about women," Nunez winked at me. "They break your balls or they break your heart."

Paris stopped half-way out of the car. "Don't worry, Nunez," she said. "I'll never break your heart."

After she left, I asked Nunez about Gedde.

"Smoking coke, guy goes gray," Nunez said. "She's partying with the poor bastard. He's run out the clock. No more rubles. So it's time for her to pull up her panties and go home. But she sees how he's sweating. A walking heart attack. So she says to him: *You got someone you can call? Someone who can come get you?* Gedde says he's got a sister in Queens, Astoria, somewhere. Paris says, okay, call her. She'll wait. She's got no reason to stay. Every reason to split. Cause if he dies with her there, she's looking at hard time. But she stays. And stays. The sister is a no show. Paris calls nine-eleven. But Gedde dies. And some winnie-wagger down the hall tells the EMS she was there."

Nunez shook his head.

"What do they say? No good deed goes unpunished. The El-tee tells me, talk to her. Find out if she's got an alibi. The whole nine. So I talk to her. No one said nail her to the cross."

We'd started circling again. Nunez was checking out the guys in the doorways, the money-for-bindle handshakes, the mooks and the floaters...

"It's all a rehearsal anyway," he said. "The show doesn't start until much later..."

A GIFT OF MAGNOLIA

Margaret B. Ingraham

> An image is "that which presents an intellectual and
> emotional complex in an instant of time."
> —Ezra Pound

As we study Pound—
poetry of another century—
I ask my students if they understand
his definition, and pointing to the gift
one of them brought, inquire what,
if any, such a complexity this common
southern blossom might present.
While they seem to ponder quietly
I am convinced they can perceive
magnolia as something more than flower
but their uneasy silence makes it clear
"instant" means a wholly different thing
through the lens of their chronology,
that they see time as nothing more
than a succession of numerals flashing
across a liquid screen, something
that they must bide impatiently
until the next dismissal bell.
As they wait for that reprieve
in status, where I stand in the midst,
I sense the consequence
of their uneven exchange
of "instant" for "immediate,"
immediatus, that is, the nothing there—
that loss of the time and space between
the then and now, the only place
for image and its nuances to reside.
The sun has moved through afternoon,
low light falls at right angles
across my desk toward the bloom
whose creamy tone is easing into beige

as petals catch its pollen in their cups
and ageless fragrance of magnolia,
for an instant, assuages my concern
as it awakens the whole room.

Il Faut Aller Voir

Joe Francis Doerr

I remember the sea and the salt on my lips,
Odysseus in my head & biceps,
and you, my Penelope, patient on a beach towel;

Calypso, too, confederate with twilight,
arranging diversions on a boat
from St. Tropez,
her argent kisses hidden
by the hand you curled against your smile.

Ocean and horizon, the almost nothing
in between: archetypal triptych
for our couched *ménage a trois.*

I held you at the Citadel,
still wish you'd bought the hat
you wore so well,
remember our nakedness
and the breeze beneath umbrella pines,

found a sign
in the stone relief:
the saint who lost his head

for love,
patron only of his own
fortuitous landfall's end,

and places
he now occupies—
tripartite, their soliloquies.

But for headless saints and *grand chapeaus*
this world is sadly lacking.

And if not for you, my love, chameleon I
would find no joy in changing.

But of missing heads and changing hats
and of saints with many lovers:
I'm out of one, one's off to you,
and I fly the other's colors.

—For Mary

Tocayo

Joe Francis Doerr

> *Come, all ye tribes of serpents and foul fish!*
> *Beetle and worm, I have a feast for you!*
> —Alistair Crowley

The first strains of *Tannhäuser* made by a Sawzall—
Specifically B/E/B/G#—before
Ascending into approximations of whale song,
Ground their way through a stubborn length of rebar
On that *Miércoles de Ceniza*—
Consequently I
Rejoice[d], having to construct something upon
Which to rejoice when the Roach Coach's wheels
Came crunching through the damp caliche
Abaft of its breakfast-announcing cuminous stench.

Toting a plate of beans and chorizo, my coffee
Lightened by unsweetened milk, and a centipede
Curious about the gray flecks on my boot heel,
I commandeered a stack of 2X4s and sat
Anxious not for company, but for morning solitude.

But he sat too, having first asked permission,
His coastal Texas accent flat and green and smooth,
Though his features gave the lie to all of this and more.

The Rastafarian tam of Garvey colors—
Red, black, green, and yellow bands of yarn—
Worn Pericles high and pushed off the brow line,
Made him seem less politic than refined.

He called me *tocayo*, shook hands as *Joseph*,
Talked of carpentry, women, Melville, and time.

The last he claimed to be done with killing;
Having done it had smothered his yen to hang fire.
And murder, to which he no longer cottoned,
Was anathematic to his new moral code.

I'd heard the rumors; he was no angel,
An anti-*santo* and apoca-prophet, yes,
But one whose company was the picture of peace.

Prior to the prolix of his conviction and sentence,
He had made it his business to furnish the dead:
Great slabs of purple heartwood,
Spalted tamarind, wengé, and mun
Became in his hands the bedsteads of the breathless,
Terminal fixtures for those whinnying with us not.

He'd made a simple living, so he claimed,
And called it *Queequeg's Coffin*,
Selling to those who wanted something
Uniquely final, or finally unique.

He'd made his own as well; or rather,
Made one for himself—it was carefully worked
Of Yaje and Cocobolo in the classic coffin shape:
An elongated hexagram with a simple sliding lid,

On which he'd carved a personal charm:
A white rose blooming from a thorn-encrusted cane.

When finished, he'd placed it in the attic hollow,
A space above his living place of rest—
The bed he shared with a woman who'd betray him—
Ready to receive him, ready there and waiting for his time.

Impassioned men are prone to crimes of passion,
And by some trick of nature find it difficult to bear
The same propensity for passion found in others—
Or such was Joseph's theory; and as theories go, it's fair.

He'd killed the man who for a time at least
Had lain beneath his coffin; had lain beneath,
Above perhaps, the woman he desired;

Had come, at any rate, between
Two objects of his passion—his words, not mine.

Fifteen years of punish and appeal,
Fifteen years of contemplating time,
Fifteen years of books and conversations
Had placed something like redemption in his grasp.

The woman who'd betrayed him never gave up
In her efforts to secure him an appeal,
To secure him his realease.

She'd worked three jobs and gone through all her savings;
Lawyer after lawyer threw his hands up in defeat,
Till one agreed to take the case
For a most unusual fee,

And managed to make a fine appeal
Before a sympathetic judge.

The sentence was reduced to time served—Joseph
Had no idea who had been responsible for this.

The day he was released he saw her standing
Near the entrance, near the exit, nearly frantic in her joy.
She embraced him, he forgave her, they remembered who they were.

After the marathon making up, and over a bottle of wine,
He'd asked her how she'd paid for such
A brilliant, young attorney who had argued
His appeal with success.

Your coffin
she had answered
it brought you back to me.

My coffin
he kept saying
it took me back to her.

The coffin
I repeated
it raised you from the dead.

BEGINNING

Jay Rogoff

A week in Italy
makes one free to
adore divinity
in art—say, Orvieto

where the tang of astringent
bianco at a caffe
cuts sharp as the legend
in Maitani's relief

on the Duomo façade,
his sixteen-pointed sun
eclipsed by God
already bearing down

on his little clay planet,
stars on his shoulder
showing day chased by night,
spirit on the water

streamlined as a dove
with a plummeting heart,
carved marble to give
us a fitting stone start,

while, gazing at the moon
the sun falls in love
as if with its own bone
and not the image of

its flame, like God's delight
in his own delicious earth,
his blue ribbon dessert
fixed to go off.

FALL

Jay Rogoff

Eve and Adam go
to a dance,
a courtly fandango
without chaperones,

hand to hand, hot glances,
cool steps; the muscle
in Adam's calf tenses;
Eve throws back a shoulder

while one supple leg coyly
coils around the other.
Carlo Blasis,
Italian dancing master

and author of sober books
on the subject would mention
that exchange of amorous looks,
the certain immodest motion

in the hips while dancing,
the way their breasts press
together, as if commencing
a final embrace.

Why did the angels disappear?
Changing their gowns?
Shedding coats of sexy gossamer
for flames?

For this is just the start
of the end. The tree
has shed its part-
ridges and lovebirds, who spy

from every prurient bush
on this Valentine's dance,
this coarse subterfuge
for the intercourse of hands,

this passing of subtle fruit:
peach, pear, or tangelo,
fig or pomegranate,
clementine or mineola

(scholars disagree);
maybe a canteloupe or a
cherry tragedy;
an apple opera.

A hissing vine coils
around the tree trunk,
grinning through its scales
with a scissory tongue,

casting a marble eye
on the first lady
(it glows like the cherry
on a hot fudge sundae).

Stamp! Stamp on the ground!
Where is God,
who's generally around?
He's letting things slide:

see the rivers escape
to the earth's four corners
so the tree will dry up
and love will abandon us

to harvest our thorns
and thistles, and fruit
to render our bones
compliant and mute.

MEDITATION ON A LINE FROM HAFIZ

Jane Satterfield

An afternoon given to walks
along the Arno, to shaded medieval alleys
where maps said we'd find the poet's home,

One regret

& we found, instead,
walls scaffolded, the *Casa di Dante*
wrapped in painter's plastic.
No tours the whole
of that fevered season.

Dear world,

we found, instead,
the tiny church
where Dante first
saw his Beatrice;
the pocked walls
from when the Arno
escaped its banks, and rising,
left its visible mark—

I am determined not to have

the light of searing conviction—

when I am lying on my deathbed

drifting back to the ghostly square
where one black-robed 'hound of God'
called forth a corps of moral spies
for public denunciation and ordeal

is that

under the dark palm
of the Tuscan sun

in the flutter of *Pace* flags—

I did not kiss you enough.

ENDSVILLE

Jane Satterfield

Based on The Grim Adventures of Billy & Mandy,
a Cartoon Network Series; the Grim Reaper speaks

I love games and I never lose
so, yes, I am "Grim"
now I've lost a bet for a hamster's soul and am stuck in Endsville
Best Friends Forever! with Billy and Mandy,
a mean-spirited girl with humor so black
it splits the skull.

Sure, I'm a walking skull-
and-bones but don't I have dignity to lose?
Billy thinks it's a dress, this black
robe which adds to my grim
appearance. "Kiss, Kiss," says Mandy,
to *me*—the Reaper (held hostage) in suburban Endsville!

How strange it is to watch days pass in Endsville:
"Grim's 'it,' " shrieks Billy, that numbskull
while he hides in the curtains with Mandy.
How I miss the simple pleasure of cutting a soul loose
from this world. Gone is the guise of my former grimness
now I drink coffee each morning, black.

I'd like a party, on the boom box a little *Back in Black*
as the goddess of chaos arrives at the Endsville
Mall. That ought to up the ante on this grim
destiny. With a bit of skullduggery
I could end this purgatory as loser
extraordinaire, countermand

a little respect. A swing of the scythe would send Mandy
to Nirvana or Lower Heck, a land black
as murder. Let her lose
face for a change. A fiend like me could go mad in Endsville
which has, by the way, no chapter of Skull-
and-Bones to fill my social time. A grimace

suits me just fine when I've no grimoire
in hand. That's a text best hidden from Mandy
who calls school
a *duty dance with death*. A black
sheep in Endsville?
Or does someone have a screw loose?

"Grim," she says, "Lose
the gloom and learn to groove the Mandy way in Endsville."
She hands me her guitar, black Fender with a skull.

Film Versions

Robert Gibb

i.

MOBY-DICK:
Leona Theater, Homestead, 1956

The runnels of the curtains parting like the sea.
Then a rucksacked figure making his way
Among the trees and fountain spray
Of a waterfall, diagonally down the screen,

When all at once from the darkness
A voice says "Call me Ishmael."
I'm still trying to account for the thrill
Of those syllables on a boy as clueless

As me. But even before Queequeg, the *Pequod,*
Or Ahab appears, before the stark masts fill
With St. Elmo's fire, the film with Pip's

Revelation that the whale was a great white god,
I'm hooked, just blocks above the sullen mills
That will in time become my whale ship.

ii.

BILLY BUDD:
Squirrel Hill Theater, Pittsburgh, 1962

Five years from now, when I'm drafted,
It will seem a different movie, playing on TV,
One in which Stamp might pass for a hippie,
Cherubic and too innocent to last.

Even now the ship-of-state's a gallows
And sways creaking upon its seas—
The waters beneath which Claggart has seen
"gliding monsters preying on their fellows."

His eyes glint like dead bits of anthracite
Billy can't fathom, nor me. Later,
I'll be thinking harder about power and hate

And flowers being threaded beneath rifle sights.
About the severe captain, Vere,
When the sights fell on Kent and Jackson State.

VERBATIM

Robert Gibb

i.

The broken-record hectoring I grew up with:
You're in for a rude awakening
And *better stop that belly-aching.*

There was *mend your ways* and *rue the day,*
And, coming home after school,
I've got a bone to pick with you.

ii.

Rue and *ache* and *bone*, each word bearing its Scots inflection, whetted on the Kirk of the stone my stepmother lived by, but *rude* (*Sc. a.*)—"marked by unkind or severe treatment of persons, etc."—can also mean "deficient in literary merit," for which the *O.E.D.* gives this example: "The Apostles used freely a rude version of the Old Testament" (**1861** STANLEY *East. Ch. viii.* [1869] 271). Now, that, she would have approved of. Her rendering of it: *No place to escape the wrath of God, save heaven, and not even there.*

City of Sand

Jackson Bliss

I. Génamé, Mali.

Honorine licked the envelope and pressed down on the porous texture of the flap, impressing traces of rust-colored soil with her chapped fingers. This letter was eight years of English study condensed into the first and only envelope she would ever send to America, the address painted with slow cursive letters, intermingling like the hands of pre-school children on a field trip.

Siddhartha Palash,
21 West Camino Merano, apt # 3B
Cardiff-by-the-Sea, CA, 92007
Les États-Unis.

She felt intense pride and then tingling jealousy: why did air-mail envelopes get to see so much of the world? They were just thin planes of coarsely constructed papyrus, little blue airplanes rising up from their corners. What was so special about *that*?

Thrusting her feet into her flip-flops, Honorine stood up from her *petit bois* chair and stretched her arms in the militant sunlight: long celery stalk shadows danced in slow motion on the crumbling wall, splitting in half as she brought her hands to her side.

—Don't be long, her Mom said, we're going to the *Moulin*.

Honorine grabbed the handlebars and walked through the compound door to the main road, wiping a tiny congregation of sweat beads from her temples with her forearm before she hopped on the banana seat.

On the dirt road, Honorine navigated her bike through a herd of goats that were grazing on weeds sprouting from the dry earth before she made a detour around her three brothers. They were enraptured in game of morning soccer, their bare feet, stomping the mustard soil in pursuit of the deflated soccer ball, their steps were a séance of sand ghosts. Honorine continued pedaling, her bike, now rusty and wobbly with age, the tires, flat and yellow like the dirt road connecting Bamako to Ouagadougou. But there was at least one redeeming feature: the bike had a lunch basket in the front. Granted, there was nothing to put inside the basket, but Honorine found it charming anyway. An empty stomach was an appetite without rules; an empty basket was an imagination without limits.

Honorine turned left, peddling against the dry Harmattan wind, slowly passing the outdoor mosque—actually, a simple rectangle drawn with a stick—where shoeless men and a few veiled women bowed their heads in rows of perfectly uniform devotion.

—Alaaaaaaaaaaaaaaaaaa...hu. ak...bar. Alaaaaaaaaaaaaaaaaaaaaaaaa...hu . ak...bar.

The bike wobbled like an amateur Scotch drinker but Honorine kept pedaling on the road, greeting each villager as if it was the first time, until she arrived at the post office. Sitting in wooden chairs underneath a tree shaped like an Afro, the Chef de Poste was drinking tea and chatting with several men Honorine didn't recognize.

—I ni sogoma, the Chef de Poste welcomed.

—I'm fine, she answered. —Here sirewa?

—There is peace, thank you, he replied.

—Bamusodo?

—Mother is fine.

—Facè do?

—Father is fine.

—Denbayado?

—The children are fine.

When his turn came, the Chef de Poste asked Honorine the same questions in exactly the same order, and then she greeted the visitors in a mix of French, Bambara and Bwamu, each in his turn giving the same responses and asking the same questions. Twenty minutes passed in this way, jumping from one genealogy to another.

When they were finished, the Chef de Poste walked inside the post office with Honorine.

—Tangara, she said, I want to send this letter.

—Ah bon?

—It's to an old friend. He lives near Japan.

—Le Japon?

She nods, pulling two crumpled bills out of her front t-shirt pocket. —That's how much?

—690 CFA.

Honorine gulped, weighing her decision. She only had two 250 CFA bills and that was already a great sum of money. 500 CFA was four days of tô or three weeks of courier travel, it was a choice between fighting the armies of famine or cultivating the luxurious dreamworld of a seventeen year-old girl destined to clean latrines and sweep classroom floors, the same classrooms where she once excelled as a high school student destined for a university scholarship and a promising career in Bamako, or so she was told, before Monsieur Keita fondled her during lunch break.

—I only have 500 francs Tangara.... Can I bring the rest tomorrow?

—Rules are rules Honorine. If they found out, I'd get in trouble.

—Je t'en *prie* Tangara, she said, pleading with the elastic part of her eyes.

He looked sideways through the post office window and then back again at Honorine. —D'accord. But please bring it as soon as you can.

—Merci bien, Tangara. You are so kind.

He smiled faintly and opened a drawer, pulling out a cluster of green, yellow and blue stamps, licking them, and placing them delicately on the envelope's top right corner. He inspected his work before handing the letter back to her. She walked to the drop-off slot and slid the envelope through the opening, narrow like a salvation parable.

—Merci Tangara.

—Give your family my regards.

—And yours mine.

Honorine walked back outside, her dress clinging to her protruding spine, and then she said goodbye to the languorous men resting underneath the giant tree. Finally she could go home. She slowly pedaled her way down the dusty road, a road much like the village, like a city of sand, evaporating with every pedal rotation, blown away by the Harmattan Wind, submerged by the Rainy Season, and swallowed whole by the cannibalistic sun.

Honorine's letter slept in a shallow cardboard box for fifteen days. When it was finally retrieved by the National Postal Service of Mali, it was covered by new correspondence:

Konaté Amadou
B.P. 2556
French Teacher of the lycée mixte de Yako
Yako, Burkina Faso.

Monsieur le directeur
O.P.A.E.E.M.
3428 Rue Républicaine
Bamako, Mali.

Coulibaly Ahmed
B.P. 30

21 Rue Djémila
Ségou, Mali.

A lanky man in pressed grey pants and a chambray button-down placed the letters in a canvas bag inside the truck that had seen three Presidents and several military coups d'état, the letters on its side, sun-faded and lost like a dead language, still haunting the memories of elders.

The driver turned on the ignition and began his bumpy return back to Bamako. Usually the trip took twenty hours of non-stop driving. But today he made good time. The trip took only fourteen hours, including three bathroom breaks on the side of the road, and one pit-stop at a *buvette* to gulp down two stout bottles of crisp orange Fanta and eat two avocado sandwiches, and a second to buy bags of peanuts and sesame wafers through the window from a little girl dressed in a used Diana Ross t-shirt.

He finally backed his wobbly truck into the loading dock in Bamako where several clerks carried the bags inside. Local mail rows 1-4. Monsieur le directeur and Coulibaly Ahmed disappeared into the pile. South and West African Mail rows 5-9. East and North African Mail rows 10-16. Europe rows 17-27. Honorine's letter was dropped onto a small pile of envelopes covered in bright, colorful stamps. These letters were known as *Harlequins* because of the bright, garish stamps used for international postage. Four days later, the Harlequin Pile was moved into a dirty cart that looked like a massive laundry hamper on wheels and then pushed into the back of a rusty airplane, eventually surrounded by other canvas hampers that arrived in fleets of two. Calloused clean hands with abrupt white fingernails appeared out of nowhere to push the hampers into place like a Tetris game where all the blocks are the same color and only envelopes with money disappear from the screen.

Both Konaté Israël and Ouédrago Adaman looked at Honorine's letter, but at different times and for different reasons. Adaman, the younger clerk, picked the envelope up and shook it in his hand before placing it directly against one of the cabin lights, searching for 10,000 CFA bills. He turned the envelope around and read the destination out loud, sounding out the syllables with his diffident English. Adaman imagined all the exotic places the envelope would travel to, pretended to calculate its journey, even though he could have sworn that California was in Mexico. Then he tried to imagine the reader's face, tried to imagine what she would look like after noticing the Malian postage of endangered animals hiding from predators in the Savannah. Finally he threw the letter into a nearby pile like a lopsided discus and walked away. The truth was, Adaman wished he could turn into a little bug and crawl inside one of these envelopes and travel half-way across the globe to America where all the women were blond and fertile, where people, even *poor people*, threw perfectly good TV's into the trash when they moved. But that was just entomology. Besides that, Adaman could have used the money to pay for a moped. With a *moto*, he could take his sister to the *collège*, pick up yams and guavas for his family and most importantly, meet girls in one of the larger villages. They always noticed a young man with a sparkling new *moto*. How could you miss it?

A few minutes before the loading was completely done, Israël, the older and bulkier clerk, noticed Honorine's letter, placed in the wrong pile. He weighed the thin envelope in his hand for a second, tried guessing its contents, and then repatriated the course paper in the right pile.

In the late morning, the airplane accelerated down the runway until it crept slowly into the air like a guilty boy raising his hand in the classroom. Adaman and Israël watched as the little blue airplane soared through the sky, bound for a world they knew they would never see in person. Everyone knew the sky was forbidden to Africans.

At least the honest ones.

II. Paris, France

Eight heavily bundled men in matching blue, red, white and gray uniforms rushed out to meet the airplane courrier as it was taxing into terminal 38-F. Their arms, swathed in layers of cotton, wool and silk, looked practically Michelin. They clapped and rubbed their gloved hands together in anticipation, the P. N. F patches, jiggling in the crisp air.

—Putain de merde, Jean-Marc shouted, it's fucking cold man!

—Ah mec, don't even get me started, Benjamin complained, I'm not even supposed to *be* here.

—Vite, François said, let's finish this job and eat, I'm fucking starving guys.

—Oui, ça va, Saïd agreed.

—Oui, oui, ça va, the other men grumbled.

Jean-Marc, François, Benjamin and Saïd waited impatiently in back for the plane to finish docking while the other postal workers stood near the front or side doors. The four men opened up the rear door, pulled down the loading ramp and began moving mail carts from the back cabin to the general loading room. Every time Jean-Marc, François, Benjamin and Saïd made a trip outside with a new cart, their breaths bellowed out into the brisk afternoon air. And every time they came inside to dump the contents of one of the glorified laundry hampers on to the moving rubber surface, they sighed as their skin defrosted in a moment of reprieve.

Honorine's letter was sleeping underneath others from Sénégal, Burkina Faso, Côte d'Ivoire, South Africa, Cameroon, The Gambia and Togo. The letters traveled on a conveyor belt, falling down a stainless steel ramp before shooting through one of ten high speed tubes that branched off in ten separate directions like a miniature freeway that split off into a separate system of exits and detours. For 3,500 meters Honorine's letter was a pink and purple blur as it raced to the North America room at the blinding speed of one hundred eighty-five kilometers per hour, streaking through the glass cylinder until it finally nosedived into a snowbank of fresh letters. Written on the wall were these words: *En Route à New York.*

When the unloading was complete, Jean-Marc, François, Saïd and Benjamin joined their other colleagues and walked down the street to Café de St. Barthes, a favorite haunt of theirs. They ordered plates of:

Port Fourguereau,
St. André
A Norman goat cheese flavored with mushroom and thyme,

And sides of:

Endive salads drizzled in red wine vinaigrette and truffle oil
Panini filled with marinated Artichokes, fresh basil or prosciutto.

The men began talking about the AS Monaco-Olympique Lynnonais game. Saïd drank a second *café au lait* while his friends finished off their first bottle of Bordeaux. After scarfing down his sandwich and saying good-bye, Saïd walked back to the international hub. He walked into one of the North America rooms and then checked the hefty plastic boxes waiting for him, their stomachs, overflowing with veiled letters, squiggly addresses, all shrouded in envelopes that resembled rectangular-shaped *hijabs* and assaulted by pompous stamps of posturing local heroes and postal codes in every permutation. Saïd's hand flipped from envelope to envelope mechanically without soul or conviction.

—This silly 35-hour a week rule is kicking my ass, he muttered. Until three months ago, Saïd enjoyed his two extra hours of freedom each week at the café. But since then he's felt restless and troubled.

Café de St. Barthes was the last place he wanted to be right now.

For the past month, he watched the news in his cramped apartment.

And over and over and over again, he kept seeing the same surreal clips, the same replays of science fiction flooding the TV stations: two planes crashing into the world trade center. Two explosions. The towering twins that once looked over the Manhattan skyway like vigils of the New World had been completely disemboweled, their torsos, sliced in half as humans spilled out like precious hemoglobin. People were holding hands and jumping out of windows in groups of two's, leaping from the 102nd floor to their death, their mass suicides consecrated forever.

Saïd felt hopeless. Guilty. He didn't know whether he was a victim of terrorism or of infidelity, violent desperation or silent metamorphosis. He needed to process the Dadaist destruction by himself. In silence. The drone of tireless machines in the dissemination room and his bickering colleagues at the café didn't give him the sanity he needed to consider Josephine's riddle: who was this girl he loved once? Was she different than the person who'd vanished from his life like wind blowing away a dirt road? Did he really have the right to say he *knew* her? After all, she'd never sent him any postcards from Belize or Honduras like she promised, never called him once she reached port, never picked up her phone when he called her a month later, never even answered his love letters. Not one. In fact, she never came back into his life again except in the REM stage.

Saïd walked into the New York Room. As of late, it had become a sort of pilgrimage for him, a way to feel connected to a city steeped in its own tragic mythology. He began skimming letters again, but for some reason, he couldn't see the words today. The letters was melting together, his eyes drooped, addresses morphed into zigzags, into tiny mazes, into pieces of sheet music. He opened his eyes again and shook his head, exasperated. When Saïd's insides were freezer-burnt, when his nostalgia for his Algerian family became an affliction, he knew the only way to get back to the human center of his job was to *read* envelopes. True, they were standardized in size and color, but it was the names people wrote on those envelopes, it was the insinuation of human life that gave Saïd hope, it was actually the only meaningful thing about his job. His fingers had touched the hands of Tanakas, Alis, Smiths, Duponts, Romanovs, Hernandezes and Lees in every country in the world; it was only time that staggered their connection. Letters brought the entire world together and the world didn't even know it. But he did. Saïd felt the world in his hands every time he read an envelope.

Blaine
798
NY

Aiko
D Street NW
Coulibaly
Apt # 29
Svetlana
4237
El Paso
Édouard
Bridgeport
Nova Scotia
Québec
ME
7th Avenue
Simpson
Mobile, AL
IL
Lindsey
1212
Hotchkins
Cardiff-by-the-Sea,
Muncie
CA, 92007
Les États-Unis.

Saïd stopped: How did this Malian girl know a guy from California? Why did he have such a strange name? What did 'Cardiff' mean anyways? What language did they speak to each other in? Were they dating? Friends? Had he been a volunteer in Mali? Was she an exchange student in the West Coast? How often did they use sign language to fill their gaps of fluency? Did they scream at each other when the words didn't come out right, the way he and Josephine had? Did they laugh at each other at the little mistakes they made? Were they in love? How were they dealing with separation? Did he find her exotic because her skin was darker than a bottle of Chanel Antaeus? Did she find him exotic because his skin was lighter than the teeth of a French professor in Dakar? Was he running away from the law? Did she view him as a Genie Lamp? Had he returned to America after an unexpected pregnancy? How had they met? And *why* did they choose to live so apart from one another when they could be together?

Saïd wished he had no principles, he wished he were some kind of moral anarchist, just another disgruntled postal worker—he would have torn open the envelope and devoured its forbidden contents, dislodging Honorine's words from her gumline like an oral surgeon removing perfect teeth. And afterwards, after Saïd had read and re-read the letter, savoring the words like a piece of hard candy, he would have simply scrunched the evidence into a concentrated little ball of curvy lines and graceful intentions, and made a three-point shot into the paper shredder. A miracle: to know someone's deepest feelings without knowing who she was or what she looked like. Saïd decides that tyrants and postmen aren't really so different after all: they both have the power to spin, cover up and airbrush history by controlling how news is delivered, at what speed events happen, and which information becomes public knowledge. This juxtaposition upsets him.

But he knows himself. He couldn't do something like this because his greatest fear was that another postal worked had the same power over him. His greatest fear was that Josephine had actually written him not one, but several letters, several long, lyrical, glowing letters full of vain promises and idle flirtation, and the great enigma of her disappearance lay in the hands of some frustrated civil servant in Belmopan or Esperanza who had simply kept her letters as payback for the two months of withheld salary. Saïd could picture the whole scene perfectly, he knew how gifted people were at justifying deceit when they were living in slums. He'd lived in an Arab ghetto for seven years before he got this job, so he knew how good poverty was at picking out scruples out of people's brains like a mother removing lice from a child's scalp. But in case he was wrong, in case there was the slightest possibility that one of Josephine's letter was lost or misplaced as so many letters were but recently rediscovered, for that reason, and only for that reason, Saïd stopped himself from reading Honorine's letter. This simple idea, this invested hope was the only dam stopping a turbulent river of desperation from bursting into chaos and self-destruction. He felt a loving jealousy as his hands gripped the dust-stained letter.

The simple beauty of knowing where to direct your love was itself, a privilege.

He thought of New York, he thought of Josephine's freckles, especially the ones evenly spaced apart and connected by invisible string, dangling above her slender shoulder blades like a necklace, he thought of Josephine's promise to take the RER train directly to his place when she returned, he thought of Claudette, Josephine's best friend, who had invited her to go on a cruise after catching her boyfriend with the maid. Saïd thought of the two explosions and the thousands of people buried underneath two hundred feet of cement blocks, electric wires, splintered window glass, a complete world sleeping in the chalky detritus of human tragedy, helpless underneath a pile of crushed and severed human bodies that once blazed in addiction to life, now, just cold shells of the human soul, sleeping eternally in the makeshift graves of a paraplegic city. And maybe somewhere in that dead valley of depleted energy and ruptured dreams was Josephine, smothered in a makeshift necropolis, frozen in chunks of rubble like petrified flowers frozen in a transparent paper-weight.

It was simply too much to bear or imagine or ignore. Saïd didn't know whether to cry or not because he couldn't figure out whether she died loving him or lived by avoiding him. Saïd had loved Josephine once. And now he wondered whether he would ever be able to love another woman again, never knowing who the victim was, never knowing whether he was divorced from, or married to, 9/11. He knew he had to go on, he understood his fixation as a product of confusion, but he harbored irrational hope without justification because he could at least understand hopelessness, it was the sibling of infatuation, after all.

As he walked outside and down the street, Saïd thought of his favorite line by Catullus, and he recited it as if it were a Surah:

Only deeds bring
Words to eyes and fingers

III. New York City, New York.

Alain Rothmann, José Santanto and Freddie Bryant were taking it easy, because they could. They were watching a Knicks game on TV lounge, eating sandwiches and sipping on cold sodas from Kurtz's Deli.

—Oh, *come* on Camby! José shouted, you gonna let some white guy stuff you like that?

Freddie laughed.

—Yo, Alain said, their defense is fucking wack !

—Man, I can't look at this, Freddie moaned. *St. John's* looks better than the Knicks. At least *those* mothafuckas can pass the goddamn ball, you'know'what'I'm'saying?

—*Yeah*, José said.

Alain nodded.

Freddie took another bite of his sandwich. Mustard squirted out of the bun as he sunk his teeth down on his pastrami on rye. He wiped the Dijon off his pants with his vacant hand and continued eating, shaking his head at the game.

Suddenly, the night manager walked out of his office and into the TV lounge.

—All right boys, the Frenchies are here. Let's get this shit done and get the hell outta here, all right?

—Sure thing, Alain said.

—Kay boss, José added.

—A'ight bwoss, Freddie said, his mouth full of sandwich and scorn.

The three men put on their gloves and their patriotic red, white, blue and gray postal jackets with rectangular USPS patches on the chests.

They walked down a long hallway and through a back door with plastic streamers hanging from the doorframe before descending a ramp towards the back of the air courrier. With the help of two French postmen, José, Alain and Freddie emptied the airplane's stomach of its contents five carts at a time until the airplane was completely empty. Then, the French-American quintet fed the cargo plane again until it was stuffed to capacity with white airmail envelopes in blue and red trim, glossy photo postcards and multifarious packages, all bound for Western Europe, the Mediterranean and North Africa.

—Merci bien et au revoir! the Frenchies said.

The airplane engines grumbled to a roar, finding their voice again in the busy din of Manhattan fugues.

—Yeah, thanks guys! Alain shouted.

José waved goodbye.

The three of them walked back inside and removed their winter jackets and gloves. All of them began dumping carts on to a conveyor belt where each parcel was X-rayed, inspected by DEA canines for Anthrax, and spot-checked by FBI agents for bomb residue. Honorine's envelope finally entered a spinning Ferris Wheel that flung letters into twenty separate branch tubes according to their zip code and size until it was sucked into tube # 16, soaring at the blinding pace of ninety-five miles per hour. The letter reached the California room and slid down a stainless steel gutter, falling into box #4.

Freddie walked into the room and checked the first three boxes, scanning zip codes. Then he noticed Honorine's envelope.

—Cardiff-by-the-Sea? He asked. —Only in California man. Nothin' but surfer dudes and fucking hippies.

Freddie tossed Honorine's letter back into the box #4 and then shook his head. He verified boxes #5 and #6 and then stood up to leave when he caught sight of Honorine's letter again. It was dirty as hell, and had pictures of crazy animals and shit, but the zip code was a dream for him. Looking at the 92007 he had to admit to himself that a few weeks in Southern California, bathing in the relentless sun, gazing at top-heavy women, a few spliffs in his hand, just relaxin' on the beach with his homeboys, fuck, that would be slammin,' if only they didn't have to deal with any Cali*forn*ians. But that seemed unlikely. As far as he was concerned, they were *all* Lakers fans, which made them traitors for life.

IV. San Diego, California.

Te adoro cariña, eres mi estrella excelsa. Brillas como un ciudad o una húmeda rosa.

Sheryl Mattson and Julio Gonzalez zipped up I-5 protected by sunglasses and water bottles. After making stops at Chula Vista, SDSU's university station, La Jolla and Del Mar, they were practically done with the day's drop-off when they arrived at the Cardiff Post Office. The sun was a warm yellow paint smudge in the grayish blue sky. In the distance, the ocean was a diapason responding to itself in gentle drones as the waves curled on the shoreline hypnotically. Sheryl and Julio's sandals climbed calmly out of the delivery truck, landing on the warm pavement with a soft plop. Dressed in custom gray-blue shorts and matching USPS short-sleeved shirts, they both looked up at the epic sky, a blue poem of pouring sunlight and translucent clouds. Then they walked to the back of the truck and opened the door.

They carried plastic boxes from the truck to the back entrance of the post office in imitation of the Pacific Ocean, their feet, moving in a series of waves, slowed down to human speed. Julio, carrying the last mail in his arms, bumped the box against the wall as he backed his way through the door. Honorine's letter spiraled onto the ground like a platform diver committing suicide:

4.2 4.3 4.7 4.5 4.3 4.7

—Is that the last box Julito? Sheryl asked.

—Yep, he said, smiling.

—*Rad*, she said. They said goodbye to Nickie who was busy sorting through the daily delivery. Sheryl walked outside, stepping on Honorine's letter before turning around to look at Julio.

—You wanna drive?

—Whatevs.

—Seriously?

—It doesn't matter to me, just as long as you stop by Juani—Hey chica! Look underneath your foot, he said, pointing. —You've got something there.

Sheryl looked down at the stained envelope, crushed under her Danskos like an old love note. She picked it up, brushed off the dirt and then read the address to herself.

—Siddhartha? Julio asked

She nodded.

—You know, that guy's name reminds me of something my mom told me when I was a kid. We don't pick our names. Even our parents don't pick our names. Our names pick us.

She held the envelope in her hand, and then walked inside the post office, placing it inside the postal cradle with a maternal gentleness that surprised even her. Then she walked back outside, following Julio to the truck. A teenage breeze was blowing erratically through the windows as they drove to Leucadia, listening to a Mexican radio station. Their day was done.

Two hours later, Nickie started going through boxes, separating letters into two distinct piles: his letters, and everyone else's. It was as if the other letters were hallucinations, well traveled hallucinations touched by a thousand hands, the story of their names, unopened and kept secret to him forever.

Once Nickie had finished sorting piles, he loaded his tiny mail truck, put on his sunglasses and made his daily rounds, pausing in the middle of his delivery for a cup of coffee and a veggie *omelette* croissant at Miracles Café where salty surfers, smoking UCSD students and local troubadours sat outside in the soft part of the afternoon sun. He finished his sandwich, wiped his mouth with his napkin, threw his plate in the dirty dish bin and then walked to his mail truck, listening to the sounds of frolicking seagulls as they flew in giant parabolas above the café.

He paused for a moment. Another beautiful day.

At 21 W. Camino Merano he stopped in front of the aluminum mailboxes with his postal stroller, whistling a commercial jingle. Nickie unlocked the frame and began stuffing the empty rectangular boxes with scented letters, trading magazines, junk mail, receipts, rebates, mysteriously wrapped pornos, bills, affidavits and coupons of every size and color.

With envelopes that traveled more than the people who sent them.

With envelopes that traveled in all the forbidden spaces: the African sky, the field of lingering memory, the lantern of physical proximity, the crumbling landscape of time, the defiant airwalk through time zones and technology.

As Siddhartha stood underneath the tepid shower, he listened to the echo of a million water droplets falling on the bottom of the bathtub, occasionally spraying the plastic shower curtain when he changed positions. He liked to think when he was in the bathroom. He stood motionless, his head resting on top of his crossed arms as he stared out the open window with the warm cascade running down his naked back and then circling his legs, stopping at his pruned feet.

Running water was a miracle to him. After taking bucket baths for four years, a hot shower was a miracle in the afternoon. Running water cleansed Siddhartha of his present tense. Running water was simply his life in America, falling into the basin of his collective experience in Africa, it was simply his own memory crashing down on a village of sand, back when the only dirt road in his village used to blow away during the Harmattan wind, or during the biblical floods in the Rainy Season.

Every time Siddhartha was underneath running water, he started reminiscing about the 1,460 days he used a blue plastic cup to rinse the baby shampoo out of his hair. For four years, he'd fantasize about taking showers back home. But now that was back in the US, he found himself fantasizing about dust instead of water, disappearing roads, not paved highways. An odd twist: running water now reminded him of Mali.

Siddhartha stood there, washing his body with a bar of lavender soap, his eyes pointed upwards towards the forbidden sky and then down again at his arms, little beads of water entangled in the dark hair of his arms. Finally his gaze came back to the wall of mailboxes across the courtyard. He watched as the local postman folded, bent and inserted bundles of letters into boxes as he hummed. Siddhartha watched the silent miracle of correspondence unfolding before his eyes and wondered how many countries the postman carried in his hands today, how many miles his envelopes had traveled to inhabit aluminum boxes, where one day they would hibernate forever inside old shoeboxes, spongy minds and expansive landfills. It seemed like such a waste of language.

To Siddhartha, envelopes were like paper passports: they allowed people to travel 1,000's of miles without moving at all; they created memory and also helped to preserve memory by documenting the experience of movement and proving the existence of space: they gave the reader (traveler) the ability to see the unimaginable, taste the impossible and feel the unknown; they were paper passports that bridged the gap between human culture and personal knowledge. Paper passports: the tangible emotion of a concrete experience surrendered to the alphabet. A letter: a message: a messenger: an invitation of conflicting symbols. An envelope possesses: a sealed one-way conversation. An letter is: a tangible snapshot of space and time, an elegant docket of fleeting monologues, an emotion immortalized in the personality of crossed T's and capital D's. A letter is nothing but: paper inside of paper like an unborn analogy inside a poet's womb. Together, letter and envelope are paper with this privilege: they contain the human mind between its two sides like a parenthesis: unsolicited pathological confessions, shared perversions, Syrah-induced epiphanies, 3:am shopping compulsions, minor moral victories written in the I-told-you-so script, politically-motivated death threats by hostile born-again Christians, generic thank-you notes, rejection letters typed on delicate Ivy-League paper, belated birthday cards with bright cartoon animals on them, sloppy love letters in marauded Bukowski tones, long-distance promises to lovers with blurry faces, collection letters written in thuggish legalistic stationery, networking to tight-fisted alumni. Together, a letter inside an envelope is the ultimate reification of memory, the last and only hints of the self, the only proof that we are not alone even when we live in solitude. And this great secret, a letter hides faithfully like a locked diary picked open by a ravenous gossip.

Postmen are like dictators: they control the love letters that never reach us, they hoard postcards from Belize, and they ignore the subtext of correspondence that is always rejected by language. What's more, they deliver the letters we cannot stop reading, even when we know they're not true. And what is history except a series of letters that we read in secrecy, simply the order in which we read them, simply the words that are available to read, simply the mind's appetite for order in world of shifting narratives and lost voices?

The sun sank into the horizon like a week-old birthday balloon. Siddhartha turned the shower off, sliding the blue plastic curtain with its swimming tropical fish and coral reefs to one side. He placed his feet in flip-flops and grabbed the last dry towel on the rack, wrapping it around his waist, tucking part of it inside. Down the hallway he heard a muted shout.

—Siddharrie! He paused, looked at himself in the mirror and wiped cold water droplets off his smoothly shaven face and armored forearms.

Siddhartha opened the door slowly. —What is it Tash?

—Come here.

—Huh?

—There's a letter for you.

—What? He asked again, raising his voice. —Whajjew say?

—Just come *here*.

Siddhartha ambled into the kitchen table. Natasha was typing on her laptop and drinking the remains of her kiwi-banana smoothie. He looked down and saw the pile of letters. He shuffled through them, stopping.

—Fucking rad! He said.

—What?

—It's my friend Honorine. She…she finally wrote back. He opened up the stained envelope that was barely sealed anymore and pulled out a white card with a silkscreen print of a farmer tilling broken, yellow earth. The sun was erupting in the background, glistening like the back of a whale. As he read, his eyes were smiling and his lips leaked a crescent delight. When he had finished the letter, he laid it down on the table.

—Well, what did she say?

—Oh, nothing really.

Natasha glared at him.

—She just wanted me to know that she'd finally learned to ride the bike I gave her.

—Oh, she said, slurping the straw.

Siddhartha looked at the letter again. He had a dreamy look in his eyes. —God, I wonder what she's doing *right*...*now*...at this *very* instant?

Natasha looked him in the eyes searchingly, and then wrapped her arms around his half-naked body, pulling him close. He kissed her cheek and then rubbed his nose against her soft fragrant neck, breathing in her scent of ocean waves, deodorant and perfume. Behind her back he saw his trip to Ghana and Burkina Faso, the twenty-five days he spent on the coast, the three perfect days he spent in Ouagadougou and then his return to Génamé where he remained until the day he left Mali forever. The letter in his hand was provocative—it ignited a hunger for the simple village life he'd had in West Africa, spitting out images of a lost world, a city of sand, a village with one dirt road that disappeared in the Rainy Season. It was a life no longer his own, a calm and silent picture captured in snapshot and petrified inside his mind forever like lavender stems frozen inside soap glycerin, like sea shells stuck inside a transparent paperweight of stone.

He could see Honorine's bike wobbling back and forth as she made her way down the dirt road with flowers in her little front basket, saying hello to all her neighbors again as if it was the first time she had seen them.

As if it was the first time they had seen her ride a bike.

As if it was the first time she kept her balance on it.

As if there really were flowers inside her basket.

<u>ISMENE</u>

Alison Armstrong

[Music selected from: *Carmina Burana* (San Francisco Symphony Orchestra) by Carl Orf. Also ancient Greek music from *Musique de la Grece Antique*, Gregorio Paniagua (Atrium Musicae de Madrid; Harmonia Mundi, 1979/HMA 1901015]

DRAMATIS PERSONA: Ismene
VOICE-OVERS: Antigone, Creon

[Opens with Orf's Carmina Burana, *"O Fortuna" [approx. 2.33 min.], then silence as light slowly comes up on stage, rose-magenta brightening to pale greenish yellow. Sudden opening with ancient Greek music, "Anakrousis."*

PROLOGUE: The plays Oedipus Rex, Oedipus at Colonus, *and* Antigone *by Sophocles, have ended. Oedipus had been cast into exile out of Thebes by his brother-in-law Creon and the two sons of Oedipus and Jocasta, wandering as a blind beggar with the aid of his young daughter Antigone; he finally met the gods who reward him after his ill-fated life in a transformative death at Colonus. Antigone, back in Thebes, has chosen suicide by hanging in the cave to which Creon had condemned her for burying her brother Polynices, after he laid siege to Thebes with an army from Argos to wrest power from his uncle Creon who had sided with his brother Eteocles. Antigone's death was followed by the suicides of her lover Haemon—Creon's son—and of Creon's wife Eurydice who bitterly blamed her husband for the deaths of both their sons.*

Now, Ismene, alone in the dark on the marble palace roof at Thebes, illuminated by a single beam of light, does a slow street shuffle, moving her feet in a child's dance (as does Helen of Troy in W.B. Yeats' poem "A Long-Legged Fly"). She looks inward, thinking of the dead: her brothers Polynices and Eteocles, her parents/siblings Oedipus and Jocasta, her sister Antigone, the fiancé Haemon, and his dead mother queen Eurydice. And of mad king Creon who still lives in the depths of the palace. She begins to speak to herself as the ancient Greek music subsides....

<u>Ismene</u> *[seeming to talk to herself]:*

Darkness fell, the plays were ended. Yet I remained....
And so I went to him, after a time. I was so frightened.
Creon, in a frenzy of grief, a wild beast raging when I called

out his name from the doorway, while I, as usual, cowered.
But this loss is *our* loss, not his only. *[pause, walks 2 steps, a harp sounds]*
Or, his alone *and* mine alone. If he has lost his self esteem, well so
have I—although his fall is the greater, being king, and I only
a woman, a princess in name only, his prisoner.

He suffers for his impossible vain decree that forced him to condemn Antigone (as my father suffered, forced to condemn himself). But I, too, suffer—from my wretched ambivalence, my vain love of life, womanly fear of the state, fear of death, fear of Creon! I did not fear the gods enough.

My fear was no match for hers, Antigone's! Her fear gave her strength. She feared the gods and respected their immortal unwritten laws, and the gods gave her the help needed to accomplish her task.

[Sound of cymbals clashing, as in Carmina, "Ego sum Abbas" followed by *Voice-over of Antigone sounding laconic or stoic:]*

> "Leave me to my own absurdity, to suffer the
> dreadful thing I alone dared do. I alone defied
> your Creon, the state, his laws that forbade proper
> burial to my dear brother Polynices to whom I had
> promised this in the sacred grove. I alone would not
> choose to suffer death without glory... as you have!"

[Ismene turns to address the audience]: And so I went to him, finally. For comfort, although I hated all that he had done, had become, had caused to occur. But I was so alone! Rejected by Antigone, I could share neither her death nor her victory over him. She will live on in the memories of countless generations. While I have become nothing. A No One. *Me tis.*

To comfort myself as much as Creon, I went in to him.

For company. *[Turning away to talk to herself again]:*

The elders have fled, the servants too. Even our old nurse brings him only his food and wine once a day and makes up his golden inlaid bed in the evening with soft furs and a priceless cloth woven by myself. He will touch nothing, only some watered wine and his old cloak where he sleeps on the floor away from the windows, away from the light.

He was as a father to me all those years when Antigone roamed, guiding our father Oedipus. Finally, when war threatened and Apollo's warning came, I left and found them at Colonus by the sacred grove, riding my shining Sicilian colt all the way from Thebes to Athens in my best cloak and broad-brimmed hat, into the land of skilled horsemen, pride of Poseidon.

I was of some use then! It was I who would perform the sacred rites in that grove! I found them to say that he, Creon, was searching…and to tell them of the quarrels of our wicked brothers. Polynices was no better than

Eteocles. They did nothing for their father, except insult him at home. And, although his heirs, they would not share power. Creon, seeing his chance, had pitted one against the other. As he would have pitted me against my sister, and our city-state, once noble Thebes, against the heavens.

[To audience]:

Hah! Sister won out as did the gods, her avengers.

Yes, he was a sort of father, this king, this nothing who once had been so prudent, so loyal, so modest in his ambitions. *[Shouting, turning toward doorway into palace]:*

But you kidnapped us, Creon! Yes, your brutal men laid hands upon Antigone and me at Colonus, do you remember? At the sacred grove where you tried to seduce our poor blind father back to Thebes after all his painful years of wandering. But he, by then, was beyond your power. Theseus' noble Athenian horsemen restored us to his side. And then our blind father walked as swiftly as a man possessed by a god, through the trees to the bowl of stone near the brazen threshold...and vanished! Into the thunder! Beyond man's reach...

[Addressing audience again]:

When we were children (fruits of that unholy union) and our parents were happy (understanding nothing), Creon as brother to the Queen our mother had all the privileges he could want—and no responsibilities except those my dear father bade him carry out. Running on that fateful day back from Delphi and Apollo's oracle, after the plague had come upon Thebes... the last task this Creon was to perform with a pure heart.

[Paces back and forth]: Oh...the gods have had their way with this family. The spiral of destiny has closed upon us tightly, and we two who remain are trapped within a chambered nautilus' shell with no escape, no future open to us. Remorse. His remorse, *that* is what entraps him—and me! Yet he now thinks to wage war on noble Athens. But I know our father's sacred corpse will drink the blood of Thebes. Shall I live out what remains of my useless life with what remains of this man—my mother's brother? My sister-mother's brother, thus my half brother, half uncle, as well as foster father! Here, in this shell of a palace, this empty husk of a doomed city, where even the sworn elders have retreated in shame and dismay, we are living shades... mere ghosts.

Horror and grief we leave as our legacy, we of the house of Cadmus, yet redeemed by Oedipus' gift, his gift to Athens, another shining city, not his own. The shades of my beloved family visit me in the early dim hours, before dawn spreads her rose and apricot and palest green across the sky *and* on that barren land out there where reeking death so recently reigned. Too soon a burning light reveals this place of desolation, and we hide our faces from the sun. Apollo spoke, and we did not understand.

Creon has forgotten that I exist, still—a living spectre—haunting his halls of madness. Oh, Creon, don't you see why I could not choose so adamantly as my sister did? You blamed me for my sympathy, but I could not *act* as she did—the gods must have put that into her head. Nor could I, in equal measure, defend your position. I, *I* had no divine inspiration, nor help! And neither did you! But it was for *your* sake—and my own—my own woman's nature so like my mother Jocasta's, that I did so little, tried to keep all from changing, tried to resist too much understanding. I wanted life and safety—for *us*! And I wanted time, too, for you to relent, you who in your king's vanity set up the impossible choice. But the gods helped Antigone—I'm convinced of it—in her self-appointed task, to bury our outcast brother, Polynices, the one you wouldn't honor, the one slaughtered on your battlefield by the brother you favored!

Yes, it was she, so like our father in her rigid determination to press the point, to honor gods above men, who salvaged the soul of poor ravaged Polynices to whom she had promised proper burial, that Polynices who had beseeched our father for aid and was doomed to the death he found in the arms of his cursed brother. Her belief, that without gods man is nothing, was to me only a religious saying, not reality.

But see, how neatly the gods tidy things up! With what perfect logic. Their justice is unbearable.

[She turns and paces towards a door into the palace]:

And now you, "king," here in the palace that was always your home, are estranged from all you were determined to uphold, your mighty laws of the State. Now you and I both understand that your laws are like sand and *not* the building blocks you claimed.

And now you, here, are left to me only, here on this shore of the river between life and death. *[Lights brighten]*

[Voice-over of Creon:

> "A twisted mind is the worst affliction known!
> I shudder with dread. Whatever I touch goes
> wrong. Here, my power ends? Enough!
> We've wept enough… Time, the great healer…."

[Music: Carmina Burana, *"Blanziflor et Helena" and ""Fortuna Imperatrix Mundi."]*

Final scene: *looking outward from the wall of Thebes toward the Plain where her brothers died, then turning toward the doorway into the palace. Music:*

"Anakrousis," as in the opening of the scene, from Ancient Greek Music]

My mother my sister; my mother *your* sister… *[Ismene whirls around, screaming into the palace doorway]:*
Creon! I know you are capable of relenting. Remember how you gave in, in the end, to Tiresias' ecstatic warnings of doom if you did not change your thinking? Yes, you relented—although too late to save my sister, your son, *or* your wife. And now I know it is in your nature. You have proven it! The degree of your harshness will be matched by that of your remorse.

[*Her voice softens*]:

If we…if we were to…come together…. If I could lure you out of your despair, if I could help you to love life again…even a little…to restore some hope with the prospect of making a new life…. Yes, yes the contamination would still be there, my tainted lineage. But the line would live on! Then all our terrible losses would not be entirely for nothing.

Oh hear me out! I, too, like Antigone my sister, have a mission!

But mine is not to move toward death, no—not suicide, not death. No! Let me bear a *new life* for us. Let us not fade out of existence for nothing!… Hear me, love me. Uncle!… Brother!

[Ancient Greek Music: *"Second Hymne Delphique a Apollon" and "Epilogos-Katastrophe." Ismene wraps an arm around each of the doorposts, swaying, then enters into the dark interior. Lights dim as music increases in volume.]*

Text reference: Robert Fagles' translations of Sophocles' *Three Theban Plays* (Penguin, 1984).

From The History of Sight

Charles Tisdale

i. Io

Rooted in Old English *bystinge beesting* udders from Io just after calving. Argus squints his hundred eyes. No son just before his mother's flow *keens* sweet *colostrums* assuaging every hurt until after she weans him. *Wen* begat *entwöhnen* begat *awenian,* for to be satisfied with the maternal nipple is to utter the same word as cognate *Venus*. A Freudian and Grimm kinship, sucking at the fairy's tit, milktooth and labial explosive. Twice blessed is this *nostrum* from the paps that gave thee suck. *Remedium*? Squeeze the breast on a Roman tongue down the runneled streets to the end of hunger where King James listens to a Swede speaking Old Norse to his scriptural midwives. Schoolboy *keens* mothermilk her jugjuice *kenning* from neither's cleft his muse-freshet, latching on to twin-handled Helicon.

ii. Oedipus

Apollo invokes the first ophthalmologist, his arrow's sister Athena *opthlamitis*, sharp-sighted *oxyderkis*:

In the Forest of Arden sight's *exits and entrances* ingress and egress on the *infant* stage. How can a swollen-footed prince nursing at Iocasta's breast–
–cheeking the brooch he gouges to the socket with—know he must tie the knot his feet are twisted with? For three months his focal length only scans a spondee's libation from elbow to nipple towering at the top the mound the shepherd leaves him on. Six million helices fire off seven-sided photoreceptors from optic Hellespont to his brain on Mount Olympus. Not what his Fate is but never to surrogate the Queen's breast of Corinth, or having done so, remember his first view of Thebes.

The *schoolboy* with his *shining morning face* and *satchel creeps like a snail* to read the handwriting on the wall on the eye chart. He has astigmatism. Horny cornea tests oblong rather than truly spherical until eyeglasses on the fourth line finally focus on the grammar of what will be or not be. He traces with his finite compass Fibonacci's golden spiral from dialectic's beginning point past the seven visible planets to infinite astronomy. The number of the notes of harmony beneath the black piano's lid are seven, too, but the scales go on either way beyond the human ear. Earth is a geometric starting place but the arc spirals exponentially forever.

In which case spiraling down the chambered nautilus, *sighing like a furnace*, the son of Peleus sings a woeful ballad to Phthia's *eyebrow* who blinds him with a ditty sprig of deadly nightshade. Why cannot *at sixteen* the end of an optic nerve not see clearly enough that seducing a father's concubine is off limits? Either to die like Romeo in Verona's mind or to live like Hal is all about gaining focus. All said and done, a good father like Peleus takes Phoenix to optilian Chiron who extracts Cupid's dart and makes him King of Dolops. While backstage of vision Hamlet has no Centaur whose binocular perspective governs the horse in him. Only Ophelia, her sunny eye, her optic helium, her nunny nonesuch.

Thus love surviving seeks the *bauble reputation* even in the *canon's mouth*. Bombs burst in air revolving disco balls. *Vasopastic* Diomedes hemorrhages when the spear strikes his shoulder and Athena spreads a mist over his eyes. As does Achilles with transient *hysterical blindness* when Aeneas finds his mark. But neither like Troilus nor King Richard in whose kaleidoscope *Old Troy doth stand*. In Helen's ship-launching face the national disease is being blinded by love's mirrored maze.

Ferdinand hews *cambium* for change. For usurped Prospero surveys from war's lookout *with eyes severe and beard of formal cut*. The old soldier within begins to notice behind the concave lentil lens his tendency to *hyperopia*. How clever-minded Odysseus in search of prudence contracts *kynzosis* from wisdom. How the man who can say *my revels now are ended* must in the professional orbit of an island kingdom first suffer itchy eyes to foil the suitors. After twenty years at forty his aim is still good but the vitreous milky gel in which the floaters have detached are flashing their little dust particles.

After slaughtering a hundred offenders hospitality's *lean and slippered pantaloon* wears spectacles on his nose. His *shanks have shrunk* and cataracts cloud the horny surface. Lower eyelids fold back *entropion* or sag down *ectropion*. *Herpes zoster* accompanies shingles. *Glaucomic* pressure is everywhere as with Glaucus an aqueous fluid caught between horn and rainbow. If it were not for Asclepius in Aristophanes' *Plutus*—who performs the licking treatment from the tongue of two serpents—Melampus would endure *keratitis* forever. For which Jacques *as he likes it* has no cure.

Second childhood is oblivion, Oedipus says, a *macular degeneration*, from too much sugar *retinal pigmentosa*. He thinks for what were the scores and ten wise years he was Panoptes, all seeing like a god, surrounding his field of sandy vision *without eyes and sans everything*.

iii. Narcissus and Echo

In which case St. Paul instructs Narcissus to look *through a glass darkly*, thereby escaping anachronism. But all he sees himself he sees staring back at himself. Mirrors run deep, not so much different from theology, but he should be able to guess, being the son of the River Naiad Liriope and the River Cesiphus, the *phi* in the middle being something like *chi—alpha and omega Ces* before and after *us*. Narcissus bends over the pool and spots only twin stars, his eyes, substance only shadow, *dimly face to face*, drowning in his waking orbs. He becomes his own god and that is why even in the underworld of his unfulfilled desire he never reaches the bottom of the River Styx to gaze in. Just as that other Narcissist Paul wishes not *to see himself* ever again *as he* knew himself but deeper even as he *is* seen. Or *known*.

Teiresias says Narcissus will have a happy life if he never knows himself. For the difference between knowing and loving is the running current and the stagnant pool. To know as Narcissus knew or St. Paul hoped is to see through all the way down to the absence of desiring any bottom. Only a memory or a hope a lover can never dwell in the dark chthonic womb he comes from or the one he seeks, the breast he sucks or the one he wants to. Love is rushing down stream ever being born with every *pebble*, and knowledge is seeping through the bottom of the *clod* down, down, down the grave into the *Acheron* he pays Charon for. *First movers unmoved* God and Satan only know their own encyclopedias. Narcissus overhears himself saying the same thing he has heard himself saying just before. No wonder Echo loves him so much. Like a creed in the *blackened church* few ever show the nerve to never want to be a flower.

iv. Iris

For seven days God and Perseus look into their brazen shield creating Andromeda's Galaxy with Pegasus birthing from Medusa's severed neck. Parthonogensis makes the world in a single parent's image, but centaured from the brow of Zeus Athena sculpts a horse further down. God does not say but sees that it is good. But since he has to speak what he is just looking at, he pronounces poetry upon the earth with his rainbow.

But from the first much damage control. Medusa's hair grows snakes in the form Satan first assumed. The speculum is Perseus' shield, his magic forceps, being a gynecologist, a sickle. Does he swipe at his own image? Or only Medusa? A good god question because after the generations mounted up to Noah God starts all over again this time two by two, prefiguring like Jesus somehow he needs a dove looking through his beak in Mary's ear. In her blue auriculum, the divine semen somehow lodges there the image of now I will finally get it right. Through the fifth color of the visible spectrum—cerulean to azure—a dove flies back with an olive branch and the pot of gold at the end sits on Ararat. Not a palindrome AVE EVA, ROY G BIV still reversing themselves anyway at dawn—violet, indigo, blue, green, yellow, orange, and red—like God did, the question.

What else can forgiveness be but a flower, or a prism of white light reflecting Perseus' own face so various? Noah looks in quite a muddle of a puddle of water, too, every morning and evening over the side of the ark at an ocean full of his two eyes floating in the world's debris. Two orbs, two human planets, snakes of seaweed, floating inundated among ocean and river, sea and stream, beck and brook, tarn and creek, spring and pool, lake and pond, one underwater world the land mass continentally drifting among them lapping the edges like waterlogged sin. And the two eyes staring back.

In the puddle God is looking from the bottom up, the same two eyes backwards at his own image. Knowing himself even as he is known? Narcissus becomes a flower because he had rather see Iris rather than Medusa's snaky flotsam, a better sounding name than Elohim his jetsam. Not mud now at the bottom but smooth stone at first the mirror is. Later obsidian's volcano erupting like an angry Jehovah, a mistake in Pliny who thought the polished surface derived from Noah's second cousin Obsius. Kind of obvious peering even later in polished copper, the evolution of looking glasses, coated with tin, finally silver wed to melted silicon by the bonding glue of theology.

Pliny was mistaken because the pagan need is not Yahweh but Iris, flip side of beauty to Eris, Goddess of Discord, *chrysopteron's* messenger, golden-winged, *podas okea*, swift-footed, *Podenemous.*

She, the rainbow, builds her colors swiftly blending in and from each other in the breaking day or dusk of earth's prismatic atmosphere, each evening and each morning of her first and only day. Wondrous she is, Daughter of Thaumus and Elektra, the amber one, according to Hesiod's *Theogony* an Oceanid, who marries Zephyrus who begets *spring not far behind* and *his showres soote the droughte of March hath perced to the roote.*

Her mist supplies the clouds with rain, her arc unites heaven and earth, the real one not reflected. Beside Hera and Zeus she stands serving nectar like divine love from a jug of ambrosia. Her colored wand sweeps clouds *kerykeion,* a winged staff, her caduceus. Her arm pours as from an ewer cloudbursts, *oinochoe* from Styx, putting to sleep all those who perjure themselves. In his *Genealogia Gentilium Deorum* Boccaccio says poetry and pots of gold at the ends of rainbows are beautiful lies.

For she like Jesus born of virgin, herself a virgin, descends unto death's adulterated house where light gets its colors the hard way and that is why no one sees one very often.

Sister of Harpies, born out of swift turbulence, Aello and Ocypete, birds with girlish heads who befoul the back yard of Noah's-Flood-God's-Flood, she showers down each of her seven mnemonic letters on each of the first seven days of their defilement.

She beseeches the seven Winged Boreads to drive away her sisters from the prophet Phineas. She reveals to argosies how to shoot through the clashing rocks Symplegades to reach her pot of gold. Where Jason Jesus splits the difference between yellow and blue, angel's hair and Mary's, Medea's seven-colored sin and her salvation.

For an Argonaut must face the teeth of the dragon, suffering from his Medea as much as any eating apple gets and gives, soldier of sin and Aeson, scouring the earth after the flood, transfusing his old blood with rush and flood, throbbing back youth *redivivus* in the herbs and fillet of a finny snake.

God said he would never drown the world *next time the fire.* But why did he have to threaten not just one serpent but Medusa's hair full? Why did he have to make not just Narcissus but Milton's darkness visible, Samson in Agony, his cropped hair full of braided Delilah's? Why Styron choosing Sophie's choice his personal apocalypse? Adam's Perseus worthy of his rainbow ends up holding the collateral damage bust and stump, her dead eyes nictitating their membrane across *the first stage of* triumph's *sexual development,* in which the self and the world are the objects *of so much sensual pleasure.*

This excerpt of *The History of Sight* is taken from a larger piece in nine parts. The premise is that the primary vocation of human life is learning how to speak in the tongue of the Gods. Its arc travels from first infant sight to end with Odysseus' twenty-year old blind dog Argus waiting for his master's return. Many instances in classical mythology where eyesight looms large pinpoint the journey and the utterances of great poets sprinkle these episodes with poignant phrases. Numerology, especially the number seven, is explored as providing a mathematical and transcendental basis for verbal harmony. The form employed seeks to emulate the way eyesight and speech operate within a manifold cacophony of sight and sound, how the hoof of Pegasus and the rainbow of Iris select beauty from multifarious chaos and empty void. Thus *The History of Sight* is not only a *theodicea* but also an *ars poetica.*

From The Bar Book

Julie Sheehan

Tom Collins[1]
Vicious is too mild a word, *mon* Gabe.
He shredded you, talked "every word you write's
a lie including *and* and *the*" type stuff,

precision tongue lashing like a pastry chef.
He even called you a bored English major,
yes, he did, girlfriend. What did you do

to rile him so?
And I'm like, sweet pea, homeboy,
listen up Queen Mab, you shush your lip
before Gabe rams a fist through those pearly white

fangs of yours. And he's like, "Oooooh, you know
him?" Know him! Mother of Mailer, I'm meeting him
in twenty minutes at the Slaughterhouse.

---

1. My husband was the storyteller, whereas I was drawn to formal matters, the rules, the orders, which is why I'm documenting my craft, however abject its thesis. Our first summer, he tried to employ me as the fabricator I'm not, asking me to pose as an interested buyer in a sting operation he'd set up to prove to himself a former business partner was thieving his intellectual property. "It's an outrage," he'd say. I said little, hoping he'd cast someone else in his drama, which he eventually did.

Though I could make a Tom Collins today, I could never have pulled one off back in 1874, when it first gained popularity not as a cocktail, but as a practical joke. To play it took planning. You had to recruit a network of bartenders in advance. You'd also need a friend who was excitable but ultimately forgiving to be the butt of the joke. You'd tell him, "Some bounder name of Tom Collins is down at McSorley's slandering you!" Once you'd gotten him sufficiently primed to duel this fictional personage, you tailed him while he burst into McSorley's demanding to see Tom Collins. At that cue, the bartender would set him up with a drink, say, "Tom Collins? He went that-a-way," then direct the hapless soul onward to the next stop in his search for honor. Who knows what the bartender served, a flip, a sling, a julep? These days "Tom Collins" is code for gin, sour mix and club soda, honor being in short supply.

I would not have been a successful perpetrator of the hoax, but I see now I could have been the bartender. It would have been immoral, but then so are all complicities: laughing at cruel jokes, serving alcoholics, napping in wartime. I would have played along, I was that desperate.

Anyhow, I thought you ought to hear
the pulp fiction that hack is hailing down
on your fifteen-dollar haircut. Honestly,

why don't you see Marcello? I gave you his card
eons ago. Run, do not walk. Your bangs
are begging for some quality revision.

So that's the poop, it pains me to report.
He's probably still there, still up the street
at Don Iago's, if you care to tango.

Warning Label on Bottle of Boodles

This gin is flavored with JUNIPER berries, giving it a POISONOUS reputation. CONSULT your pediatrician. Call the HOTLINE. Juniper has ABUSIVE properties, many imagined, some real. RABBITS should avoid swallowing its needles, berries or stems. Also PREGNANT WOMEN, who should AVOID SWALLOWING needles, berries and stems altogether. INHALATION: get fresh air immediately. Contact your representative. CLEAR and HOLD. You will be instructed. DO NOT use passive tense. Americans, this gin has been engineered to WARD away curious CHILDREN while cleansing the target area.[2]

---

2. When I was pregnant, I worked, hoisting cases of Amstel Light and garbage cans of ice right up until the point when I realized the sous chef was interrupting his fricassee to help, busboys were staying late to stock the bar and waiters were steering their customers away from the few decent wines on our list, the ones kept in the tiny back cabinet made inaccessible by my ballooning midriff. I was costing them, so I took my leave.

At home, I helped my husband clean out the crawl space behind the stairs where a previous tenant had left, amazingly, a car engine and some long pipes that might have been useful for off-shore drilling, all of which we dragged piecemeal at four a.m. to an adjacent building where a dumpster, that urban rarity of large-scale disposal, had appeared, a miracle, like life itself.

How to Make an Old Fashioned

For once, success depends on making a muddle. Use the AO for mortar, a heavy-bottomed old fashioned glass, so that you won't have to transfer the remains. Improvise your pestle. Call up a sugar cube and dash of bitters, the human condition. Then a maraschino cherry. Then a few drops of water. Then a slice of orange. Mash them until the solids crash. The Old Fashioned winks nobly at its own vanishing appeal, as if a prisoner before a firing line, but it won't see any action until orange flesh merges with red, liquids and solids converge somewhere between liquid and solid, and entropy reigns over the mutual antagonism of the ingredients. "Surely that rough paste is how we look to God," cries the chaplain, who forgives us our infections as we forgive those who infest against us. The Old Fashioned is ready.[3]

(*Interior Life of Tumbler:*

Spare me the sweet sediment. Spare me the instant sour mix. Spare me
the flat beer of your sympathy. So I'm young, big deal, so I still weep in terror
at the insatiable whine of an Electrolux vacuum cleaner. I've got rent to pay,
extravagant emotions, a noisome hereafter grander and greedier
than you'll tap in our two days' acquaintance. Big deal,
my parents call Sundays, spare me, send mittens and clippings of high
grade grubbers no thanks rubbing up to Security's leg like the one-eyed cat
I sat for two weeks of Ramen spare me Noodles. Nose bleed East Siders, spare
me the change from your Bencharong teacup, your Boshanlu censer, no sense my Bunsen
burner can't compete for hard wire heat I seek I seek I seek
truth and ye shall bruise.)

Pack ice on top of this mess, a medic with a terminal case, and dress it with whiskey, bourbon or rye. Work gently so as not to disturb the muddle. The customer decides when to stir, not you. Lay a thin blanket of club soda on the very top, a General Issue version of tucking in a grown man's body.[4] Service is not a form of communication, since

---

3. I am nostalgic for a past I've never actually *had*, for 17th-century craft guilds, spelling bees in one-room schoolhouses, gloves over the elbow, for the wind in Genesis moving over the face of the waters, all before my time. If I leave my foxhole, there is no Beforehand to which I may return, only out-of-reach histories and childproof folkways.

4. Early in my courtship with disaster, he took me to one of the few bars where they know how to make a proper Old Fashioned. How I lied about hating the taste. "I love it," I said. No wonder his aim suffered.

the server gives attention without asking for any in return. Service is a subset of myth and therefore ominously unilateral, creative but prone to bellicose stealth and friendly fire.

How to Cure a Hangover

The only cure for excess is moderation, but hard drinkers reject such diplomacies. They seek salvation after the fact, the power of the placebo effect. Look it up and you'll find that *placebo* in Latin is the first person singular future indicative of *placere*, to please, and translates to "I shall be pleasing or acceptable," exactly the words a hard drinker wants to hear the morning after. (*Placenta*, by the way, comes from the Latin for *cake*.) Those who face hangovers have developed a variety of faith-healing measures none of which shall be pleasing to the taste, a whiff of punishment being essential to their faith: drink a big glass of milk and Coca Cola before bed, eat tripe or deep-fried canary for breakfast, drop a raw egg into a glass of tomato juice, or, by far the bitterest cure, have some Fernet Branca. Only the hard core dare ingest it, or rabid believers in the medicinal value of revulsion.[5] Black and slightly thick, it begs, like motor oil, not to be consumed. Brits, who brought us Marmite, another substance of alarming appearance and consistency, swear that a shot of this foul substance first thing in the morning cures a hangover.

Fernet Branca

"You're pipes are caustic, ma'am." The plumber spoke
with courtesy reparative. Yet she knew
just what the handyman meant. Why, they've been through
so much, so much through them, no wonder they're broken,
she thought, or bitter. "Honey, after the highballs
they channeled last night, my pipes, no doubt unstinting
in their disregard, can't help their hinting

5. Given these properties, you'd think Fernet Branca would be in the speed rack of every seedy rat hole worth its neon sign, places like Paul's Lounge, where I'd go to meet a certain out-of-work drummer before wedded bliss and motherhood asphyxiated my Lucky Strike-toting wild girl image. At Paul's Lounge, the hard core and the rabid mingled freely with urban anthropologists like me under the penurious owner's gimlet eye. Nobody felt the need to keep up appearances, because nobody could see, the light was so dingy. And yet I never heard a single call for Fernet Branca, though there was plenty of moaning about hangovers. It's in the sort of upscale bistro where I tended bar that you find the kind of person who would order it: gallery owners, executive directors of foundations, Brazilians on their marathon holidays, anyone who wears a Windsor knot over a secret history of TV dinners.

at character defects in their low-pitched squall."
They suffer, but suffering's so tedious
one can't make a living at it anymore.
Why don't they try stand-up, or Literary
Criticism—that smart-mouth esophagus,
bowels labyrinthine as a Borges library,
fallopian jokes. Hilarious, the gore.

As with raw emotion, serve Fernet Branca in a sherry glass far daintier than what's in it.

Leaves

Bruce Snider

My brother, in jail, grows thin,
a boy again, who cannot find the things
he's lost—a job, a wife, grow lights
rusting in a shed. Magazines
spill from a trunk in his garage:
an article describes the flowering phase,
the dark period should not be violated
by any light. When my mother reads it,
she cries. The doctor can't
get her medicine right. She works
her garden to relax. Morning glories
scale the fence, a fevered network
where we used to sit watching
her mulch tulips, bulbs pushed in
with her whole fist. Lately, she dreams
clematis so thick over the house
she can't open the patio door, red leaves
like strangers' faces. My brother
once told me it's not leaves
you smoke, but the resin crystals
on the buds when it flowers, a good buzz
just THC and dopamine receptors.
Now he says three days straight in a cell
can make anyone crazy. Everywhere
I go I see his face, imagining
the bottle rockets we used to steal
arcing over neighbor's houses, birds lifting
like our shared childhood fevers,
how we fought, fist to fist, pushing
each other in the dirt, one cell
translating feeling to the next. Lately,
his yard grows wild, dirt alive
with seed, symmetries of leaf and stem.
My Mother says it's not her fault.
She visits him on Sundays, later
working her yard with instruments

she's been given. Her old shears snip wild
greenery along the house, no will
to temper their pruning, so much sun
astonishing the brickwork.

Planetary

in memory of Miss Jane

Bruce Snider

Today they lowered you, shovels
charting your descent as you once
charted the solar system, strips of dark
blue crepe and glue sticks, yellow
construction paper for Saturn's rings.

The temperature of the moon,
you said, varied on its sunlit side,
a comet's tail not a tail at all, just a ribbon
of fiery ice. Leaning over my desk,
you smelled of drugstore perfume

and moisturizer, your hair a stunning
peroxide blonde, as you told me about
Ham, the Astrochimp, who rode a shuttle
to the stars, then died eating an apple
in his cage. At the planetarium,

you stepped off the bus, your face,
even then it seems, composed
of memory and the same compounds
that make up a distant star: hydrogen,
carbon, ash. For years I remembered

how a giant sun spends the last days
of its life forging an iron heart,
transmuting hydrogen into helium,
oxygen into silicon. How to master
such a feat, willing oneself to metal?

Even the telescope couldn't explain
everything, its lens making the whole sky
blaze as you stood in your lime silk blouse,
poised to take the next step and the next,
satellites passing overhead like theories

of the soul. The truth is most meteors
burn out, smaller than drops of water,
hurled by friction to dust. If you were here,
you might explain how each minute
photons from a great supernova

are tearing towards us, moving
through the Oort cloud, its cemetery
of icy bodies. You'd say not even
light can penetrate the deepest recesses
of space, that time and distance

are always relative, that outside,
even now, people pass under some dead
star's flicker, so much taken on faith, grief
and the moon's dry filament forged
in the still dark spaces between the trees.

North Sea Doldrums

Henry Hart

Knowing no-one in the city, I wandered to the beach,
the day a windblown mist, trash flapping like gull-wings
from the park's roller coaster and carousel.

A brown bird squawked, its accent unintelligible.
Waves tippled oil
from a whiskey bottle, retched.

I followed a helicopter beating through smog toward the invisible
offshore rigs, an oil tanker dragging
its shadow over the elephant-colored bay.

"Why are you here?" the crab claw asked,
tapping its code on a coal pebble.
A syringe hid in a Medusa-clump of seaweed.

Ghosts no longer rode dolphins from the harbor channel
toward islands once graced by literate monks.
The wind was salty, cold, down-in-the-mouth.

Surf broke the bird song *who are you, who are you?*
with monotonous caesuras,
stained the sand with bilge and backwash.

On the sidewalk, a slug hunted for its shell,
spitting a line of asterisks and apostrophes
toward the hiss of car tires.

The lighthouse turned its blind eye
toward the park's chimes and rattles.
The sun dowsed its match behind the horizon's steeples.

Like a sentence afraid of periods, I kept going
past stop signs toward the moor's yellow torches
burning in forsythia and gorse.

By a bracken patch, I gathered the sticks of my name
wind had scattered over eroded roots,
built a small teepee, lit it to warm my hands.

An Oil Rig West of Aberdeen

Henry Hart

The moon tolled like a church bell.
In the bare nerves of trees
crows cried all day

against mist blowing off the sea.
A lady bug adjusted her crampons,
scaled an ice cliff

on a photo of the Cairngorms,
then billeted to the calendar's date:
February 8, 2007.

Why hadn't windows cracked years
before from the constant *thrump*
of helicopters flying to offshore rigs?

One thrashed the air toward a lorry
parked on a football pitch,
its blade gusts hurling a goal into the hedge.

Later, a man in an orange monkeysuit
rang the doorbell. "Don't worry," he said.
"We're just practicing search-and-rescue."

On my bed, one arm crooked over my eyes,
I rocked through sea winds to a rig
like a birthday cake,

its one candle lighting the constellations.
I wanted to know what it was like
to work with nothing around but waves,

a diamond-studded drill grinding
toward buried reservoirs
the world couldn't survive without.

I wanted to know how it felt
to fly home after days of not knowing
where the horizon began or ended,

how you found your way
when clouds erased the compass points
of stars and the wind sang:

"Just lean back and let the darkness flow."

ZURICH, EARLY FALL

—for John Peck

Bruce Lawder

Zurich's cloud cover stays
locked on the lake for weeks. But on clear days
the peaks, like sails, launder the air,
a postcard garden calm descends,
even the twisted trees
budding their small sour fruit
seem no more than graffitti,
the painted scrim of an arbor
preparing some theatrical scene.

Think of the breach in the wall
when the light went and the dark
loosed at last seemed the soil
to root in, the blood arc
skulled to a vision, not that gap
the sun narrowly reaches, free,
too, of the tribal call
that claims the boat full even empty.

You know the guards of the day
shut the temple and curb
the streets like horses time and again.
Go through the gate now,
it does not matter who you are,
the star stitched to the skin,
life's difference,
only to walk on stone
as if on water,
and tell yourself alone
what happens, atrocious
sunset, silence,
blood of another
confession, another lie.

Hate, like the haze settling upon the lake,
will settle nothing. In the narrow stone valley,
the houses gleam corruption.
Hope is the catch in the breath.
What you hold in your hands
now is an absence
still to flower, the light
more than that of a match.

HOLZWEG

Bruce Lawder

—"alltäglicher muss
die Frucht erst werden...."

I still lose myself in the wood,
threading an old goat song
even on these rocks, seeing
the wind silver the olives
or light veil the blown trees,
and the gold cuts of grain
on the altar's stone wheel;
but in the branching dark
of this ribbed northern light
what unmarked trails I find
bring me up to a wall....

Namely unjust, you said,
are the ways of this world,
condemning even then the paths
bound like the reins of the horse
that riderless now hauls
the black carriage through sleep,
following still a trace
drawn in the dirt the wind
had not yet erased, your bridge
a bird's flight, and the fruit
brought back ripe from the fire.

Ruined familiar wood, the light
darkens the way here, and
lodged in the mountain the shepherd
ledges and legends slip back....

When the city went under
that time, the split whiteness
spilt into the petals and fell
with the ashes, the crystals,
for more than a night, and no one
remembered the name, the number,
nothing, and that, too, still
even now breaks into the song.

Betrothed, Liebestod

Kevin T. O'Connor

Betrothed from birth, dark one, we were bound
feet of fear and love, though romantic soul
denied our affinity, to be unwound
like Plato's primordial egg, broken whole;
born of honeyed lust, ravenous with need,
who found delight in polymorphous dreams
where the hungry body seemed to feed
itself, relished its own erotic means
to merge and make meaning beyond the flesh
of others promising fidelity—
but waking to the same redolent scent
and feel you always breathing within me—
abiding half-life of love, fading light,
I felt how cold the sun is without night.

Directions to the Afterworld

James Doyle

The coma wound him tighter and tighter
like a cocoon cynical about a future
of change. Soon there would be
nothing left but residue.

The family around him saw themselves
as castoffs. Curlicues and atoms
spun into thin air by a whirling
center intent only on burrowing.

Each religion, like an endless line
of nurses, carried in its words
on a tray. The family took language
seriously, sipped the various mints

in an elaborate tea ceremony,
but he wouldn't disappear
as all the words promised. Perhaps
they could carry him to the grave

just as he was. If the afterlife
wouldn't have him, surely
the world could nudge aside
its dead by the millions

to make room. They smeared
earth on him for easier passage.
The heavy blood would carry
its message to the brain

and he would shed himself like leaves.
The hospital room would be a bare plain
with its soft flurries of wind
and pilgrims standing hooded in a circle.

Photos of the Dead

James Doyle

The wallet-sized offerings, nickel
portraits tinted in bronze,
held the shape of his face
until the last. The incense peeled

away the rest of his life except
for his widow who broke
the ashes down by years,
the markers of her flesh turned

luminous with grief. She declared
herself too rational
for freedom and was
committed to the marble institute

of survivors. She pinned her family
album to the walls
in her cell, white-
washed against the presence of ghosts.

The charred edges of the photos
refused to fit
together snugly.
There is no satisfaction like a completed

jigsaw puzzle, so she filled in
the gaps with random
promises to suspend
disbelief until all the facts fit.

His eyes followed her around
the room. Even
when she worked
so hard to pray him into

heaven, she knew he winked
the moment she
turned her back.
Finally, there was nothing to do

but laugh. The staff was used
to confusing
a sense of humor
with mania, and the ashes were

taken from her. The prognosis isn't
good, they wrote,
as she went on
enjoying the rest of her life and his.

CHELTENHAM: A BLUE STATE STORY

Mary Kalfatovic

What did you say? -- Yes, I live here in Cheltenham. -- Okay, sure, I can give you a minute. -- Well, I've got my own business. A little second-storey enterprise located above a coffee shop just a few blocks from the main gate of the Great University. -- I am a body worker. -- Yes, one might say masseuse but that's so open to negative interpretation and, besides, it's not English. -- Yes, one could also say massage therapist but that's so clinical, so like something obtainable only if you show your Blue Cross card -- What I do, ultimately, is help people. The musclo-skeletal system is where the woes of individuals manifest themselves. When I came to appreciate the profundity of the mental pain/body pain connection I decided to do something about it. I would help release the anger, the suffering, the confusion, the frustration, and in doing so help make the world a better place. -- As it happens I do have some free time. My next client isn't due for half an hour. Come with me to my studio. This way. -- Yes, we're walking but don't worry. Distances in Cheltenham are short. We are the fourth largest city in the state but our state is small.

-- No, the weather isn't typical of this time of year. Normally, it's colder. What magazine do you work for again? -- I've never heard of it. *City, Town, and Village: A Journal of Community Affairs.* Is it American? -- But we don't use the word village in America except for some pretentious suburbs that insist upon it. -- Of course I realize you didn't name the magazine. What got you interested in community development issues? -- The paycheck! Ha! So you're a journalist for hire. I like that. It's so, what shall we call it? So adventurous sounding, so resourceful, live by your wits, Mark Twain-ish. Have pen will travel. Can I ask you something else? -- It's a question I like to ask people I've just met. What's your dream? That's my question. Your loftiest goal? If you know that about someone you know the essence of all there is to know. -- Really? Your dream is to be a reporter for *Look at Us.* Well, I've certainly heard of that magazine. Nobody who's been in a dentist's waiting room hasn't. -- No, I'm not mocking. Reporting on the activities of prominent persons has a long and noble history. Think of Boswell. Of Einhard. -- It doesn't matter who they were. I'm just blabbering. I must admit, though, that I've not read *Look at Us* in years and years. I don't read any newspapers or magazines. I don't own a television. I've decided to retain the essential integrity of my being in every way possible. I used to attend the Great University and while matriculating there I came under the influence of Dr. Harvey Goldfield. You may have heard of him. He wrote that much talked about book, *Find Mauritania*, in which he decried the average American's lack of general knowledge and asserted that this ignorance will eventually lead to the nation's political and economic collapse. Dr. Goldfield was a bully who wielded his erudition like a bludgeon but still I cling to some of his notions. That's why I keep away from television and movies and even magazines and newspapers. Mental pollutants, all of them, in Dr. Goldfield's opinion and in mine.

One more question, please. And it gets us back to the subject of your community affairs article. Why did you choose to write about Cheltenham? -- Okay, then, I'll change my question. Why were you *assigned* to write about Cheltenham? -- True, I suppose we *are* a good example of a down and out industrial city that's made something of a comeback. -- Yes, I suppose that having opened a business here, I am part of the revival. I might possess, as you call it, insight into the situation. But keep in mind that I was part of Cheltenham's decline, too. I was born and brought up here. I was a runny-nosed ragamuffin, a sass-the-teacher troublemaker, a shoplifter, a street vandal, a truant. A walking, breathing reason why the Cheltenham public schools were once ranked among the worst in the north and why you could, at one time, buy a ten-room Victorian house on the eastside of Cheltenham, an area that was then considered the least awful part of town, for less than the cost of a Chevy Camaro. When I was sixteen, for no particular reason, I shattered the front window of a Polish bakery that used to be over on Wolverhampton Avenue. I still remember the thrilling smash, the fascinating disorder. I was the most dangerous kind of vandal there is, one who acts alone. Apparently the window was the last straw for old Mr. Bronkolowski or whatever his name was. He never had the glass replaced. The window was boarded up and the bakery closed up soon after. The place stayed boarded up for a decade or more. Then, a couple of years ago, a store that sells five-thousand dollar French racing bikes and two-hundred dollar German tricycles opened up in that spot. That's what our revival is mostly about. Gadgets and treatments and food. Look around you. That gourmet market sells ninety-five kinds of cheese. And that wine bistro used to be a hardware store. The Tibetan imports boutique was a barber shop. We're not a city any longer but a combination of collegetown and upscale suburb without an urb. Did you know Cheltenham used to be the shoe capital of America? The shoe factories were all along the river. The Great University was just a quiet, stuffy little sideline hardly noticed by the local people.

-- Yes, it's hard to imagine now, isn't it? Some of the old buildings, as I'm sure you've seen, have been renovated into condominiums and lofts and offices for high-tech companies but most of them are just gone. The factories are gone and most of the descendants of those who worked in the factories are gone. Our little city used to be loaded with Italians and French Canadians and Poles. What we attract now are sullen Central Americans who sweep the floors at the Great University and collegetown sycophants like the would-have-been hippies who run a roast-our-own-organic-coffee place below my studio.

Let's cross here

-- No, I'm not old enough to remember any of the shoe factories actually operating. -- I'm thirty-eight. And you? -- Really, I'd guess younger. -- No, no, forty-nine *isn't* high time you gave up your *Look at Us* dream. A person without a dream dries up inside. Getting back to shoes. Have you ever worn a pair of shoes made in America? -- I don't think I have, either. The pair I've got on now were made in Brazil. -- No, I'm not complaining. Cheap foreign goods give us the good life. We've got a Bullseye's in Cheltenham now. Out on the highway, naturally. I shop there often. Of course, unless I want a llama wool yoga mat, flaxseed bread, or finely aged Stilton, there's really no practical alternative in town. Once I thought Bullseye's represented capitalism gone demonically awry. Back when I was a student at the Great University I marched to prevent its coming to Cheltenham. I used to be a very pessimistic person.

-- No, locals very rarely attend the Great University. I was an unusual instance of town putting on gown. We locals, we real locals, not these new people, if we go to college at all, go to Cheltenham State, which used to be known as the State Teachers' College at Cheltenham, and was originally called the Cheltenham Normal School. Founded in 1839 by Horace Mann himself. -- Yes, indeed, American history was my academic field. I got as far as an unfinished dissertation. Formidable Dr. Goldfield was my dissertation advisor. An ugly little man. He looked like Stephen Douglas. -- No, not Stephen Douglas the actor on *Peyton Place. Peyton Place*? Are you sure you're only forty-nine? Actually, Dr. Goldfield wasn't so very ugly. He did have one good feature. His hair was shiny and dark with a dramatic grey streak across the front. It's gone all grey now but that makes it even more impressive. I see him around town now and then. He glances at me with no sign of recognition. But I've been told more than once that I'm not a memorable person. My guidance counselor at Cheltenham Vocational High advised me to join the Army. She said that blending into the ranks was something a shade of a person might do well. And I did join. That's how I ended up at the Great University. When I got out of the Army I decided to think big with my G.I. education benefits. And, of course, the Great University needs a certain amount of underprivileged types as protection against charges of snobbery.

We're almost there. -- Being across from the main gate of the Great University *does* seem a good location but in reality most people use the side entrances to the campus. The ones off the parking lot and so forth. Still, I do alright. I'm planning to take a cruise in the Greek islands later this year. The beach. The sun. Stuffed grape leaves. Retsina. No ruined temples or musty museums. No history. None of that for me. 'History, shmistory,' my mother once said. 'Why study that? If I want to know history I can just read a book.' But she never read a book. And how wise she was. What a torment history was to study. Utterly demoralizing. History is the true dismal science, offering neither the emotional consolation of literature, art, and music, nor the pristine intellectual pleasures of philosophy nor the speculative amusement of economics, the supposed dismal science. What history does offer is just a long, sad story. Almost nobody wants to hear it. The majority of that small number who do take an interest in history are set on changing it. Expurgating, propagating, and obfuscating to support some agenda, some set of patriotic or political or cultural beliefs.

We've got a Revolutionary War battlefield here in town. On the southside. The Cheltenham Skirmish of 1774. A small but pivotal engagement. -- No, the Revolution wasn't my period. I focused on the twentieth century. The dissertation that I never got around to completing was on the foreign policy activities of the vice-presidency of Richard Nixon. -- You heard right. *Vice*-presidency. -- Sometimes, only sometimes, I wish I'd sat down and finished that dissertation. I had it all planned out. I was taking a dramatic approach and beginning with Ike Eisenhower, in 1952, asking 'Who's this Don Dixon everyone keeps pushing at me?' and finishing up with the Kennedy inaugural on that famously snowy day in 1961.-- Yes, I've heard that JFK slept with Angie Dickinson on the night of his inauguration. -- No, of course I wasn't going to put that in the dissertation. -- Well, for one thing the focus was on Nixon. For another thing, who slept with whom is not relevant to an examination of foreign policy. -- I know sleeping arrangements are the kind of thing most people prefer to read about but I never had any illusion that most people were going to read my dissertation. Nobody at all was going to read except Harvey Goldfield and two other professors who had to because it was part of their job. But let's forget all that. And forget history. It's a profitless enterprise. It's crying over spilt milk. I look to the future now.

You should step back a little so the Great University shuttle bus doesn't hit you. Since your true interest is show business celebrities let me tell you that we do get the occasional star here in the Cheltenham area. There's a Vegas-style casino-resort hotel a few miles outside of town on the shores of Lake Momassen. It's run by our local Indians, the Witictics -- W-i-t-i-c-t-i-c-s. -- M-o-m-a-s-s-e-n. This is the off-season so there's no headliner there now, just a *Star Trek* convention in the main ballroom. -- How do I know about the *Star Trek* convention if I avoid all media? Good question. The answer is I happened to see a poster on the bulletin board at the would-be-hippies' coffee shop below my studio. -- Yes, I agree that posters are part of the media and should, if I'm being consistent, be avoided. I *do* avoid them. But sometimes I just don't turn my head quickly enough. Things like that happen. I can't help it. I take in information I don't seek. There's only so much control a person can achieve. Everything can't be deflected.

What's most disturbing is the lack of control we all have over what goes into our heads during childhood when our brains are most absorbent. When I was little, residing in a rundown house on the northside of Cheltenham, nobody wanted to talk. A pleasant conversation would require more good will than anyone in the family possessed and contentious conversations led to sometimes violent arguments. So the television was always on. Two televisions, in fact. One upstairs, one down. Therefore, when I happened to find out via the poster that Janet Wilkenson was appearing at the *Star Trek* convention, in an instant my brain produced an image of Janet Wilkenson, effortlessly dredging it out of what must have been layers of muck because, I assure you, I hadn't given a thought to Janet Wilkenson in years. Yet, in a nanosecond she appeared in my internal screen. Such a clear image it was, too. The puffy blond hair and garishly colored clothing exactly as they were. How efficient the brain is. It can even run episodes of Janet Wilkenson's big hit situation comedy *The Best is Yet to Come*. I see the three young working women -- one tall, one short, one in between; one blond, one brunette, one redhead, one Catholic, one Jewish, one Protestant, Janet Wilkenson being the tall, blond, Protestant one – lounging in their unrealistically spacious San Francisco apartment and spouting out what was meant to be provocative feminist rhetoric. It was a Sherman Foss production and, as I'm sure you know, facile social commentary was the Foss niche. Janet Wilkenson's tall, blonde, Protestant character was called.... -- Don't tell me...I've got it! Becky... and she worked as a cocktail waitress. The other two...okay, now I need your help. -- Of course, Roxane and Amanda. Roxane, a law student or something, and Amanda, a photographer or something, were always trying to raise Becky's feminist consciousness. My favorite episode was the one in which Becky has an abortion and the other two take her out for a champagne brunch afterwards.

I need your help again. What is Janet Wilkenson's connection to *Star Trek*? -- Oh, a pre-*The Best is Yet to Come* fame appearance she made as an inhabitant of an all-female planet where everyone looked like a human fashion model except for having a yellow line down the middle of their faces. Okay. But tell me, do you think that the beings on other planets look like humans except for some relatively minor detail like a line down the face or pointy ears or green skin? My guess is that our neighbors in the universe, if they are further evolved than us, have entirely gone past a physical manifestation. They've broken off the albatross of the body. Are pure thought and spirit -- Alright, I'll stop. And we're almost at my studio anyway.

-- Certainly I have professional training. One needs to learn certain things in order to be a massage therapist. Of course, these days even things that can't be learned are taught anyway. Educational credentials are all the rage. Poets and novelists earn university degrees for writing poems and novels. The place of the artist these days, it seems, is the grad student lounge. All this formal instruction, this degree getting, is just timid bourgeois validation. Listen to these two statements and tell me which one a parent can deliver with more pride –'My son Jonathan is getting his MFA in creative writing. He's going to read from his work at a conference at Middlebury this summer' or 'My son Jonathan sits in a Starbuck's day after day writing something, nobody knows what, then goes to another Starbuck's where he's the assistant manager of the evening shift.' Tell me which... -- Okay, I'll stop.

-- My training? The Northeastern Institute of Physical Maintenance. -- Possessing a high school diploma or GED, filling out a one-page application, and submitting a single letter of recommendation. For that letter, I had the temerity to ask my former advisor, the brilliant and irascible Dr. Harvey Goldfield.

'I have no idea how well you massage,' he told me. And that was true. He didn't know. There was never any crossing of the line in our dealings. Dumpy little Dr. Goldfield exuded asexuality. I can't envision him even being conceived through intercourse. He was spontaneously generated by the New York Public Library.

'Then you could write about how prompt I am,' I suggested.

'Are you prompt?' he asked.

For nearly every one of our meetings over the years Dr. Goldfield was late. I would stand outside his locked office door until he un-apologetically arrived. For how long had I been waiting? One minute or twenty? He never asked.

'I'm dependable, too," I said.

'When I have I ever depended on you for anything?' he said.

Harvey Goldfield (could there be someone, somewhere, who calls him Harve?) depends, I suspect, upon nobody. He lives in an isolated old farmhouse on the edge of town. A house filled, I imagine, with great books. I can only imagine because I never came close to being issued an invitation to stop by. He never invited anyone over. Dr. Goldfield is an historian but literature is his true passion. Back when I was a student I witnessed him use his verbosity to subdue a visiting professor of literature, some neo-Marxist, who claimed that all literature that isn't political is irrelevant and that Henry James, for example, is trivial. The neo-Marxist asserted that the greatest novel of the twentieth century is *Darkness at Noon*. -- What? Oprah thinks the greatest novel of the twentieth century is *The House of Sand and Fog*? Oprah. Please. You and your celebrities. I dread to think what Dr. Goldfield would do to *you*. You would be a sobbing heap on the floor. Anyway, difficult as he made himself, Dr. Goldfield finally wrote the recommendation letter I needed to get admitted to the Northeastern Institute of Physical Maintenance. Or NIPM as it's called.

Here we are, at last. My studio. Come on up -- This room we're in, as you can see, is the main office slash waiting room. Over there, in that room, is the chair where people sit face down while I work on their back and shoulders. And in that other room is the table used for the full body massage. -- The place is a bit cramped and in need of a some new paint and plaster but I do alright. Small businesses are the spine that keeps this nation standing tall. Or so it was said in the local Chamber of Commerce material sent to me the other day. Sit down. Would you like a glass of spring water? These five gallon jugs come from the Great Smoky Mountains. There's a spring water plant five miles away from here, over in Roehampton Falls, but water from hundreds of miles away is cheaper. Explain that? -- Yes, it was just a rhetorical instruction. I know economics isn't your forte. Gossip and ephemeral schlock are your areas of expertise. But I don't judge. I'm not Dr. Goldfield. I won't strip you of every shred of dignity.

My client is late. But she's often late. One of my semi-regulars. In fact, she's my old high school guidance counselor, Ms. Stromboli. Of course, she doesn't remember me, shade that I am. While we're waiting, I'll wipe down the chair with disinfectant. -- Sorry. But it's not toxic.

-- Headaches. That's the main complaint I get. Eighty-five percent of all headaches are the result of constriction in the shoulders and neck muscles. Many of my clients just need a little time up in the chair. Lots of body workers operate out of a spa, like the one they have out at the Indian gaming resort hotel, where they slather bodies in oil for an hour while new age music plays softly in the background. At the end of this little rub down they wrap you in a terrycloth robe with the spa's logo on it then tell you to help yourself to green tea in the waiting room. That's not my style. I get them in the chair and get down to business with their muscles.

-- Ah, that must be Ms. Stromboli -- Well, to be honest, yes, you might be in the way. You can sit over in the full-massage table room or you could go downstairs to the would-have-been hippies' coffee place -- Good. Try the chai. No foam.

‡ ‡ ‡

-- I got the chai, without foam, like you suggested. Sandra Bullock likes chai *with* foam. -- Are you mocking me again? -- Yeah, I got more material for the article. I talked to the couple who own the place. The people you called the hippies. They're not hippies, they're Pentecostal. -- All I know is what they said.

"Pentecostal?" I asked. "Would that be like Aimee Semple McPherson?"

"Who's Aimee Semple McPherson?" they said.

So I suggested they take a look at the TV movie where Faye Dunaway played Aimee Semple McPherson. It might be available on DVD.

Most of the time talked to a short, grey-haired guy. He was all excited about the *Star Trek* convention out at that Indian casino. But it's not *Star Trek* he cares about. It's Janet Wilkenson.

"She's one of the great actresses of our time," he said. "Most people don't realize that but most people are stupid."

He told me that he was once a lonely young bachelor living, for professional reasons, in Bloomington, Indiana, and renting a furnished apartment with a nine inch black and white television. He watched the primetime original broadcast of that *Star Trek* episode about the fashion model planet.

"*Star Trek* is third-rate science fiction that pales beside Wells and Verne," he said. "The episode Janet was in was without sufficient character development and dramatic tension but Janet's brilliance shone like supernova of 1054 over the Aztecs."

Except he didn't say Aztecs. He said something else -- Maybe Ananazis or whatever. -- But I got the picture. He's going next month to see Janet play *Mame* at a dinner theatre in North Carolina. I wondered whether she can handle the singing and he reminded me of how Janet got to show off her voice in the episode of *The Best is Yet to Come* when Becky gets a job as a lounge singer but quits after one night because Roxane and Amanda convince her that it would be more personally fulfilling to be a singer-song-writer like Janis Ian -- What? -- Harve. He said his name was Harve -- He wouldn't tell what he did for a living.

"I add to the world's confusion," was all he'd say.

SPEAKING OVER GRAVES

—for John Berryman

James McKenzie

Cemeteries are ideal sites for gestures of reconciliation—secluded, open, green, quiet—yet crowded with granite, cement, and other reminders of individual humans, their lives and kinships: chiseled names and dates, fragments of biblical or secular verse, crosses, angels, Marys, Stars of David, the occasional photograph under plastic. If a person has soldiered, a flag, an insignia, their military rank cut into the stone. People leave flowers at gravesides, favorite foods of the deceased, fake, paper money in Buddhist cultures, rocks atop the tombstones of Jews; I've seen cigarettes, cans of Budweiser, swatches of colored fabric, notes and letters; on the graves of children, pinwheels spinning, stuffed animals, balloons—bobbing or pan-caked, collapsing more quickly than their placer had hoped.

A graveyard is a place where someone mourning, remembering, missing, or just vaguely searching, can focus spirit. A place for reflection. The nearness of the dead one's remains, six feet below earth's lid, sealed in a vault, or resting in an urn, can loosen the tongue, clarify lingering mysteries, or reveal nuances of feeling and understanding one might not otherwise identify. Things happen in cemeteries, for all their apparent, timeless, stasis.

Never having visited graves of family members in my earlier days, except at their burials, I was startled, in Hilo, Hawaii's old Chinese cemetery when my wife began to speak, once, for no apparent reason. We were staring down at her mother's grave, having spent an uncomfortable time looking for it, lugging a sloshing pail of anthuriums and orchids cut from a sister's yard, with increasing fear we would never find the stone. Leong See was thirty years dead and, calming into solemn reflection after the anxiety of our search, I was trying to conjure something of this woman I'd never met, born in nineteenth century China, come to the Territory of Hawaii for menial labor when the great sugar plantations were getting underway.

Suddenly, Elaine's voice broke the silence. I turned to see what she wanted, but she wasn't talking to me; her tone was off and her head, like mine, was still tilted toward the ground. Her words had nothing to do with our search for her mother's grave or anything else we'd been discussing; I was momentarily confused, had no response. Then I realized she was addressing her mother—several phrases, maybe a sentence or two. I don't remember what she said: spontaneous words, wistful greetings, an update, perhaps, yanked unbidden from her spirit by the dynamic of the moment. She spoke to her father too, once we located his grave a few rows further up the hill; he'd died when she was two, her name still Sau Kwai; there was no family plot, so her parents were not interred together.

‡ ‡ ‡

I too have spoken over graves now, usually alone. Not long ago, I was back at Sacred Heart Cemetery, near Donora, Pennsylvania, where my parents are buried. I had trouble finding their headstone until I realized the "McKenzie" was obscured by a couple of spreading lilies my sister Lois had planted since my last visit. The stone is flush to the ground and I'd walked right by it several times, seeing only the bushy growth. I don't remember whether I said anything or not there, but words popped out a few minutes later at another grave, several rows back.

At mom and dad's stone I wedged five small sunflower heads I'd bought at a nearby Giant Eagle into Lois's lilies, weaving them among the stems and leaves so they'd stand up better in wind. My parents both liked sunflowers, exclaiming together over the miles of blooming fields they'd driven past, visiting me in North Dakota—thousands of acres of bent, golden heads, all tilting east, the drama of their bright yellow contrast to the leafy green of beet tops, the blond-brown of all that wheat, wheat, wheat. Mom used to grumble about how finicky cemetery managers were about any loose, stray, plant: "too many rules; they'll confiscate stuff if they don't approve," she warned. It was a sunny, August, weekday morning, the whiz of distant traffic in the valley below the only sound, and I hoped my hybrid creation might go unnoticed by fussy workers; with luck, my bright gold additions would fade, turn brown, and remain in their temporary host plant long after I was gone. Mom would have appreciated my effort at camouflage; dad—obeyed the rules.

Leaving their graves, I turned on my cell and phoned our last relative living in Donora, Aunt Nell, battling cancer in her late eighties, to see if I could visit. Aunt Nell is not a blood relative, technically no relation at all, her formal connection to McKenzies broken by Uncle Johnny's awful, drawn-out, pneumonia death in the winter of 1943. But when she married Tom Petrus after the war, he immediately became Uncle Tom, their five ensuing daughters joining Marilyn, her daughter by young John, as cousins. Our families remained close through the roughest times, my various sibs going to school with a succession of Petrus daughters. But at the core: Nell a long-time confidant and comfort to mom.

"I just changed out of my jammies," my aunt said, "but I don't have any treatments today, so come on over. Where are you anyway?" When I told her, she said Tom's grave was nearby. "It's over at the end, Jimmy, just a few rows back from your mom and dad; I haven't been out there for a while."

"I'm sure I can find it, Nell. I'll be by in a half hour then, if it's ok."

I'd never visited my uncle's grave, could not pinpoint the year of his death, and presumed he'd been buried at Saint Dominic's, the Slovak parish cemetery; time to catch up. I returned to my parents' grave, lifted a sunflower head from its new lily home, and set out to locate Tom Petrus's stone. That's when I spoke. "Glad you're close by," slipped from my lips when I found it. Now *I'm* doing it, I thought, chagrined at the gap separating reason from the needs of spirit.

It was Uncle Tom who'd helped arrange for the police the night John and I kidnapped dad, forcing him into the alcoholic ward of Pittsburgh's Saint Francis Hospital, its huge psychiatric department. I'd talked with Tom about what we were planning the day I snuck back into town to see Doc Rongaus and Phil DiRienzo. Tom Petrus was Borough Secretary, sharing a crowded little office with a police dispatcher and other functionaries in the Borough Building, across the street from where I'd picked up my newspapers. Sometimes, my newsboy's bag stuffed with *Sun-Teles,* I'd check out the fire station, then hit their water fountain before heading out on my route. Uncle Tom's office was off to the right, and if he had a minute, he'd engage me, warm, genial, supportive, even—I now understand—knowing more about our home life than I ever guessed as a child. His having a desk job, the coming and going of blue uniformed policemen, and the crackling voices over the dispatcher's radio, all magnified the importance of his work to my inexperienced eye. Uncle Tom also served as a Justice of the Peace and sold insurance, jobs I now realize were cobbled together to support his large family, not indications of the important man in the community I once imagined him to be.

Our talk was brief that late fall day, 1961. All Uncle Tom had done was promise to let the police know we might be calling for help, the night of December 8th. Still, he'd been a steadying influence, a trusted older man, an outrigger for the flimsy craft of our scheme. His immediate cooperation must have assured me that what I intended was right; otherwise he would not have agreed to speak with the police. I couldn't have been in his office ten minutes—nervous, trying not to be overheard, eager to catch the next bus back to Pittsburgh before too many people saw me in town. By the time I got to the shabby little bus station in the abandoned Princess Theatre, one street over, the whole scheme felt more legitimate. Safer.

"Thanks for helping out," I blurted, laying the sunflower on his brass name plate. I placed it over the words "M. Sgt.—World War II," leaving his "Thomas Petrus" itself visible.

"I come here because no one talks back to me," a middle-aged woman in running shorts sang out as I approached my rental car, the jogger and I still the only people in Sacred Heart Cemetery. Sheepish, I looked back across the stones to Uncle Tom's grave; too far away—she couldn't have heard me. My audience had been only the intended one, the fragment of Tom Petrus' spirit within, the memory of my uncle.

At Aunt Nell's house a bit later, I asked her what Tom may have told her about our kidnap plot, always hungry for more information about that harrowing event, greater insight and perspective. She laughed. "The girls and I called him Gluejaws;" she said, "he was very discrete about anything at the Borough. I never knew your dad was going to the hospital till it was over.

"But yeah, Jim, Tom was in combat. He was in a mechanized division off Normandy, so he didn't go in on the first wave. They went all the way through France, Belgium, Holland, and Germany." Warm peals of laughter, always a part of my conversation with Nell, break out again as she tells me of the pictures she found of Tom with various women as their unit made its way across the continent. I talk with Aunt Nell several times a year, usually by phone, so it felt especially good to end our visit as I have sometimes concluded our calls, thanking her in person for her support of mom during the bad times—the most intimate example I know of the everyday, supporting, solidarity ordinary women offer each other.

‡ ‡ ‡

Not all bodies rest in peace; bones locked in underground boxes can summon vengeful gestures as well. A cousin's husband once told me how he and some friends, sons and grandsons of steelworkers and coal miners, pissed on the grave of Henry Clay Frick on more than one occasion. Dead two decades before any of them were born, the former King of Coke (the purified coal that fuels steel-making, not a beverage or narcotic) lives in the memories of some Pittsburghers still, not as patron of the arts or dedicatee of parks, but as Carnegie's enforcer, the man who turned the world's largest steel mill into a fort, "Fort Frick", workers called it—complete with a three mile long, barbed-wire-covered, twelve-foot, stockade plank wall (200 rifle slits), gun towers at strategic points, searchlights, and water canons—hired 300 Pinkertons, and launched a private military assault against striking workers from two barges in the Monongahela River. Ten people died in the day-long skirmish, seven of them steel workers. The people of Homestead and the workers captured the Pinkertons and held out for several days before the Pennsylvania state militia subdued the uprising and seized the mill. The political, social, and historical toll was high, as Frick and his associates intended: the 1892 Homestead Strike led immediately to already low wages being cut in half, and set union organization back for decades, part of a legacy that made him one of the first to be called "the most hated man in America."

The Homestead strike crowned a career of villainy, as far as steelworkers and miners were concerned. The year before, 118 immigrant laborers died in a poorly run Frick mine, Mammoth #1, a few miles from the owner's Westmoreland County home. Grass had no time to cover the trench of their mass burial before the grave was opened again, this time to receive the bodies of nine coke oven workers, striking for safer, more humane, working conditions and higher pay; gunned down by deputies of H.C. Frick Coke Co. in what came to be known as the Morewood Massacre. "Riot" the business, and upper class, community called it. It took more than a century before the Pennsylvania Historical and Museum Commission placed two detailed markers at the site, one for each catastrophe; a 1996 study of the event mentions "divisions which are, to some extent, still present today" in the community. So much coal out of the earth—that Pittsburgh Seam—so many bodies back in, all just a short hike from Frick's Scottdale birthplace and home; and never any sign that he felt any discomfort over those proximities.

And, two years before those disasters, one county east: the Johnstown Flood, Frick the organizer of the exclusive club (called "the Bosses Club," by a Pittsburgh newspaper), a vacation retreat up and away from the heat, smoke, grime, stench, and people who turned all that mineral wealth into enormous fortunes for those bosses. When the club's illegal, ill-maintained, faulty dam—lowered unevenly, for example, to allow their fine carriages to pass one another—burst, it destroyed the Conemaugh Valley's largest city, killing more than 2200. Frick again a leader, deflecting all law suits, keeping his South Fork Fishing and Hunting Club out of the spotlight, his lips forever sealed about any responsibility for that calamity.

Never a man for nuanced communication, much less reconciliation, Frick's bitter, final words to Andrew Carnegie at least betray some awareness of why others might later piss on his grave: "Tell him I'll see him in Hell, where we both are going," he told an emissary for his long-estranged, dying, former partner. Having had his favorite architect, Daniel Burnham, design a building that to this day keeps Carnegie's earlier, smaller, structure in permanent shadow (Pittsburgh), then built a Manhattan mansion to "make Carnegie's," as he said, "look like a miner's shack," Frick remained—like the sound of his name—cold, hard, abrasive to the end. So much more incomplete a human being than even the easy name-rhyme that still comes so readily to some Pittsburghers' lips connotes.

Most historians agree that anarchist assassin Alexander Berkman's attempt on Frick's life in his downtown Pittsburgh office, just after the peak of the unrest—two bullets to the neck, a third deflected by a Frick associate; four stab wounds from a dull, eight inch, stiletto; even an attempt to blow them all up when Berkman, still short of his goal, chomped down on a mercury fulminate blasting cap, which had to be pried from his jaws—that this savage attack quickly drained away most national sympathy the striking Homestead workers had awakened. Far from rallying to his, Emma Goldman's, and the workers' cause, people reeled backward in horror. "The ruthless brutality of Frick," may have been "universally execrated," as Berkman writes in *Prison Memoirs of an Anarchist*, and "the tyrannical attitude of the Carnegie Company...bitterly denounced," but after his bungled assassination attempt, even the union condemned his act.

I doubt I would ever have visited Henry Clay Frick's grave but for my in-law's tale of youthful, symbolic, vengeance. Some odd desire I had—oldest of nine, in a family that owed much to unions, likely its survival—to connect with the larger web of events, to see for myself how the biggest union-buster of all, one of the most unrepentant of robber barons, had tricked out his mortal remains for the rest of us to gaze upon. When I finally made that visit, later on the same day I'd called on Aunt Nell, a nephew joined me, sister Kathy's younger son, Nick.

Our trip was spontaneous—a typical instance of my cramming as much as possible into a return to the region—so all I knew about the grave's location was that it is in Homewood Cemetery's famed Section 14; "Pittsburgh's most prestigious neighborhood," according to their website. For five dollars each, I later learned, we could have scheduled a one hour tour the Cemetery calls "Taking It With You." I like the independence that the cemetery's humor reveals, but I'm glad Nick and I were unaccompanied that August afternoon.

Still, there were problems. We had no trouble finding the general area: the highest hill in the cemetery, crowned by a row of story-and-a-half, columned, granite and limestone, Palladian mausoleums; but Frick's grave eluded us. We enjoyed our search, however, calling out familiar Pittsburgh names as we discovered them, making several, erratic, zigzagging, circuits around Section 14: Heinz and Mellon, Baum and Bigelow, Benedum,

Jenkins, Schoonmaker, and Pitcairn, bankers and big shots, steel men and industrialists, "all the big boys," as my nephew said; "it looks as if each was trying to be better than the next." But we kept missing Frick's grave. Finally, I hailed a skinny runner in red spandex and asked for help. "You've passed it already," he said; "Frick's up on that slope you just came down, past all the Greek Temples; he's behind that hedge."

My difficulty had not been searching for a single stone, lost in a maze of similar stones; we'd been distracted by all the ostentatious granite, stained glass, and ironwork of the other multi-millionaires, assuming "the biggest boy" would have a similar structure, only grander. It turned out Nick and I had passed the chest-high yew hedge surrounding Frick's site several times in our comings and goings, looking past it at all the other, taller, structures: obelisks, a pyramid, the arches, pilasters, and pediments of the many temples subduing that hill. But what Frick lacked in architectural ostentation he made up for in dimension—4200 square feet, "large enough," a cemetery publication says, "for 125 graves," three times the size of the renowned Henry Adams grave in Washington's Rock Creek Park Cemetery. Frick had carved out his own cemetery within the larger one.

Not that his grave was especially humble. A huge, 47 ton cenotaph "of pale pink Westerly granite…the Cadillac of granites," the word FRICK chiseled into its base, commands the center of his little colony of graves. Also designed by Daniel Burnham, the gigantic marker required twenty-two horses to haul it from its rail car to the grave site where Nick and I found it, well into its second century of duty, pristine still, a long way from its inevitable, Ozymandian, ruin.

Frick had long since mastered the harnessing of men, animals and machines to labor for his various dreams, but a Carnegie Library photograph of the stone's progress up Homewood Avenue, circa 1892, still rouses a sense of spectacle: a monstrous, wooden crate, listing to the left, dwarfs the humans in attendance. Seven pairs of eyes, two sets belonging to children, gawk back at the camera; people line the far side of the street. The entire neighborhood must have watched its imperial progress. Paused in front of Clayton, Frick's Pittsburgh mansion, the enormous box dwarfs too the horses hauling it, stretching to the right edge of the photo, awaiting their next command. Perhaps Nick and I would have spotted Frick's monument ourselves that August afternoon, had its identifying, single word, FRICK, been chiseled into its top instead of the base, or if it had not been set apart by that rectangle of thick hedge.

Once there, Nick breached the yews and was inside before I found the intended entrance and joined him; soon we were inspecting names and dates together, I adding what scraps of information I could, Nick ranging around, asking questions, speculating on relationships, enjoying the hunt for whatever all we were after. I told my nephew of those earlier, family-connected, urinations, offering explanations of why young Pittsburgh men might piss on the grave of Henry Clay Frick so many decades after his death.

Only nine Fricks are currently interred there, most in identical, granite structures with open centers, planted in pachysandra. The plants were long past their spring blooming that August day, so their waxy leaves formed a uniform, coffin-sized, carpet inside each tomb, dark green life embraced by the pale granite box, as if each Frick were sprouting. None of the built-in, bronze, vases had been pulled out of its granite sleeve to hold any flowers.

Nick noticed the two shorter stones first, obviously the graves of children: Martha, a six year old daughter, dead soon after the Morewood Massacre, and a new born son, Henry Clay Frick Jr., born two days after the pitched battle in the streets of Homestead, dying a month later in the bedroom next to the one his father lay in, still recovering from Berkman's attack. Information that softened my judgmental mood. Noticing daisies in the infant's tomb, I bent down to see if they were real. Their petals were cool and living to the squeeze of my fingertips; no one alive could have remembered him, but someone had made the gesture of planting them.

I didn't know then that the immense central stone had stood alone for seventy-three years, nor that his daughter Helen had encased her father's tomb in "over a foot and a half of concrete," as a protection against vengeful desecration. A cemetery historian mentioned rumors that a guard had been posted at the site in the early years. Nick and I saw no one but that skinny runner that August afternoon. If there had been any recent urinations, there was no sign of them on Frick's pale pink cenotaph.

On our way back to the rental car, we stopped at the nearby Heinz mausoleum. Someone had woven two thin strands of ribbon into the iron grillwork, making an awkward, irregular heart, fading and fraying since what we decided was its weaving the previous Christmas season. "Oh that would have been for John," the cemetery office voice told me later over the phone, referring to Senator John Heinz. "The family has an endowment for upkeep, but other people still come and leave things from time to time; we don't know who they are, but it's always for the Senator."

When I phone Nick at his auto body shop, trying to reconstruct how our visit had ended, he teases me with an immediate answer: "I remember exactly how it ended: you were really low on gas for that rental car; you were kinda panicky, Uncle Jim. You asked me which way to turn when we left

Homewood to get to the nearest station." Then, more reflective, he begins to speak of "how Pittsburgh would never be what it is without those names; they did a lot for the city. But here's the thing: if we know what we do about them already, just think what kinds of things they must have done in private, things we'll never know."

‡ ‡ ‡

Peeing on the grave of a long dead robber baron, even if it temporarily yellows the raised letters of his famous name on the Cadillac of granites, doesn't approach the desecration John Berryman imagines inflicting on his own father's grave in his penultimate *Dream Song,* number 384; as if it took the previous three-hundred-eighty-three poems to power up for the outrage he has in mind. That poem, trailing Berryman's fury, anguish, venom, and despair, keeps bobbing into consciousness as I have thought about reconciliation and the consequences of an inability to heal, of being imprisoned by past griefs and wrongs, large tracts of inner life frozen in the grip of extreme emotional states, here, the effects (and affects) of his father's suicide when young John was a boy of eleven. Berryman's disturbing poem, with its primal imagery of the poet standing "above my father's grave with rage," spitting on "this dreadful banker's grave/who shot his heart out in a Florida dawn," then "scrabbl(ing) till I got right down/ away down under the grass"

> and ax the casket open ha to see
> just how he's taking it, which he sought so hard
> we'll tear apart
> the mouldering grave clothes ha & then Henry
> will heft the ax once more, his final card,
> and fell it on the start

has unsettled me since I first encountered it: a haunting, a caveat, a radical emblem of the power of festering wounds, and what it might mean to be completely unreconciled with a deceased family member, a father. More than the ax itself, chopping ha at his dead father's bones—a horror all its own—it's the image of Berryman clawing at the grave with his bare hands that keeps returning: a mad cartoon figure, Wile E. Coyote in human form, rag of a beard strung out behind him, glasses sliding down his nose, attacking the ground in a frenzied blur, arms whirling, so energized by his mania that he churns through the earth, unstoppable, mounds of dirt gathering around him, a maniacal digging machine; until a hollow bonk announces his success. Recalling this poem, I sometimes feel dirt under my own nails.

I cannot separate Dream Song 384's electrifying impact on me from my first encounter with it, hearing it from the poet's lips, Notre Dame, 1969: Berryman frail, wobbly, uncertain, trembling, hiding, it seemed, behind his horn-rims, his tangly beard, the podium, the pages of his text itself, then exploding with poetry once his mouth neared the microphone, one of those *Dream Song* readings that cast such spells over so many audiences those last few years. "His powerful voice keening and filling the auditorium," his biographer writes, describing another reading a few weeks later at the University of Washington; "'by the time he reached the last poem," Mariani's source reports, "'the overflow crowd was breathless, most eyes were wet.'"

I'm sure I didn't weep at that Berryman reading; at twenty-eight, I was still a decade from adult tears, having clamped down hard on such displays sometime early in grade school, whether in imitation or defiance of my father, self-defense, or plain, numb, emotional exhaustion, I cannot say. I was a new father myself by then, and having just passed a two-day, fourteen hour written exam in 20th Century American Literature, squirmed, hiding, inside a clunky armor of three years' professional study; two more to go. And even though I was soon to write a dissertation on the poetry of Theodore Roethke, I had never heard a poet read.

A fellow grad student, a writer less devoted to the isolation of his library carrel than I, invited me to that Berryman reading. I'd read my Rosenthal, so had a school boy's knowledge of Berryman's work: he wasn't a major, 20th Century American poet yet (that category, according to my doctoral program, reserved for Frost, Pound, Eliot, Stevens, Williams, Crane and a few others—the white, male, high Moderns), but I knew something of "the confessional school of poetry," and had prepared to discourse convincingly on Berryman's place in literary history, should my examiners ask: how he'd moved, like Lowell, from classic late Modern (mention *Mistress Bradstreet*) to a more personal, intimate, voice; Plath, Sexton, Snodgrass, and Ginsberg the others I could say a few things about under that rubric, if required.

Seymour Gross, who taught a year-long pro-seminar in American Literature for first year grad students, a winnower for the program, announced, before handing back our first papers, irritated, that if love and enthusiasm for literature had brought us this far, we were now to bury that and become professional scholars and literary critics. Professor Gross's staged pique, the breeze of that winnowing fan: your next papers had better be a quantum leap in substantive, documented, analysis, or you'll need to find some other career path. Relieved that, approaching thirty, I'd finally gotten both direction and traction (I'd been recruited, barely knowing what graduate school was) I embraced Professor Gross's exaggerated dictum; I would not be found among the chaff. Enthusiasms out; hard, scholarly, work in. By the time of Berryman's reading, I'd become a studying, researching, paper-writing, machine—twelve to fifteen hour days in an endless stream, with the occasional half-day break: parts of Saturday, Sunday mornings.

But something had already touched me about Berryman before I heard him read. I'd roamed the *Dream Songs* beyond mere study, enjoying their distinctive, fragmented syntaxes, breezy slang, their comedy, and the sheer wild energy unleashed by their fracturing into multiple voices within the same, short, poem. The reader never knew what might be next as the poetry swerved abruptly from high culture: Galahad in 2, Rilke in 3, St. Stephen, Keats, Aeneas, and Abelard, in 6, to the Vietnam War: "A Buddhist, doused in the street, serenely burned./ The Secretary of State for War,/ winking it over, screwed a redhaired whore." Anything might find a place in this exciting, ongoing, high-wire-act of a poetry sequence.

It meant a lot to me that poetry could join contemporary events with larger histories and the world's literary canon. Poetry not for English study but as a thread of consciousness, weaving through centuries and cultures, documenting, expressing, and making mind itself; keeping score, but raised to a higher plane. An activist against the war since my Army discharge, I was buoyed up by the opposition of poets and writers: Levertov and Rich, Lowell and Mailer at the Pentagon, Bly turning his thousand dollar National Book Award over to fund draft resistance. Berryman too was on our side, attacking Rusk and McNamara, moved by self-immolating Buddhist monks half a world away. In those days I believed most sources of my distress were external: political, social, historical—other people. A new outrage every week.

But Berryman's *Songs* connected at a deeper level too, intermittently—occasional jolts, minor shocks of recognition. I empathized with the splintered, central speaker of these poems—his chaotic urges, entrapments, grievances—though I recognize my identification, mostly in retrospect, by the uneasiness, and the speed, with which I'd veer away from the *Dream Songs*, afraid to get too close to the consuming fire of their central energies.

Song 29, for instance, in Rosenthal, with its evocation of guilt-wracked insomnia, all the more paralyzing because its source cannot be located; the often quoted opening lines:

> There sat down, once, a thing on Henry's heart
> So heavy, if he had a hundred years
> & more, & weeping, sleepless, in all them time
> Henry could not make good.

and its awful conclusion:

> But never did Henry, as he thought he did,
> end anyone and hacks her body up
> and hide the pieces, where they may not be found.
> He knows: he went over everyone, & nobody's missing.
> Often he reckons, in the dawn, them up.
> Nobody is ever missing.

The revelation of that humble adverb, 'often': those countless, wakeful, early morning hours of obsessive self-scrutiny; that dark down-spiral of compulsive, tortured rumination.

Or "Life, friends, is boring. We must not say so." (Song 14), with its expression of bootless craving: "After all, the sky flashes, the great sea yearns,/ we ourselves flash and yearn," yoked to spiritual bankruptcy:

> 'Ever to confess you're bored
> means you have no
>
> Inner Resources.' I conclude I have no
> inner resources...."

These, and other fragments, lodged in me as I read, not the way I memorized and yellow-highlighted the lines of other poets, hoarding them to buttress answers for possible exam questions, but of their own doing, like Velcro, adhering on contact, because they corresponded so closely to my own, roughened, inner surfaces. I loved Berryman's kaleidoscopic voice scattered over the 385 poems—the unnamed speaker, Henry, Mr. Bones, and the minstrels—shifting with each, frequent, shake or tumble, all of them mirroring the fractured poet, a new configuration for each poem. Contemporary, hip, frantic, and learned, the *Dream Songs* voice—sometimes comic, always dark—was also seductive, almost familiar. But, hemmed round by professional worries about Affective, Intentional, Pathetic (might as well be alphabetical) and other Fallacies, boiled in New Criticism, I'd ignored, if I even recognized, my identifying with that central Berryman persona.

My academic distance took a direct hit at that Notre Dame reading. The poet's immense, obvious suffering was on display, excruciating to witness, this man of such accomplishment, fumbling his cigarettes, the ice-clinking in his water glass as he bumbled it awkwardly around the podium—couldn't tell if he were getting drunker or sobering up—utterly dependent on the people around him, holding him together, it seemed; but once he began to read, becoming a raw, focused, force of nature; a master of consciousness itself. I remember thinking Berryman must be a man of great courage, forging on, no matter what:

> Hunger was constitutional with him,
> women, cigarettes, liquor, need need need
> until he went to pieces.
> The pieces sat up & wrote.
> They did not heed
> their piecedom but kept very quietly on
> among the chaos.

The ultimate dedication to one's work, a consummate pro. The poet in extremis, still at his post, shaping thought and feeling, soul-making—his own, and part of the culture's.

I did not recall the story then, but my awakening at that Berryman reading was like that of "the correspondent" near the end of Stephen Crane's "The Open Boat." Drifting all night with three companions in a tiny dinghy, their ship having sunk, the four of them cannot reach the safety of land as the currents keep sweeping them back into steeper waves, toying with them; a shark threatens. All the while the little boat bobs about within sight of shore. Someone on the beach waves at them, unaware of their mortal danger, an idle greeting when they require immediate rescue. A cosmic joke; classic Crane.

Suddenly, near dawn, utterly exhausted, unclear whether any of them will survive, the correspondent remembers a stanza of verse "he had forgotten he had forgotten," a popular, Romantic poem, "A soldier of the Legion lay dying in Algiers." He'd memorized it in school, "but the dinning had naturally ended up making him perfectly indifferent." That poem "was less to him than the breaking of a pencil's point.

> Now, however, it quaintly came to him as a human, living thing. It was no longer merely a picture of a few throes in the breast of a poet, meanwhile drinking tea and warming his feet at the grate; it was an actuality—stern, mournful, and fine.

Listening to Berryman reading his *Dream Songs*, I heard his poetry become that "human, living thing," a stern, mournful, fine actuality of a kind I had not encountered before. It went further. My poet was not drinking tea and warming his feet on the grate, these were not emotions recollected in tranquility; this poet was writhing in front of me—a one-man spectacle. If the speaker performing these poems had donned some 'persona,' his mask looked uncannily like the suffering face of John Berryman. I read Berryman, read all poetry, a little differently after that evening; I remained a budding academic, but felt "physically as if the top of my head were taken off," as Emily Dickinson defined poetry to her Higginson. Now I wanted more from poetry, more from all literature.

‡ ‡ ‡

By the time Berryman jumped off the bridge at the University of Minnesota less than three years later, I'd read all the *Dream Songs* more than once; and awaited, hungry, any new work from this genius of my time, bulletins from the front lines. Teaching poetry myself then at North Dakota, a few hundred miles further up the road, I felt close enough to Berryman—the man and his poems—that his suicide seemed proximate, if not intimate, a personal loss: not Hart Crane plunging over the rail of the *Orizaba*, 1932, or Sylvia Plath in a cold, faraway, London winter, her head so deep inside that oven, but someone whose struggles I'd identified with, admired, a nearby poet I felt I knew, cashing it in.

Berryman's death in Minneapolis, a news flash from the darkest regions, struck like a sledge hammer and came with a warning: something about the dangers of too much intensity, too many secrets—"Huffy Henry hid," the whole sequence begins (the gulf of that pregnant white space, that blank Berryman did not fill in)—the lethal power of unfinished business. Without realizing I was doing so, I immediately began to soften Berryman's suicide by constructing a story founded on erroneous assumptions: for years I believed he'd drowned in the cold Mississippi that January day, and took comfort in the river's iconic status: Father of Waters, Twain's river, Melville's *Confidence Man*, Faulkner, "Over DeSoto's bones the freighted floors/ Throb past the City storied of three thrones." So much literary lore already for so young a country. The poet who'd spoken so thoroughly to my own inner life at least wrapping himself in the shroud of those myths.

But it was not so. Learning details of his death much later—how high the bridge was, that ambiguous wave of his hand to passing students (hello/ goodbye), the fact that he'd not disappeared in water, like Icarus, Virginia Woolf with her heavy, pocketed, rock, Hart Crane, or those innumerable, anonymous, Golden Gate plummeters, but had smashed onto the bank (clearly a deliberate choice), his broken body rolling ignominiously down the slope—stripped away the thin fabric of comfort I had woven, however unconsciously, out of American literary history. That mythmaking was all my own, a delusional, literary, construct, a dodge. Protection. I live in Saint Paul now, find myself on the Minnesota campus several times a month.

I cannot walk that Washington Avenue Bridge without feeling the waste of Berryman's death, mourning him, hearing the sickening whump of his fifty-seven year old, intelligent, gifted, poet's body landing on that West Bank knoll. Berryman's death was alcoholic, despairing, suicide, not mythic transformation; the poet of the *Dream Songs*, and so much more, ended in protracted nightmare.

A few years after Berryman's death, I ended a class early when, discussing *Song 384* and other of those Songs, I could not answer an older student's question about how a person so affected by his own father's suicide, a gifted poet, expressing that pain and loss so memorably, could then take his own life, leaving children behind, including a young daughter. My student had lost a brother to suicide years earlier and Berryman's poem (we may well have read some Plath and Sexton too that semester) brought her terrible loss back with fresh vigor. I was shocked at the strength of that student's anger so many years after her brother's death—her face red with fury, her body trembling, as she silenced our classroom with the challenge of her accusations.

Whatever else I told my students when we reconvened two days later, offering hope without any definitive answer to such a question, I took shelter in the lame safety of the poet's own words; I owed Berryman that. I remember supplementing our anthology's choices with photocopies of a few of his "Eleven Addresses to the Lord," and ended with the final line of the posthumous *Delusions, etc.* from "King David Dances": "all the black same I dance my blue head off," another Berryman line that had Velcroed itself to me. I added something about the blues too; Berryman's line always evokes such associations: that long, ongoing, American musical tradition, now global, rooted in African-American music and history, field hollers, gospel, minstrel even (hello, Mr. Bones), Lead Belly, Robert Johnson, carried here all the way back to the court of King David. Dance and sing one's blackest sorrows, no matter what they may be; keep on keepin' on.

Had I known it then, I would also have given my students Berryman's answer to the first question Richard Kostelanetz reports from a conversation with the poet after *His Toy, His Dream, His Rest* (Dream Songs 76 to 385) won the National Book Award, 1969.

> To what extent, I asked, did the poet resemble "Henry," the dominant character of the Dream Songs? "Henry?" said Berryman; "he is a very good friend of mine. I feel entirely sympathetic to him. He doesn't enjoy my advantages of supervision; he just has vision. He's also simple-minded. He thinks that if something happens to him, it's forever; but I know better."

By the time Berryman tilted off that bridge rail, Berryman's supervision had disappeared; he and his persona had become indistinguishable. No reference to Henry or any of the other fragments of Berryman's voice appears in the Dream-Song-like poem fished from his wastebasket after the poet's suicide, a line drawn through its text.

> I didn't. And I didn't. Sharp the Spanish blade
> to gash my throat after I'd climbed across
> the high railing of the bridge
> to tilt out, with the knife in my right hand
> to slash me knocked or fainting till I'd fall
> unable to keep my skull down but fearless
>
> unless my wife wouldn't let me out of the house,
> unless the cops noticed me crossing the campus
> up to the bridge
> & clappt me in for observation, costing my job—
> I'd be now in a cell, costing my job—
> well, I missed that;
>
> but here's the terror of tomorrow's lectures
> bad in themselves, the students dropping the course.
> the Administration hearing
> & offering me either a medical leave of absence
> or resignation—Kitticat—they can't fire me—

Whatever the sources of his despair, Berryman felt, like his Henry, that they were forever so, two days after writing this poem, he made his own irrevocable act. He no longer knew better than his Henry.

‡ ‡ ‡

When I learned last summer that John Berryman's grave lay only a few miles from my Saint Paul home, at Resurrection Cemetery, high above the point where the Minnesota River joins the Mississippi, I paid a visit. Remembering Dream Song 384 but not knowing quite what I wanted to do, I cut some flowers from our little prairie garden— sprigs of hosta, a few day lilies, three white yarrow—plus some pink, gaudy, 'weed' plucked impulsively from the edge of the back yard, and headed out. It was a sweltering August day, and I was picking my wife Patti up at the train station after work before heading up to Resurrection, so I put them in a clear glass vase; no wilting flowers for Berryman's, or any, grave, if one can help it.

Song 384 opens, "The marker slants, flowerless, day's almost done."

Berryman's own marker, it turns out, will never slant since it is flush to the ground, convenient for the industrial size mowers, one of nearly five thousand such graves in Resurrection's Section 60, "a small city in that section alone," the gracious office assistant said, handing me a map. She filled Berryman's little square in with red ink. "They're buried chronologically in our 'next available' section. If he died in January, I'm sure his would have been pre-dug. That's how we handle winter burials."

Not knowing the grave stones in that entire section were flat, we drove past them all on the first pass. But once oriented, I quickly found Berryman's plot, head to the ground as we read the graves, moving backward in time, dodging long, arching, jets of water from the sprinkling system. Only two symbols besides his name and dates mark Berryman's ordinary grave, an IHS Christogram, fitting, I guess, given "Eleven Addresses to the Lord" and his efforts to embrace a more personal God those last years, and a Celtic cross, less stark, with its interlocking curves, than the plain Latin cross chiseled on my parents' grave.

Patti stepped back several rows towards the car to leave me alone there but I wasn't sure what, if anything, I wanted or needed. Dropping the flowers onto his stone, I heard "Rest in peace, John Berryman" escape my lips, an echo of the many "*Requiescat in pace*s we'd both heard as altar boys at other burial sites, he in Oklahoma, I in Pennsylvania.

On another impulse, seeing the water in the clear cylinder vase in my hand, wondering what to do next, I dumped it on his stone. I'd already dropped the flowers onto his name; no point leaving that vase for the grounds crew to confiscate. "You should have drunk more of this," I heard, my brother Damian's voice saying from the spring before, as he'd spilled mineral water from his plastic bottle onto Grampa Jerry's grave.

"Might as well get all of them," I'd said. "They all could have used less alcohol." So Damian, approaching thirty years of sobriety himself, doused Grandma Elizabeth's, Uncle Johnny's, and Aunt Stell's identical stones as well. He, Lois, and I had a good laugh at that splashing.

But I'd said all I wanted to at Berryman's grave. I stared at his flat stone as my cascading water lifted previously unnoticed dirt from the stone, swirled it with bits of mown grass, and drained off the edges into the lawn, leaving Berryman's wet rectangle of granite to glisten in the setting sun. The next prairie thunderstorm would wash the stone better than anything I could, or would, do.

A Lord of Limit

Geoffrey Hill. *Collected Critical Writings*, ed. Kenneth Haynes. Oxford University Press. 2008.

Kevin Hart

One can imagine a book by Geoffrey Hill entitled *Collected Critical Writings* that contains both his essays and many of his poems. It would include, like the volume under review, *The Lords of Limit* (1984), *The Enemy's Country* (1991), *Style and Faith* (2003), and two previously uncollected series of lectures that were conceived as books, *Inventions of Value* and *Alienated Majesty*. Yet it would also gather together individual collections of verse from *For the Unfallen* (1959) to *Canaan* (1996). For they too are "critical writings," their imaginative reach being one with their criticism of life in general and their criticism of poetry's longings to speak beyond its proper limits in particular. Despite individual lyrics in the more recent collections, Hill's later poetry does not exemplify, as his best earlier poetry so splendidly does, Pound's dictum: "The poet's job is to *define* and yet again define till the detail of surface is in accord with the root of justice" (quoted, p. 4). Were we to suppose that the later criticism falls off at the same rate as the later poetry, though, we would be very much mistaken. As a writer of critical prose, Hill at his best remains as tough-minded and incisive as he has ever been. It is as though Hill the older poet is only half-listening to Hill the mature critic when the latter tells us that, "the great poem moves us to assent as much by the integrity of its final imperfection as by the amazing grace of its detailed perfection" (p. 477). A poem such as "September Song" or "Funeral Music" or "Lachrimæ" is eloquent in its "final imperfection" as well as in its "detailed perfection." One cannot say the same for the poems of *Speech! Speech!* (2000) or for a great many that have come after it. Here the notion of "final imperfection" has become a gesture, not a hard-won consequence of moral inquiry.

The young Hill was as gripped by perfection in his prose as in his verse, and was accordingly sparing in his production of both. *The Lords of Limit* contains nine essays, only five of which had appeared in print before he gave his inaugural lecture "Poetry as 'Menace' and 'Atonement'" on assuming the Chair of English Literature at the University of Leeds in the December of 1977. True, Hill had also published short pieces in little magazines, several reviews and review essays in scholarly journals, and his first three collections of poetry. Nonetheless, it is hard to imagine today how a scholar forty-five years of age could be appointed to a Chair on the basis of only five solid essays. Yet those five essays—on Jonson, Shakespeare, Swift, the diverse world of nineteenth-century British writing, and the idealist philosopher T. H. Green—remain astringent, probing and illuminating, which can scarcely be said of the first essays of most professors of English thirty years after they were written. Not only is Hill's critical acuity evident in every paragraph of these five essays but also they reach, with impressive ease, from the seventeenth to the twentieth century, and deal with drama and poetry, prose fiction and prose non-fiction. When one adds the other four essays that make up *The Lords of Limit*—analyses of Southwell, John Ransom, and J. L. Austin, not to mention the inaugural lecture—it is clear that we are in the presence of a mind of unusual power and scope.

It is also a mind that is unusually self-conscious. The inaugural lecture shows Hill at both his best and most characteristic as a critic, which in his case seldom converges with best and worst. There are no moments of bad criticism in Hill, although there are times when one could have wished him to be less crotchety, less tangled, and less inclined to take his own poetic practice as a norm for all poetry. Consider the first piece in *The Lords of Limit*, "Poetry as 'Menace' and 'Atonement.'" It is a wide-ranging essay in which several chords we will come to recognize as Hill's leitmotifs are played by way of quotation. First, we hear Milton's statement that poetry is "more simple, sensuous and passionate" than rhetoric. And second, we are reminded of Coleridge's observation, "Poetry—excites us to artificial feelings—makes us callous to real ones." In the *Collected Critical Writings*, though, one will not hear the first chord: Hill has lightly revised "Poetry as 'Menace' and 'Atonement'" and removed the quotation from *Of Education* (1644), doubtless thinking that he has cited it sufficiently often over his writing career. The emphasis on "atonement" and "menace" remains, and serves to guide us through the thirty-three essays that follow it. The two words in the title are important: each in its own way speaks of sin. Hill is a rare critic, even among those who work in "religion and literature," in that he affirms the doctrine of original sin in all its terrible weight. The word "sin" sounds time and again in this volume, even though it is now written with a lower-case "s." In *The Lords of Limit* Hill wrote "Sin" in the opening essay, the unnecessary capital letter turning an old concept into an allegorical figure, and suggesting a dark intensity that is now lost. The prophet has truly become a professor.

In "Poetry as 'Menace' and 'Atonement'" Hill quotes the second edition of Karl Barth's *The Epistle to the Romans* (1921). The young theologian tells us there that sin is the "specific gravity of human nature as such" (quoted,

p. 17). It is a memorable expression, but Hill leaves it unclear what he has in mind in quoting it. For his source he cites an essay by another scholar who quotes the expression, and one must assume that Hill has not read *The Epistle to the Romans*. So it is unlikely that Hill has in mind the exact cut of Barth's distinction between Grace and sin, or anything in Barth's early theology; and we simply do not know if Hill takes "specific gravity" to be the burden of original sin, the weight of actual sin, or the concupiscence that remains after baptism. In this passage, at least, we are dealing with a magpie, not a scholar. He uses Barth's line when making a large mannered formulation. "I am suggesting," he says, "that it is at the heart of this 'heaviness' that poetry must do its atoning work, this heaviness which is simultaneously the 'density' of language and the 'specific gravity of human nature' (p. 17). If Hill is really talking about sin, then "atonement" must refer to how the debt of sin is discharged. Yet he does no such thing. He never truly removes the quotation marks from "atonement," and redefines the word as "the technical perfecting of a poem...in the radical etymological sense—an act of at-one-ment, a setting at one, a bringing into concord, a reconciling, a uniting in harmony" (p. 4).

Now in the hands of a good poet, technique is very seldom just mere technique; it is the sharp point of a shaping moral intelligence. Scrupulous writing cannot atone for sin. It may, however, minimize the gap between aesthetic and moral judgments, a gap that is a consequence of sin, and produce a sense of at-one-ment for writer and reader alike. One may well wonder why a venerable theological word such as "atonement" is being evoked if it is to be used only in another sense. The best that Hill can tell us is that poetry not only provides "atonement" but also continually risks being a moral menace: enabling, even encouraging, the displacement of moral categories by aesthetic ones, and thereby calling for acts of penitence from the author, sometimes in the poem itself. It is a variation on the project of Jena Romanticism. Where the brothers Schlegel brightly insisted that the poem must include its own theory, Hill instructs us that the poem must include its own act of penitence. The one gives us the "literary absolute"; the other gives us the penitential conditional: we are never fully absolved in the world of Geoffrey Hill.

Poetry, for Hill, can offer at best limited "atonement": not salvation only for the elect but a partial closing of the gulf between aesthetic and moral judgments. This is put as clearly in the sonnet sequence "Lachrimæ" as it is in the inaugural lecture or in any of the essays that follow it in this volume. One could wish that "Poetry as 'Menace' and 'Atonement'" guarded its thesis less anxiously and devoted more time to define and test its central terms. Does Hill need to evoke theological categories in order to make his point, or could he make do perfectly well with the distinctions of ethics? Probably the latter, although his conviction that human beings are fallen creatures explains why one cannot ever completely close the gap between aesthetic and moral judgments. And so he brings a theological perspective to literature, and is not shy of criticizing others who have done the same. "The major caveat which I would enter against a theological view of literature is that, too often, it is not theology at all, but merely a restatement of the neo-Symbolist mystique celebrating verbal mastery" (pp. 18-19). Quite so; but when Hill talks with conviction of sin and then introduces the concept of atonement solely in the register of poetic technique one may well surmise that he is biting off less than he should try to chew. In pages that could situate a consequence of sin—the very gap between aesthetic and moral judgments—in a theological context, we have instead several fidgety paragraphs that attempt to display a mastery of literature. Olson, Baudelaire, Eliot, Péguy, H. A. Williams, Jeremy Taylor, Jarrett-Kerr, Stevens, Arnold, Mallarmé, Rimbaud, Yeats, Rilke, P. T. Forsyth, Steiner, and Empson: all are named in a few pages and little more than named. Perhaps it is best to say that Hill is an essayist, given to empirical criticism and suggestion, and not a writer of books that elaborate a sustained argument.

It is often in local moments of reading a text that Hill shows his highest value as a critic. When reading Swift's "A Beautiful Young Nymph Going to Bed," for example, he quotes the following lines:

> The Nymph, tho' in this mangled Plight,
> Must ev'ry Morn her Limbs unite.
> But how shall I describe her Arts
> To recollect the scatter'd Parts?
> Or shew the Anguish, Toil, and Pain,
> Of gath'ring up herself again?
> The bashful Muse will never bear
> In such a Scene to interfere.
> Corinna in the Morning dizen'd,
> Who sees, will spew; who smells, be poison'd.

Hill comments: "The perfect dryness of 'recollect', the peremptory burlesque of the eighteenth-century colloquial rhyme 'dizen'd' / 'poison'd', have complete control over the plangencies of 'Anguish, Toil, and Pain'" (p. 84). So they have, yet only Hill has seen it so clearly. Hill is similarly good in another mode: thinking how best to approach the style of an author. Consider his comments on Robert Southwell, not the easiest of poets to reckon with in this regard. "Style is not simply the manner in which a writer 'says what he has to say'; it is also the manner of his choosing not to say. There is a distinction to be drawn here between the manner of not-saying and the demeanour of silence" (p. 9). That is perfectly put, and of more general application than reading Southwell.

When we move forward to "Language, Suffering, and Silence" (1998), we find Hill still talking about "religion and literature," although his general thoughts about it seem not to have developed over the years. "If I were to consider undertaking a theology of language, this would be one of a number of possible points of departure for such an exploration: the abrupt, unlooked-for semantic recognition understood as corresponding to an act of mercy or grace" (p. 404). We have not moved far from thinking of poetic technique, when deployed properly, as "atonement," although other theological terms are now invoked. At the level of ideas, Hill prefers to stay at the beginning. He is too skeptical of systems and too attentive to literary texture to pass from literature to thinking theologically about literature. So *Style and Faith* offers only some gnomic general remarks on the subject. "With Donne, style *is* faith: a measure of delivery that confesses his own inordinacy while remaining in all things ordinate. To state this is to affirm one's recognition of his particular authority in having achieved the equation; one recognizes also such authority in Milton and Herbert. They are not, generally, otherwise to be equated" (pp. 263-64). A writer's style is one with his or her character, to be sure (which makes the desire to "change style" a moral issue), and a writer of tested religious convictions will not change styles except as a consequence of deepening his or her faith or adjusting the object of that faith. Perhaps this is what Hill means here. Yet it is odd that someone who broods over the word "or" (p. 100) and has smart things to say about the semi-colon (p. 393) relies rather lazily on italics to give the impression of a conclusive case being made in the book that follows the preface. Not even a word about *fides qua* and *fides quæ* is given, and without due attention to that distinction one will not have much that is precise to say about faith.

Hill is perhaps more deeply committed to "literature and politics" (taken broadly) than to "literature and religion". *The Enemy's Country* is dense, eloquent testimony of his sense of how literature is embedded, often in an angular way, in the common weal. "Civil polity…is poetry's natural habitat" (p. 518), he says in the later *Alienated Majesty*, lectures he once delivered at the University of Notre Dame, and chooses his words with care. Ecclesiastical polity is presumably not poetry's natural habitat. It may have been for Herbert and possibly for the Eliot of "Ash-Wednesday" and "Four Quartets" but not for most strong poets. "A system of ethics, if thorough, is explicitly or implicitly a system of theology," Eliot wrote in his dissertation on F. H. Bradley. To which Hill responds, with reason, "This is debatable to say the least" (p. 551), although he characteristically does not continue the paragraph by following the initial idea, as one could do in different ways with the help of Aquinas, Kant or Kierkegaard, to give only three inevitable names. Rather, Hill modulates to a suggestion that there is a connection between Bradley's "sceptical idealism" and Anglo-Catholicism, followed by a doubt that Eliot was truly interested in philosophical or theological *systems*, followed in turn by a condescending remark about Bradley's prose style ("the odd glissades and cornerings of Bradley's prose: 'what in morality only is to be, in religion somehow and somewhere really is, and what we are to do is done'" (p. 551)), a prose style that was the basis for Eliot's own. It is characteristic of Hill as critic that he prefers not to engage at length with ideas and looks instead for a nice quibble or a severe remark.

There are long passages in Hill's essays, early and late, when he seems continually cross. He sounds then rather like a Master in a British public school a century ago, a character somewhere in the range of the first volume of *A Dance to the Music of Time*: a fastidious philologist who once earned a decent first at Oxford and who is prone to throw a tantrum when boys in the lower fifth make a loose remark about Hooker. Christopher Ricks turns out to be one of those inattentive boys when Hill turns to him towards the end of "Dividing Legacies" (1996) to rebuke him for having the temerity to admire Philip Larkin's poems. "I would ask him to place his 'generous common humanity' within the field of Hooker's common equivocation and to determine how much weight and pressure that generous humanity can sustain" (p. 379). Ecclesiastical polity might not be poetry's natural habitat but there are times, it seems, when it can be of use to literary criticism. Yet why should one choose Hooker here? One could put "generous common humanity" in the frame of St Thomas Aquinas's *Summa theologiæ,* especially the *prima secundæ partis* and the *secunda secundæ partis*, and see how well it fares. And then one could put Hooker's treatment of "common equivocation" in the same frame and see how well *it* does. The example of Aquinas here merely helps to make a point: Hill's choice of Hooker in this context, and of one particular aspect of Hooker, is a figure for Hill himself.

What Hill dislikes about Larkin, and the Eliot of "Four Quartets" before him, is their lack of "pitch." The word comes to him from Hopkins, a poet who has always been close to Hill. In his remarkable review of the second edition of the Oxford English Dictionary, Hill chides the editors in their entry on this word. "In recent years there have been scholarly glosses on the peculiar meaning Hopkins gave to this word (for example, in Peter

Milward's *A Commentary on... 'The Wreck of the Deutschland'* [1968]), which the compilers of the O-SCZ *Supplement* (1982) appear not to have considered" (p. 267). Perhaps those poor benighted souls were indeed unaware of this fine commentary published by the Hokuseido Press of Tokyo in 1968. Milward notes the implication of "the peculiar meaning Hopkins gives to the word, when he speaks of 'this unspeakable stress of *pitch*, distinctiveness and selving, this selfbeing of my own'" (*A Commentary on G. M. Hopkins' "The Wreck of the Deutschland,"* p. 86). Hill is entirely right to point to the value of this word for criticism, although he makes very heavy weather of it and leaves the word remaining more suggestive than well defined. In the process he bypasses Derrida's sense of the word "idiom" which does some of the same work as "pitch." All he can muster in the direction of contemporary French criticism is the silly remark, "Since I do not believe that 'texts' write themselves, I am here considering a quality of Wordsworth's intelligence and personality" (p. 390). Of course, if Hill had bothered to read a page by Derrida or even Foucault he would have discovered that no one has ever said that texts write themselves, and that the claim at issue is a complex one in the philosophy of the human subject, one that deserves close inspection and not a flip journalistic response.

And yet Hill is no enemy of the complex. Indeed, he is one of our most articulate and insistent defenders of the difficult. Like Hugh MacDiarmid, he desires "A learned poetry wholly free / From the brutal love of ignorance" (quoted, p. 173). And he brings Hopkins quickly to his defense in the poet's letter to Bridges of November 6, 1887: "Plainly if it is possible to express a sub[t]le and recondite thought on a subtle and recondite subject in a subtle and recondite way and with great felicity and perfection, in the end, something must be sacrificed, and with so trying a task, in the process, and this may be the being at once, nay perhaps even the being without explanation at all, intelligible" (quoted, p. 98). My one caveat here is not to do with difficulty, or even with Hill's testy reproaches to those who plead for the "accessible" (for example, Isobel Rivers' concession not to take the reader's knowledge of seventeenth- and eighteenth-century British culture for granted, and the decision to use modern spelling in the new edition of Tyndale's translation of the New Testament). Rather, my concern is with the underlying assumption that runs through Hill's criticism that "difficulty" characterizes the best literature and the best ideas. There are times when the most telling word to use of a poem may be "rich" or (with caution) "mysterious" but not "difficult." Strong literature always requires the most its readers can give, and sometimes quite considerable effort and labor are called for on the part of the reader. But one reduces literature to just one of its many modes of being when one approaches it solely with the word "difficult" or chastises its authors for not being sufficiently "difficult" in their compositions. One reads Larkin poorly when one reads him with the expectation that his poems will give themselves in the same ways that Hill's early poems give themselves to us. One reads "Four Quartets" weakly when one expects Eliot to write his last poems in the same way he wrote "The Love Song of J. Alfred Prufrock." There are distinctions other than the one between "menace" and "atonement" that can guide us when reading poetry, although, to be sure, it is Hill's genius that he has compelled us to see so much literature in terms of that distinction and all it has spawned for him.

KEEPING GOOD COMPANY

James Agee: Selected Poems. American Poets Project, The Library of America, 2008. *Anne Stevenson: Selected Poems*. American Poets Project, The Library of America, 2008.

Kevin O'Connor

Virtually unanimous praise has been lavished on the Library of America's definitive editions of our national literature. Less has been said about the same publisher's American Poets Project, a series of compact editions of American poetry, selected and introduced by distinguished poets and scholars. Beyond the few "category" anthologies (*Poets of World War II, American Wits, Poets of the Civil War, American Sonnets*), the poets in the series range from the marginal and neglected (Yvor Winters, Kenneth Fearing, Louis Zukofsky) to the popular, but academically slighted (Edna St. Vincent Millay, John Greenleaf Whittier, Carl Sandburg, even Cole Porter), to those who should be, but have not yet been, honored with complete editions (William Carlos Williams, John Berryman, Theodore Roethke, Gwendolyn Brooks), to those recently deceased contemporaries making an early bid for some kind of canonical recognition (Muriel Rukeyser, A. R. Ammons, Kenneth Koch)—the series attempts to fill a huge void between those poets unfairly left on the shores of oblivion and those already enshrined on the peaks of Parnassus. Given the vast sea of neglected poetry around us, the only puzzling choices seem to be those poets like Whitman and Poe, who are already represented by fuller Library collections.

The most recent volumes in this series *James Agee*, edited by Andrew Hudgins, and *Anne Stevenson*, edited by Andrew Motion, (Volumes 26 and 27 respectively) assume very different positions in the Project's growing constellation. James Agee, legendary for his personal charisma and his eclectic literary passions, joins Edith Wharton on the list as a famous writer of prose whose poetry is here being re-presented (Agee's major prose, like Wharton's, is collected in a Library edition). The much less known American-British writer Anne Stevenson, on the other hand, distinguishes herself as the only living poet yet to be featured in the Poet's Project (John Ashbery is represented in the Library). Stevenson is a recipient of the Neglected Masters Award, established by the Poetry Foundation, and this volume is published in conjunction with that award. Furthermore, a good bit of the Agee volume is a reprinting of *Permit Me Voyage*, which won the Yale Younger Poets award in 1934 when Agee was just 24, and shows his overall poetry *oeuvre* to be thin, while Stevenson's volume is a selection, culled from a richer source of a dozen volumes from a poetry career spanning almost 50 years. It would be silly to catalogue invidious comparisons between the two. Beyond the flashes that reveal the seeds of a wild and profligate talent—and clues to his personal conflicts, if not demons—Agee's poetry confirms that his essential literary reputation rests with his prose; Stevenson's selection, on the other hand, makes a claim to be read with the same attention accorded to influential poets like Sylvia Plath and Elizabeth Bishop, who are subjects of Stevenson's nonfiction, a biography and a book of criticism, respectively.

A character in T.S. Eliot's *The Cocktail Party*, with a dry insouciance typical of his leisured aristocratic milieu, delivers the following line:

> Yes, I've seen her poetry—
> Interesting if one is interested in Celia.
> Apart, of course, from its literary merit
> Which I don't pretend to judge.

To adapt Eliot's character's quip to James Agee: many readers might be drawn to this volume of poetry if they are already interested in his nonfiction, fiction, and screenplays.

In fact, Agee's poetry might be evaluated much like the early poetry of James Joyce: regardless of its literary merit, it is interesting and valuable for the light it brings to the later prose. Since he wrote increasingly fewer poems in his short, tempestuous adult life—restlessly veering from the *sui generis* accomplishment of *Let Us Now Praise Famous Men,* to groundbreaking film criticism, to brilliant screenplays like *The African Queen*, to his moving fiction, including the posthumous (and recently re-edited) *A Death in the Family*—some might be tempted to dismiss the early poetry as juvenilia, or, as in Faulkner's sly deprecation of his own youthful poetry, a noble failure, on the way to manifesting his métier as a great prose artist. But, as in Joyce and Faulkner, it is the lyrical quality of all Agee's writing, his care and consciousness of language itself, that gives currency and power to his literary achievements as a whole.

In his introduction to his edition of the Agee volume, Andrew Hudgins makes the strongest case for the achievement of his poetry in Agee's sequence of 25 Shakespearian sonnets in *Permit Me Voyage*. Suffused with the vestiges of Agee's devout boyhood Anglo-Catholicism, radically tempered by his coming of age in the Depression and his early reading of Marx, and echoing Christian poetry from the King James Bible to Donne and Eliot, these sonnets begin with the death of the first Adam, but instead of appealing to the consolations of Christian salvation, they follow the conflicts of

Adam's descendants as they struggle between physical hunger and hunger for divine purpose: in Hudgin's pithy formulation, "History works itself out as theological fate." The second sonnet begins,

> Our doom is our being. We began
> In hunger eager more than ache of hell:
> And in that hunger became each a man
> Ravened with hunger death alone may spell (II)

This passage alone makes clear why Hudgins finds in Agee's poetry a world-view "as bleak as anything that John Calvin ever formulated." As much for his own physical hungers—in his brief life of 45 years, Agee's drinking, smoking, and sexual careering were legendary—as for his ultimate appeal to a Christian God for understanding, the heart and anxiety of his poetry reminds me of certain lyrics in John Berryman's *Dream Songs*, where of Henry, he writes, "Hunger was constitutional with him, / women, cigarettes, liquor, need need need / until he went to pieces. / The pieces sat up and wrote" ("311"). As in Berryman, Agee's moral judgments about instinctual transgressions may be rationalized in the light of civilization and its discontents, but the poet's ultimate concerns are religious—with guilt, sin, and redemption—even if his explorations are conceptually limited by an all too human language:

> I have known love as lowly, full of lust,
> Bent on contriving Godhead from the flesh,
> Wrought from desire and waning through mistrust,
> Starved in the sinuately carnal mesh.
> Is there indeed a God who can redeem
> The love we know as a dawn-tinctured dream. (Sonnet XII)

As much as I admire Agee for his moral passions and the achievements of his brief, brilliant literary career, I think Hudgins overstates the case for Agee as a lyric poet. Yes, he delivers intermittently the Romantic pleasures of the glittering fragment, but even the above passage reveals a tendency toward strained diction ("sinuately"?), the reliance on abstract terminology, and—rather than subtle and creative adaptations of his nativist Tennessee sermons—a tone too highly arched, sometimes even a bit bombastic. Toward the end of his sonnet sequence, even when he personalizes the burdens of history and human failing, his sonnets lack the particular intimate drama and urgency of Shakespeare's sequence. Or, to use a fairer comparison, though Agee does sometimes successfully link particular emotional or psychological conflicts to the universals of moral allegory, his sonnets lack the seering immediacy of Berryman's sonnet sequence about an adulterous affair. In short, the limit of these sonnets is located in the exact area where Hudgins finds their strength: even when Agee uses the personal pronoun "I," the speaker seems to be addressing (beyond himself, of course) a congregation from behind a formal, elevated poetry pulpit, rather than to be speaking artfully to another person—whether Shakespeare's Dark Lady or Berryman's mistress—in the earshot of overhearing others.

Those readers like Hudgins who may believe Agee's achievement exists where "the restraints of poetic form become a bulwark against the excesses and narcissism that mar his greatest work in prose," will certainly disagree with my belief that "Dedication"—a Whitmanesque, Blakean blast, part holy manifesto and part oracular howl, written in a rhythmical prose nowhere confined by predetermined form—is the best poem in the book. It is a long litany to his imagined readers, from his beloved inspirers to the venal power-brokers whom he would like to convert:

> To Mark Twain; to Walt Whitman; to Ring Lardner; to Hart Crane; to Abraham Lincoln; and to my land and to the squatters upon it and to their ways and words in love; and to my country in indifference.
>
> To the guts and the flexing heart and to the whole body of this language in much love…
>
> To those merchants, dealers and speculators in the wealth of the earth who own this world and its frames of law and government, its channels of advertisement and converse and opinion and its colleges…that they examine curiously, and honestly into their own hearts, and see how surely and to what like extent they are in themselves blood-guilty…and that they repent their very existence as the men they are, and change or quit it: or visit the just curse upon themselves.

In the cataloguing repetitive structures of "Dedication," which takes its place in an incantatory line from the King James Bible to Ginsberg, we recognize sincere moral yearning and moral outrage channeled through its own authentic diction and its own open forms. If you want this naturally expansive, somewhat disheveled poet to give a fiery sermon of poetry, don't box him into 14 lines with regular meter and end rhymes. Let him rip.

I also love the poignant, free-form "Sunday: Outskirts of Knoxville, Tennessee," where the omniscient speaker's concluding prayer that a romantic young couple will in time be blinded to his graphic images of their fall into marital conflict and disillusionments:

> Now, on the winsome crumbling shelves she loves of the horror
> God show, God blind these children!

His more formal lyrics, however, like "Permit Me Voyage," an homage to and conversation with Hart Crane, or his sonnets, which echo the Metaphysical poets, Houseman and Auden, among others, show not just the awkward promise of apprenticeship, but their essentially derivative, imitative nature. (In his more narrative poems, one hears Frost's "Home Burial" in "Ann Garner," Keats's "Eve of St. Agnes" in "Epithalamium," Byron's "Don Juan" in "John Carter.") I appreciate Hudgins' advocacy of a hugely sympathetic, very flawed, courageous, self-destructive, and ultimately great prose writer, who left so many of his ambitions incomplete. Agee's passionately lyrical, self-conscious prose does not show his missed potential as a poet; rather, this thin volume of poetry shows him finding his voice as a writer of poetic prose.

Anne Stevenson shares with Agee the inheritance of a deep family identification with Protestant Christianity, even if her relationship to that tradition seems more remote and studied. Born in England of American parents and repatriating there after university in the U.S., Stevenson is the author of a dozen books of poetry, as well as criticism and essays, but her work, as her award indicates, has not been widely read, especially on this side of the Atlantic. Perhaps best known as author of the controversial biography *Bitter Fame: A Life of Sylvia Plath*, Stevenson's reputation (or lack of it) as a poet has suffered predictably for her being neither fully fish nor fowl, American nor English, and surely her preoccupation with the influence of place—more culturally and spiritually, than geographically or nationally defined—reflects her own formative displacements and replacements. This preoccupation is hard to miss, given the titles of early lyrics selected by Andrew Motion, the former Poet Laureate of England: "Living in America," "Still Life in Utah," "Ann Arbor," "Coming Back to Cambridge," "North Sea Off Carnousie" and so on. Her affinity with Bishop is clear from the opening of an early nature lyric, "Sierra Nevada":

> Landscape without regrets whose weakest junipers
>   strangle and split granite,
> whose hard, clean light is utterly without restraint,
>   whose mountains can purify and dazzle
> and every minute excite us, but never can offer us
>   commiseration, never can tell us
> anything about ourselves except that we are
>   dispensable...

The careful description of the concrete particular, the humanizing anthropomorphic images of nature, the speaker's voice, which is both self-effacing and expressively self-defining, all show a family resemblance with Bishop. Like Bishop, her consciousness is often defined from the outside in, and poems about places, weather, plants, fish, birds, animals insist at once on the primacy and pre-eminence of nature and simultaneously on the value of human consciousness as it defines itself in the act of perception. But, more than the often reticent and cautious Bishop, Stevenson is capable of both philosophically discursive musing as well as emotional, even erotic expansiveness and self-exposure. The conclusion to "Himalayan Balsam," an effort to descriptively reenact a natural phenomenon, ends in a meditative movement from Wallace Stevens to Molly Bloom:

> I could cry to these scent-spilling ragged flowers,
> and mean nothing but 'no', in that word's breath,
> to their evident going, their important descent through red towering,
> stalks to the riverbed. It's not, as I thought, that death
>
> creates love. More that love knows death. Therefore
> tears, therefore poems, therefore long stone sobs of cathedrals
> that speak no ferret or fox, that prevent no massacre.
> (I am combining abundant leaves from these icy shallows.)
>
> Love, it was you who said, 'Murder the killer
> we have to call life and we'd be a bare planet under a dead sun.'
> I loved you with the usual soft lust of October
> that says 'yes' to the coming winter and a summoning odor of balsam.

No one would ever mistake a voice so embodied and foregrounded for a Bishop poem, and in its centered celebratory self-possession, it is even more distinguished from another important influence, Sylvia Plath. Yet, Plath, who also tried to bridge the cultural divide of the Atlantic along with the daunting chasm of gender politics, also becomes one of Stevenson's useful repertoire of assimilated voices. When, in her *tour de force* book-length *Correspondences: A Family History in Letters* (1974), she needs to speak in the voice of a desperate young mother, writing to her own mother from a mental institution in a tormented mixture of plea and indictment, echoes of Plath's "Daddy" are delivered with the ironic distance of dramatic monologue. The section begins,

> Mother,
>
> If I am *where* I am
> because I am *what* I am
> will you forgive me?

> God knows I have fought you long enough…
> soft puppet on the knuckles of your conscience, or
> dangling puritanical doll made of duty and habit
> and terror and self-revulsion.
> At what cost
> keeping balanced on invisible threads?
> At what price
> dancing in a sweater set and pearls
> on the stage sets of your expectations?

Its end resembles the signature Plath poem, reminding the reader how closely related the artistic rites of repetition and rhyming are with simple obsession.

> Come when you can, or when
> the whitecoats let you.
> But they may not let you, of course.
> They think you're to blame.
> Good God, mother, I'm not insane!
> How can I get out of here?
> Can't you get me out of here?
> I'll try, I'll try, really,
> I'll try again. The marriage.
> The baby. The house. The whole damn bore!
>
> Because for me, what the hell else is there?
> Mother, what more? What more?

I confess to being mostly ignorant of Stevenson's poetry prior to reading this volume, and this long poem, a family saga in verse spanning several generations of an American Protestant family over a century and a half, is impressive in its scope, ambition and achievement. Along with her many short lyrics, *Correspondences* shores up Stevenson's place as a major voice in Anglo-American letters. In her assuming the voices of fictionalized relatives, young and old, male and female, boorish and sophisticated, *Correspondences* not only shows off a deft ventriloquism, but shows through dialogic interrogation how traits and beliefs of the generational past are recast in the present. I am especially taken, for instance, by the way Stevenson imaginatively and convincingly re-inhabits the beliefs of a 19th Century Presbyterian minister dolling out the harsh wisdom of a Puritan faith to his bereaved, recently widowed daughter:

> Even presupposing that God has summoned you this sacrifice,
> do you deem it in the interest of The Lord to secure your favor?
> Is not sacrifice punishment of Sin?

The poem does not merely demonstrate how later generations in their evolution toward a skeptical humanism cope, or fail to cope, emotionally and psychologically with such suffering; she also dramatizes what Weber had argued in his sociological exposition: how the Puritan work ethic was twinned from the beginning with the deforming pressures of capitalism, as are the maxims of one ancestor businessman, written in his journal of 1900:

> Work is next to Godliness; a man should keep books
> when dealing with the Deity.
>
> The golden Rule of the New Testament is the Golden
> Rule of Business.
>
> Religion is the only investment that pays dividends in
> the life everlasting.

While Jacob Chandler's unadorned commitment to revealed truths precludes more poetic language, the journal writings of his betrothed daughter, about to bury her erotic imagination beneath moral duty, shows the fading coals of a language shaped by yearning plaintive rhythms,

> For now it behooves me to
> crush out all personal sorrow,
> forsake the whole ground of
> self interest, ask not,
> "Do I love him?" but affirm!
>
> If I keep every moral commandment,
> fulfill every physical requirement,
> feed mind into heart,
> proffer heart to humanity—
> stands it not then to reason
> a woman will be happy in her season?
>
> I think not.

It is left to the damaged and rebellious Oedipal descendants of the late 20th Century, Kay and Nick Arbeiter, to reemploy the language for historical self-examination and reconstruction. Grieving his mother's death, a young son poetically indicts the legacy of his Puritan forbearers:

> We accuse you, fathers,
> we accuse you of lies.
> of pouring out a smoke screen
> of high-minded fervor,
> and then setting off to murder
> under twin banners, Profit and Compromise.

His sister Kay writing back from England to New England—"dissolving like a green chemical./Old England bleeds out to meet in mid-ocean"—ends the poem with a resonant question: "Can the pages make amends for what was not said?/Do justice to the living and the dead?"

Even if this conclusion might lose some force read from the distance of three decades after the disappointed apocalypse of the late 60's, Stevenson's language proves equal to the ambitious task she set for herself in the poem. Her talent for elegy, as much as for the epistolary, characterizes her work. Likewise, because her poetry shows an uncanny ability to be literary and natural, formal and authentic at the same time, I look forward to reading her most recent long poem, *A Lament for the Makers*, not yet published in the U.S., or included in this volume, in which, according to Andrew Motion, Stevenson converses across time with those poets who have meant the most to her. "Letter to Sylvia Plath," no less than her several other elegies for friends and relatives in this book, might provide a glimpse of coming attractions:

> Let me shake
> some echoes from old balled eye Blake
> over your grave and praise in rhyme
> the fiercest poet of our time—
> you with your outsized gift for joy
> who did the winged life destroy,
> and bought with death a mammoth name
> to set in the cold museum of fame.

The echoings or mimickings of Blake, as well as the Auden of "In Memory of W.B. Yeats," are playfully apparent, but the tribute is no less sincere and worthy of its passionately literary addressee. Anne Stevenson keeps appropriate company.

MENTIONING UNMENTIONABLES

Unmentionables. Beth Ann Fennelly. New York: W. W. Norton, 2008

Mike Smith

Beth Ann Fennelly's virtues as a poet have never been more apparent than in *Unmentionables*, her third full-length collection. Chiefly, they are: clarity; humor; precision (by which I mean accuracy sustained by well-tempered thought); ambition, which springs from a wide and deep reservoir of learning and a willingness to delve, sometimes recklessly, into the depths of preceding works; an unforced and genuine sensuality, which combines interestingly with Fennelly's fondness for audacity; and the sort of earned wisdom that avoids quaintness. Formally, the poems are unabashedly conventional, so if we are to look for experiment, even audacity, we must turn more often to the subjects Fennelly chooses and the rhetorical strategies by which she makes them present to us (which isn't to say that her lines lack invention). And we will not be disappointed, though in the end not all these strategies succeed equally well.

The collection is long by contemporary standards and is divided into small groups of shorter poems alternating with longer pieces. The grouping of the shorter lyrics is thematic, for the most part, and there is a pleasing sweep to the collection as a whole without the contrived tying up of loose ends so common in contemporary collections. Two of the longer works center on famous and difficult cultural figures, which helps to color the entire collection as literary. Fennelly prefers the sequence to the cycle and the cycle to collage, and seems to be, like many of her contemporaries, most comfortable in the mode of direct address.

Direct address is certainly the preferred mode in the shorter poems, the addressees often family members, most conspicuously her young son or daughter. A common occasion for the shorter poems is the quiet moments of routine, or, more exactly, the quiet moments between routines: the taxi to take-off or brief respite during a child's playdate. And the book opens with two such occasions, in poems which also embody many of the virtues listed above. "First Warm Day in a College Town," charmingly rewrites W.D. Snodgrass's "April Inventory," as the poet drives to work and notices the (male) joggers, who have also noticed the change of temperature and the early spring of the Deep South.

Hard to recall just now
that these are the torsos of my students,
or my past or future students, who every year

grow one year younger, get one year fewer
of my funny jokes and hip references
to *Fletch* and Nirvana…

The second poem, "Cow Tipping," begins as simple recollection, as the poet sees out her plane window a "field of cows, the meek, long-suffering cows;" but, because she is an American poet alone on a plane after 9/11, it launches out at just the point this line occurs into an appropriate excoriation of her own (innocent?) nostalgia and the indulgence of wider middle-class American childhood and adolescence. The last lines of the poem make clear that Fennelly is aware that this very poem presumes the same homogeny of America that "whole countries hate."

And I, a girl at thirty-two, who likes to think she was a rebel….

who brags (isn't it a brag?) that no harm
ever came to her—what would they think of me, the terrorists
and terrified? Wouldn't they agree I've got it coming?

Yes, undoubtedly.

The four poems that begin *Unmentionables* lead into the first and next-to-finest longer work in the book: "Berthe Morisot: Retrospective," a biopic of sixteen poems, spoken in the Impressionist's voice. But is it her voice? Fennelly is no mockingbird, disappearing into her subject's song, and a large part of the success of this sequence is how obviously Fennelly—poet, wife, and mother, identifies with Morisot—artist, mother, and wife. For this reason, "Colorplate 30," with its startling and marvelous conclusion (Can it be true?) and "Colorplate 36," which I will quote in full below are my favorites of the sequence.

Soon my fellow impressionists
are praising my new style—my
"great contribution to the movement"

"Loose, calligraphic strokes
which produce the effect of spontaneity
and rapid brushwork"—

(I do not say, *I must paint rapidly*)

"Radical simplicity"—
"Exaggeration and blur"—

(I do not say, *I haven't slept*).

This rhymes nicely with Fennelly's "The Mommy at the Zoo," a funny poem in the middle of the next section of shorter poems on motherhood which should be required reading for anyone burdened with the great privilege of having to keep up with small children. "Berthe Morisot: Retrospective" is a compelling sequence, though I do wish a few more of the sections ended less like the couplet in a Shakesperean sonnet and that Fennelly worried less, at times, about communicating actual biography.

But this fondness for Laureate-like rightness and completion is less a problem for any one section than for the book as a whole. By the time I reach, in the third section, "To JC and DL on the Opening of the Sestina Bar," I find myself on my knees praying for a pantoum, a triolet, or even some linked haiku, anything but the inevitable sestina that follows, and not even Fennelly's awareness of the cuteness of her choice in the last lines can rid me of the taste of Harp in my mouth. The real problem is I like the poem quite a bit, and think it one of the few successes of the form in contemporary American poetry, which is saying something, I suppose, since you're not a poet these days until you publish one.

You're also not a poet, apparently, until you contend with the ghost of John Berryman, as Fennelly does, not for the first time, in the sixth section of the book, "Say You Waved: A Dream Song Cycle." In fifteen dream songs, Fennelly recreates, in contradistinction to "Berthe Morisot: Retrospective," not the voice of her subject, but the manner of her subject's persona, Henry. This isn't the first time Fennelly has wrestled with this particular fallen angel, as readers of her first book will remember. If anything, the family tree of Fennelly's "Mr. Daylater" and Berryman's "Mr. Bones" has been further pruned by this new record of her contention. There is much worthy of praise in this cycle, but I'm afraid this section brings the dividing lines between aesthetics and ethics a little too close for my comfort. It's one thing to impersonate a person, but to kidnap the speaking voice of a persona, a persona created in a specific place and certain time as a way of making known certain feelings—individual (original) and emphatically idiosyncratic (unrepeatable)? Hmmm. Not that Fennelly does it badly or without artfulness, but in too many places, she really does, as the book-jacket claims, "out-Berryman Berryman" in the way a certain kind of bright and contentious student might try to out-profess their Prof. (This analogy gains its freshman fifteen when one encounters all the riffs on the works of Berryman's heroes and peers that pepper the cycle, indeed the collection as a whole.) The poignancy of his (hard-won?) frenetics seems, at times, to be more the end rather than means for Fennelly.

> No sing, no sing to shay. Naughty Henry's
> gone away and if I live a peckel
> he won't be-O.
> Let's wake him. I'll call the Davids wicked, Kevin, Karl,
> & Jack Pendarvis (I'll be the only lass),
> we'll Danny-boy-O.

Of course, there are a great many moments where Berryman's manner is clearly the means for Fennelly's realization. Here's the opening salvo from "5."

> Fall'd find you mooding, brooding on turkey's fate.
> Then winter worst. If you wrote not of snow hate
> it's because you wrote not.
> Then spring your pen. March a lion. Out put,
> A ball of dough, punched down, will rise,
> double in size—

The classic (eternal?) lyric sentiments behind moments like these get close to what Robert Pinsky noted about Berryman's own purpose, something to the effect that the outlandishness of the language, its slanginess and play, actually conditions the reader to admit moments of high-art in the Songs. I'm afraid, though, that no amount of manner can admit to this reader the throwaway anecdote snuck in at the end of "6."

> "Free Willie" is the question, a U.S. flick
> about a whale I saw previewed in London,
> where "willie" is slang for "dick."
> Free Willie. Like whales the giggles breached.
> Is accountability just that, some cosmic
> inadvertent joke?

Not that all the anecdotes fall flat. "7." does it much better.

> In roadside Mexico a man macheted pineapple,
> sprinkled it with salt and lime and hellborn chili dust.
> It cost less than a buck.

> Don't eat it, a fellow tourist warned, coming off the bus.
> I ate it. So with your words
> my lips sweetburn.

I wish I had more space to talk about this cycle. But perhaps it's best if I, too, put it "in the ground." I hope Fennelly will put Berryman down now too. After all, fifteen songs, not to mention the earlier incarnations, are much more solid a block than Berryman gave even to Delmore Schwartz.

"Say You Waved" leads, quite naturally, given Berryman's own biography, to a poem in the seventh and final section of the book about Fennelly's own father, a compelling antiphonal work occasioned by Fennelly's wide reading, which engages any number of father-as-river myths, emphasizing both his power and inscrutability and the daughter's continuing (impossible?) desire for understanding. "I thought of my father's knuckles and how he threw his head back when he laughed./ *He said, Like a language studied two languages ago, this river.*" The four shorter poems that make up this last section are the most intimate but also most expansive in the book, where Fennelly seems to be writing out what her Daphne-self asks of the river: "Teach me to drift in the eddies of clouds and willows./ *Without this irascible grasping after meaning, he said.*" All four could be read as ars poeticas—two bravely, brazenly so—and, thusly, autobiographical. But these narratives have admirable gaps and while part of the lack of immediate cohesion present in the last poems is due to the fact that almost all are drawn from outside sources (so other kinds of discourse and other voices are written necessarily into the poems), part of it must also have to do with Fennelly's awareness of (and resistance to?) her "gathering/ scraps of phrases/ weaving my story of someone gone bad."

By way of ending, I want to retrace my steps to the fourth section of the book, which is, to my mind, the crown of the collection. "The Kudzu Chronicles" makes me wish I had written it from the moment it begins:

> Kudzu sallies into the gully
> like a man pulling up a chair
> where a woman was happily dining alone.
> Kudzu sees a field of cotton,
> wants to be its better half.

For me, these five lines are worth any number of copycat Dream Songs. And it only gets better. Best of all, though, is the author's (hyper-aware) identification with this fellow transplant to the South.

> Kudzu quickly aped the vernacular—most folks assume
> it's native. Thus, it's my blend-in mentor, big brother
> waltzing in a chlorophyll suit, amethyst cufflinks.

Of the longer works, it is this sequence which best blends Fennelly's considerable gifts of clarity, wit, and precision with her fondness for contending with, and evoking, literary predecessors. It is this sequence that best blends her tendency towards cohesion with her recognition that the best stories give us gaps to fill and refill ourselves. And it is this sequence that stands out to me in *Unmentionables* most, and most worthy of mentioning last.

No Waste. Many Lands.

Richard Berengarten. *Selected Writings of Richard Berengarten, vols. 1-5: For the Living, The Manager, The Blue Butterfly, In a Time of Drought, Under Balkan Light*. Cambridge: Salt, 2008.

Paul Scott Derrick

The work of Richard Berengarten will already be familiar to some readers of the *Notre Dame Review*. Under the name of Richard Burns he has published, during the last four decades, a large, and still growing, body of original, independent and, in so many ways, *unexpected* poetry.[1] His first volume, *The Easter Rising, 1967*, appeared in 1968. Since then, Berengarten has published more than 20 books, displaying a range of subject matter and technical mastery that many poets writing today would be hard put to equal.

With the publication of these five tastefully-presented hardback editions of his recent work by Salt, one of the most productive and influential poetry publishers in the UK, Richard Burns has chosen to repossess the family name of his father, the cellist and saxophonist Alexander Berengarten. It must be more than a simple coincidence (Do "simple coincidences" even exist for poets?) that the decision to return to his original family name came with his 65th birthday and accompanies the appearance of this new series, which is in effect a "retrospective exhibition" of his accomplishment to date.

The first four of these books had already been published in paperback: *The Manager* by Elliot & Thompson in 2001, *In a Time of Drought* by Shoestring Press in 2006, *For the Living* and *The Blue Butterfly* by Salt, in 2004 and 2006, respectively. *Under Balkan Light* appears for the first time here and completes Berengarten's *Balkan Trilogy* (whose first two volumes are *The Blue Butterfly* and *In a Time of Drought*), a complex and profound celebration of the cultures and history of that crucial area of eastern Europe.

Because he has travelled widely, and lived in several countries, and absorbed from those experiences a great deal of the material that informs his poetry, Berengarten cannot easily be dropped into the potentially restrictive categories of English or British poet. His interests and concerns, the influences and traditions he works from, are broader and more varied. And this reluctance to conform to received expectations is surely one of the reasons for the relative paucity of critical attention he has received in the United Kingdom. *For the Living* contains a selection of longer poems and poem sequences written in Greece, Italy, England and former Yugoslavia between 1965 and 2000, and is therefore an excellent sampling of that rich variety that is, in my opinion, one of Berengarten's deepest strengths. For those who may be acquainted with the 2004 edition, this new version of the selection offers a few notable differences. Three poems have been removed. "The Ballad of the Seagull" and "Wayside Shrine" are included in *The Blue Butterfly*; and one of this reviewer's favorites, "The Voice in the Garden," has now found its definitive home in *Under Balkan Light*.

In compensation, two previously uncollected poems have been added: "The Offense of Poetry" (written and published in 1973) and "Day Estate" (written during the 80s and unpublished until now). The former, a delicate, abstract evocation of the mercurial interplay between consciousness and perception, is influenced, according to Berengarten's notes at the end of the book, by the writings of Martin Buber and Heraclitus. The latter, in Berengarten's own words, is a "twelve-part set of variations on the Canonical Hours, composed in honour of Margaret Thatcher and published nearly thirty years later [...] in recognition of the enduring legacy of Thatcherian conservatism, which is still apparently considered fit for purpose throughout the United Kingdom of Great Britain and Northern Ireland" (222).

Some of the other significant pieces included in *For the Living* are the long, open-field contemplation on the origins of poetry, *Avebury* (1971); "Angels" (1974-6), a richly fanciful allegory on human destructiveness and the (possibly evolutionary) pathways of vital transformation; "The Rose of Sharon" (1972-3), a tightly-structured "Mandala-poem" reflecting on "the feminine aspect of the divine presence in the Kabbalah"; the narrow, trunk-like, 365-line-long, downward-growing *Tree* (1978-9); "Against the Day" (1987), an intricately-interwoven sequence of 18 nonce-form stanzas, each composed of 5 couplets, that was written for Berengarten's daughter on her eighteenth birthday and is a commentary on Jan Vermeer's little-known painting, *The Guitar Player* (which supposedly depicts the painter's daughter); and *Croft Woods* (1998-9), a literal walk through the imaginary woods where the speaker perceives that the emergence of poetry from perception, through feeling and into coherent thought and language is a natural, organic process of growth.

And, as impressive as this partial selection from the book may be, even more impressive, for my money, is the 13-poem sequence *Black Light* (first published in 1982). This small book is a brilliant response to—and imaginative collaboration with—the Greek poet George Seferis, in particular his long poem *The Thrush* and his journal entries for the year of its completion, 1946. Stylistically, the sequence is a *tour de force*, exhibiting much deftness with forms ranging from the villanelle to the prose poem. And while each one of these poems is preceded by and deeply resonates with a passage from Seferis, *Black Light* is more than an interesting case of intertextuality. Above and beyond the complicated posthumous "exchange" between a Greek and an English poet, and the multi-layered play of reflections and echoes and subtle transmutations between the Greek and English languages, apart from its profound vision of the blackness that Seferis perceived at the core of that burning Hellenic light, these poems vividly capture the very particular sensual qualities of the life of Greece that those who have been lucky enough to experience will immediately identify with.

The longest of Berengarten's poem sequences, which he worked on from 1978 to 2000, is *The Manager*. This ambitious narrative is, among other things, Berengarten's "post-modern" response to the fragmented Modernist aesthetic of Pound and Eliot and might have been subtitled "He do the police in different different voices." As Berengarten puts it in his *Postscript*, the poem consists

> of one hundred sections and three buffer pieces. It is written in a form that I call the *verse-paragraph*. This is related to the *verset* of French poetry, and is used in other European literatures as well. [...] I believe it to be a prosodic unit of great strength and flexibility, well suited both to the cadences and varied registers of modern English and to the particular demands made by a long poem. (161)

Over the course of those 103 relatively connected (or disconnected) sections, we are given a cornucopia of speech-acts, images and ideas—more than enough information to piece together the life and times of a London-based, middle-management executive (Charles Bruno, aka *Homo aspirans*, Incipient man, aka Adam Kadmon) who, as the narrative develops, is forced to invest his whole existential capital in relearning how to "manage" life—that is, how to love—in a spiritual wasteland.

In 1961, Samuel Beckett famously declared: "To find a form that accommodates the mess, that is the task of the artist now." Beckett himself had carried out that task through the gradually disintegrating form of his *Trilogy*. Forty years on, *The Manager* moves in the opposite direction, through disintegration and towards reintegration. Berengarten uses the constantly repeated, determined form of the verse-paragraph to resist the mess of modern urban life. He not only "channels" that mess through the form; the form, in a sense, disciplines (or manages) its content.

Our Modernist predecessors invented a whole rag-and-bone shop of fragmented forms to embody a conviction that the world at the beginning of the 20th century had already begun to fall apart. They seem from the standpoint of the beginning of the 21st century to have been right. Now is the time to try to put it together again. The story-line of *The Manager* may be fragmentary, but the story-line's vehicle is not. To echo the title of one of Robert Frost's sonnets, this is Berengarten's "one step backward taken"—from flux and disorder toward order and meaning—and offers the reader a model and an opportunity to construct something more than Frost's "momentary stay against confusion."

This new edition of the poem, apart from some alterations in the ordering of the sections, contains a considerably longer and more detailed list of the author's Notes on contents, sources and references, as well as a new "Editor's Preface" (written by Chris Hamilton-Emery, the dynamic "manager" of Salt), that provides an informative description of the publishing history of the poem and an overview of critical responses to it from 1980 to the present.

The third of this five-volume set, *The Blue Butterfly*, is also the first part of Berengarten's *Balkan Trilogy*. As its "Editorial Note" explains, "The book's twin points of departure are a massacre that took place in Šumarice, outside of Kragujevac in October 1941, and an encounter with a blue butterfly at the same location in May 1985. The poems are laced into their contexts by documents, photography, a postscript, and endnotes which provide references and dates and places of composition" (xiii).

Berengarten worked on this extraordinary collection of poems for around 20 years, from its first inception on 25 May, 1985, when the butterfly "came to rest on the forefinger of [his] left hand—that is, [his] writing hand" (123) until its final publication by Salt in 2006. Over the course of those two decades, the book formed itself into a complex structure: seven sections, each composed of seven poems. A number of attempts have already been made to explain the significance of this structure (which also appears in *In a Time of Drought*) and many more will certainly follow in the years to come.[2] But whatever the reasons for it may be, this close attention to structure also serves to underscore the importance of form in everything Berengarten writes. Among all the other things it accomplishes, this collection is another technical *tour de force*. From the "found poems" adapted from authentic German military communiqués in "Two Documents" in Section 1 ("The Blue Butterfly") to the seven villanelles that make up Section 2, "The Death of Children," and the seven sonnets of Section 3, "Seven Wreathes," to the regularly-rhyming quatrains in poems like "The Shadow Well" and "Ballad of the Seagull" (in Section 4, "Seven Songs of the Dead") to the modified *terza rima* of "Diagonal" (in Section 5, "Seven Statements of Survivors") to the free-verse forms used in Section 6, "Flight of the Imago," to the short, three-line stanzas Berengarten developed to mimic the structure of Chinese hexagrams (in various poems of Section 7, "Seven Blessings")—the technical mastery demonstrated here is both exhilarating and sobering (exhilarating in the context of the humdrum, free-verse, personal anecdotes that so often pass for poetry these days, and sobering for those who write them).

And yet, even more worth noting, the display of forms is not ostentatious. In almost every case, the technique doesn't intrude between the reader and the content; it participates with the sense and delivers it efficiently. Because the sense (which is also the *direction*) of this book is of utmost importance. It is probably unfashionable among the competing cliques and coteries of the poetry-game today, but Berengarten refuses to put on a cynical pose, to descend into bitterness or to yield to despair. *The Blue Butterfly* is a poetic condemnation of all-too-human inhumanity and a moving commemoration of the suffering and nobility of the almost 3,000 victims of the Kragujevac massacre. But as its section titles indicate, it also does more. This book witnesses, commemorates, laments and, whether fashionable or not, affirms and blesses.

The same can be said of *In a Time of Drought*, which shares the 7-section/7-poem structure of *The Blue Butterfly*. Here though, each poem consists of four rhyming couplets, with a chorus that varies from section to section between 2, 3 and 4 lines. Because of their musicality, their conspicuous use of rhyme and the ease with which they read, these short poems may initially appear to be simplistic, sing-song jingles; but nothing could be further from the truth. In fact, as the prose postscript, "Arijana's Thread," points out, this book is constructed on a solid cultural foundation: the pan-Balkan rain-making ceremonies whose principal figure is the rain maiden known as *Dodola* or *Peperuda*. In this specific context, the book's lilting, apparently infantile rhythms—which are based on both English and Balkan folk-jingles—turn out to be perfectly appropriate.

In addition, the compendium of detailed information in the glossary and notes reveals the thoughtful care with which these poems have been woven with garlands of the plant life of the region and enable the reader to appreciate how the myriad historical and cultural references throughout the book gather irrevocably toward the cataclysm of destruction and death of modern warfare. But like *The Blue Butterfly*, *In a Time of Drought* insists on affirmation and revival. The dynamic tension between the playfulness and childhood innocence suggested by the tone of these poems and the "adult" horrors of war and death to which they lead becomes one of the book's key elements.

Berengarten lived in what used to be Yugoslavia for three years, from 1987 to 1991. These were key years in which that tense federation of states was beginning to break apart in a series of violent conflicts. His love of the people and deep knowledge of the culture of the Balkans, forged during that period and expanded through many later visits and lasting personal contacts, are the motivating factors for *The Balkan Trilogy*.

Its third volume, *Under Balkan Light*, is a diverse collection of poems giving a much more personal response to his experiences there. It also consists of seven sections, although the number of poems in each one varies from one (the sprawling "Do vidjenja Danitsé") to twenty-one (in Section 4, "The Voice in the Garden").

Berengarten's deep familiarity with the geography and history of the Balkans is powerfully illuminated in "Do vidjenja Danitsé" (Goodby Balkan Belle), which gives the book a firecracker of an opening. This 12-page, free-verse narrative poem (with an additional 7 pages of notes) is, in a certain sense, reminiscent of Whitman; it, too, "sings" the land and its people. Through an imaginary female protagonist who personifies the region, this poem re-presents the geography of the area—literally embedding 77 Balkan place-names within the left-hand side of the text—and retells its history from earliest legends up until the dissolution of Yugoslavia.

The other high point, for me, of *Under Balkan Light*, is section 5, a suite of 17 poems entitled "On the Death of Ivan V. Lali ." Berengarten and Lali (1931-96) became very close friends; and Berengarten's comments on their friendship in his Postscript are pertinent to these poems:

> To me Ivan was a kind of wise and knowledgeable older brother. In our conversations, ideas triggered fast, and we often thought of the same things at the same time and finished each other's sentences. I learned an enormous amount from him. His poems have not only called me. They have resonated for me as tuning instruments for my own. (140)

What makes these poems so striking is not only the quality of their deeply-felt and complicated emotional response to the irrefutable fact of death. One of the central concerns of Berengarten's poetry has always been one of the central concerns that set Western culture off, something like two and a half centuries ago, into the subversive course toward Romanticism: the need to redefine—or to re-conceive—our understanding of the mystery of death and the relationship between the living and the dead. These poems might be read as a kind of culmination of that movement. If Berengarten "collaborates" with Seferis in the writing of *Black Light*, he goes even further here. These poems reach into the silence of death toward the source of that lost, responding voice; and in an intimate act of communion, become both yearning question and reply. If the irrefutable facts can be refuted, this is the only way it will ever be done.

This ongoing series of Richard Berengarten's *Selected Writings* may be a kind of retrospective (and at the age of 65, he deserves one), but not one, as often happens, that signals a summation and an ending. Berengarten continues working on a project called *Manual*, a collection of poems (all having two 5-line stanzas) that celebrate human hands and what we do with them. He has now published three small booklets of twenty poems each through the Earl of Seacliff Art Workshop in New Zealand. Two more of these will round off the total number of poems to 100. He is also working on a book based on the *I Ching*, the Chinese *Book of Changes*, that is to contain 384 poems (a total obtained by multiplying the *I Ching*'s 64 hexagrams by each one's six variant interpretations).

A prolific output, impressive mastery of forms, sweeping breadth of subject matter, depth of both intelligence and feeling, these are the components of a significant poetic accomplishment. Richard Berengarten is, in the opinion of this writer, a unique case among contemporary British poets. The publication of these five volumes should help to make a wider audience aware of this so unlikely, yet manifest and fascinating body of poetry and to confirm Berengarten's status as a major contemporary poet writing in the English language.

NOTES

1. Burns' essay "With Peter Russell in Venice, 1965-1966" appeared in *Notre Dame Review*, 4 and excerpts from *The Manager* in Issue 7. More recently, "Three Poems in Memory of Ivan V. Lalić" were published in issue 26.

2. See essays by Andrew Frisardi, John Lucas, Aleksandar Petrov and Slobodan Rakitić in Norman Jope, Paul Scott Derrick & Catherine Byfield (eds), *The Salt Companion to Richard Berengarten* (Cambridge: Salt, forthcoming). At least partially in response to that speculation, Berengarten himself offers his own suggestion in a note on the number seven which has been added for the second edition (138-9).

THE MEANS TO A MORAL FICTION

James Wood. *How Fiction Works.* Farrar, Straus & Giroux, 2008.

Anis Shivani

It is not really that great a number of questions, what makes for meaningful fiction, yet theorists ancient and modern have forever been bashing their heads against these stones. In the twentieth century, Bakhtin, James, Woolf, Forster, Trilling, Booth, Crane, Barthes, Gass, and Kundera, among other prominent critics and writer-critics, have tried to clarify some of the perennial dilemmas: What is character? Does fiction represent reality? If so, what is the nature of this reality? Is novelistic narrative different from other kinds of narrative? How crucial is conventional plot to meaning? How far can fiction stray from ordinary prose and still maintain the claim to realism? Is the history of modern consciousness the same as the history of the novel? Does and should fiction seek to alter reality? Is the fiction writer a presence above and beyond his creation, or is he to be read as submerged within it? Does, in the end, the world need fiction? Never have these questions had such urgency, as the reading of literary fiction plummets according to most measures. If the history of liberal consciousness is indeed in large measure coterminous with the history of the novel, then the prognosis is grim indeed. So there must be value in rehashing the old, familiar questions at this late date.

Enter James Wood, critic at first for *The New Republic* and now for *The New Yorker*, himself the author of a well-received novel, *The Book Against God* (FSG, 2003), and one of the most rewarding critics of our times. In landmark essays like "Hysterical Realism," "Jonathan Franzen and the 'Social Novel,'" and "Tom Wolfe's Shallowness, and the Trouble With Information," he has shown himself to be a keen analyst of the compulsions driving contemporary authors. In *The Irresponsible Self: On Laughter and the Novel* (FSG, 2004), his last collection of criticism, the metatheme running throughout the essays is the contrast between what he calls "the comedy of forgiveness" (the "comedy of irresponsibility" being a branch of this) and the sterner "comedy of correction," a wide enough rubric to enfold a vast range of innovative fiction. Like J. M. Coetzee's *Inner Workings: Literary Essays 2000-2005* (Viking, 2007), with which it overlaps considerably in subject matter and lucidity, *The Irresponsible Self* is an indispensable manual for readers wanting to be educated in the not-always-so-obvious connections within and across national styles of writing.

Now Wood has come to the explication of great fiction from another angle, using the format of the manual of craft so popular in the first half of the twentieth century—the kind of exercise to which most serious fiction writers feel drawn to at some time or the other—to not only expound the rules as manifest in the works of the greatest fiction writers, but to convey them in such a manner as to provoke self-criticism in the aspiring fiction writer about his means and methods, and more importantly, about why he wants to be a fiction writer in the first place. It is a philosophical treatise expertly cloaked as a guide book (one thinks of Machiavelli's *The Prince*, exemplar in another discipline, as a parallel), and is simultaneously rooted and diffuse enough to appeal to practitioners of fiction at all levels of skill.

The book's greatest value seems to be as a needed corrective to the reductionist approach to fiction-making found in any number of the nation's writing workshops, an important and growing part of the humanities at our universities. Whereas the ethos in the classroom seems to be to produce fiction meaningful to the writer's own moral needs, Wood, as is often true of any critic worth his salt, seeks to understand the type of fiction that writers over the ages have produced at the level of universal meaning. Individualism, it seems, is best nourished not in conditions of solipsism, but in a reach of Shakespearean or Keatsian "negative capability," the ability to leave the confining precincts of the self and stand in the shoes of low and high; the greater the courage of the writer in attempting this miracle of self-distance, the greater the writing. We must be taught not to dig deep within ourselves (as this injunction is understood simplistically), but to reach far outside ourselves. A common instruction in the academy is to write what one knows best, that is, to regurgitate the wisdom and judgment of the solitary soul. But the greatest writers have not been afraid to leap into the unknown, deploying the elements of fiction—choice of narrative point of view, selection of detail, and interplay of plot with character—as means to realize the reality of their own imaginative world.

The question comes down to confinement versus expansiveness. Wood's fundamental motive seems to be to reintroduce the lost commitment to expansiveness, of the mind and spirit, in contemporary writing. Is one's audience fellow workshop participants, or, at best, interested commercial publishers, or is the task one of connection with the vastest aims of one's literary forebears, to whom one must return again and again to replenish the will?

Along the way Wood finds a number of false dividing lines to blur again, at the same time as he must reiterate clear evolutionary markers in the history of narration. The distinction between reliable and unreliable narration might not be as clear as popular perception would have it: "Actually, first-person narration is generally more reliable than unreliable; and third-person 'omniscient' narration is generally more partial than omniscient"; furthermore, "omniscient narration is rarely as omniscient as it seems" and "[s]o-called omniscience is almost impossible." Wood argues that "As soon as someone tells a story about a character, narrative seems to want to bend itself around that character, wants to merge with that character, to take on his or her way of thinking and speaking." This involuntary merger of omniscient narrator with independent character leads to the crowning glory of narrative fiction, "free indirect style," or "close third person," or "going into character."

This represents an advance over the soliloquy of pre-twentieth-century novels, itself derived from earlier theater, because it opens up numerous gaps between author and character, allowing for greater room for various forms of irony. Wood shows how James in *What Maisie Knew* uses free indirect style to let us adopt multiple perspectives on the action. He undertakes close reading of passages to pinpoint James's choice of individual words that open up ironic distance for more generous understanding of Maisie's character. The really thrilling peak is when a writer like Chekhov coins striking similes and metaphors that the character himself might have produced. Nabokov's *Pnin* meets Wood's test of veracity here, while Updike's *Terrorist* fails. Much of the reader's engagement in the text ensues from the uncertainties following the "tension between the author's style and his or her characters' styles."

Wood fluidly converts any simple rule-making about choice of point of view into an issue of integral choice about style, or the author's personality: "So the novelist is always working with at least three languages. There is the author's own language, style, perceptual equipment, and so on; there is the character's presumed language, style, perceptual equipment, and so on; and there is what we could call the language of the world—the language that fiction inherits before it gets to turn it into novelistic style..." A stylist like Joyce or Bellow can write over his characters, depending on which details his inclinations compel him to choose. Wood takes us back to Flaubert, the originator of fictional narration without visible traces of authorship, and ascribes his success to his ability to mix "habitual detail with dynamic detail." What's interesting about Wood's method of exposition of the elements of fiction is that each room in the house of fiction opens naturally into another; choice of point of view is inextricable from style, which depends on the author's visibility, which is determined by the ability to mix the relevant and the irrelevant detail, which creates a lifelike effect, a cinematic perspective of the flâneur standing in for the author and for the astute reader.

From Flaubert onward, the literary author gives readers a great deal of credit for being above-average "noticers," which, in turn, minimizes our disbelief at encountering characters who seem to have an unnatural (author-like) facility to notice and describe. To the extent that this expectation has become part of the role of good readership, fiction trains us to become good noticers in life, ideally teaching us to distinguish between necessary and unnecessary information. The cinematic eye, Wood suggests, is never all-encompassing. It is, however, a myth modern fiction has taken over, but is always, to the extent that it is realistic, at pains to demolish, since style takes the upper hand over indiscriminate observation.

Stepping back to the function of free indirect style, its connection with teaching us to be stylists or cinematographers or observant flâneurs or invisible writers in our own right, Wood does not deviate from received consensus, from Percy Lubbock onward, in elevating Flaubert to fatherhood of contemporary fictional technique. But the history of the rise of extravagant noticing, compared to what Coetzee has called the "moderate realism" of the eighteenth century (without the imaginative, specific, strange detail), is as instructive as ever. Wood, as always, is wary of adopting the simplifying instructions of some workshops: not all detail that is important is visual, as Nabokov seemed to fail to understand, dismissing "Mann, Camus, Faulkner, Stendhal, James," because they trafficked in metaphysical detail. Another way to describe the choice is between "off-duty" and "on-duty" detail, both superfluity and impoverishment serving necessary purposes, given the author's aims of the moment.

To retreat into another room in the house of fiction, all this manipulation of types of detail has the purpose of "the management of temporality," the evocation of the "passage of time" being fiction's "new and unique project in literature." It is mysterious details, which "refuse to explain themselves," as in Chekhov's "The Lady with the Little Dog," that leave a more lasting impression of character. This is a more complex analysis than the often-cited basic rule of tying up all details in a fully explanatory matrix. Even intentional misleading, as Henry Green seems fond of doing, has its place in the construction of character.

And now that this room has been entered, Wood takes apart some of the fondest myths of the writing trade, which seem most wrongheaded on character. The partiality for likeable characters, such a staple of writing instruction, as well as editorial preference at the commercial publishing houses, is mistaken, since we can see life as well from the eyes of unlikeable characters as their more empathizable counterparts. On the other hand, there are critics like William H. Gass with too little belief in character, holding them to be never more than provisional constructions. Wood takes offense at this polarity as well. Similarly, contrary to perhaps the most pervasive prejudice of the writing business, that in favor of Forster's "round" against his "flat" characters, Wood suggests that often the most alive characters, such as Dickens's Mrs. Micawber, are flat characters, "monomaniacs," caricatures that come with easy tags perpetually attached to them. By the measure of aliveness, they, nonetheless, fully succeed as novelistic characters.

Wood goes so far as to claim that he would be "happy to abolish the very idea of 'roundness' in characterization," since it is an "impossible ideal" that tyrannizes "readers, novelists, critics." Instead, "It is subtlety that matters—subtlety of analysis, of inquiry, of concern, of felt pressure—and for subtlety a very small point of entry will do." Flat, monomaniacal characters may be interesting and alive because they may be "*consistently surprising*." Roundness is true only of Austen's heroines, but not of her surrounding characters, who are just as memorable. Of Shakespeare's *Henry V*, Wood argues that King Harry is round, but unsurprising, while Fluellen is flat but surprising. In surprise lies the "self's chink of freedom, its gratuity or surplus, its tip to itself."

Wood has here pounced on one of the secrets of great fiction, the extent to which, in the end, it is a gratuitous, not an earnest, act, and this in turn is connected with the novel's unique contribution to "*who a character is being seen by*." This uniqueness can be singled out by contrasting King David in the Old Testament, Macbeth, and Raskolnikov *in Crime and Punishment*. David has no "privacy" and "*he does not exist for us*, but for the Lord." Compared to David's opacity, Macbeth's "story is one of publicized privacy," while "Raskolnikov's story is one of scrutinized privacy." The novel's unprecedented gift to literature is that the hero is now free to be an ordinary man, liberated from "the tyranny of necessary eloquence." Since the character no longer has to "voice his motives," the reader must interpret the real, unconscious motives.

Wood immediately recognizes the new tyranny, however: "In the novel, we can see the self better than any literary form has yet allowed; but it is not going too far to say that the self is driven mad by being so invisibly scrutinized." We may use this as an epitaph for the twentieth-century novel as a whole, the unprecedented hermeneutic demands on the reader to decipher unconscious motives and make moral choices accordingly, and the semi-madness of many of the most memorable twentieth-century characters. This, in fact, is where we stand now, and if fiction stands at a plateau, it is because of the very great heights reached by Proust and Joyce in creating self-dividing characters, inviting us to probe bottomless motives.

Twentieth-century writers have deployed surprise in metaphor (its mixedness can be justified) and different registers of language, as Roth and Bellow do, for instance, to manage to be stylists without "writing over" their characters. What finally distinguishes commercial realism from literary realism is the degree of style which cannot be "reproduced" and "reduced," and the challenge for the writer of fiction is not to latch on to successful convention, which "is always dying," but in "trying to outwit it." When we arrive at realism by this definition, we escape the dead-end of deconstructionist dismissal of the novel's ability to depict reality as such.

Metafiction at the trivial level asks the question, "Does Christie [B. S. Johnson's Christie Malry] exist?", but at the more sophisticated level, asks, "How does Christie exist"? In Muriel Spark's *The Prime of Miss Jean Brodie*, the profound metaphysical question being addressed is, "Do we exist if we refuse to relate to anyone?" The successful fiction writer, like Virginia Woolf, W. G. Sebald, or Philip Roth, teaches us to adapt to his or her conventions, to accept his or her reality. In convincing us of the truth of the writer's world, he may resort, as James does at the beginning of *The Portrait of a Lady,* to extended essayistic commentary. This lays to rest another of the simplistic no-nos of many writing workshops. Essayistic rendering may not meet the criterion of exact cinematic detail, but can help make characters memorable anyway, as is true of Isabel Archer.

Poststructuralist theory has long banished consideration of the author to primitive backwaters—in its view, the creative writing departments. In the war between the supposed intellectual side of the literature departments (theory) and the unintellectual side (writing), the latter have been defended as at least upholding the belief in the existence of the author—their very purpose, after all, is to create more and better authors. Wood shows that writing departments need not feel defensive in relation to their more *au courant* competitors if they accept the depth of the challenge of understanding what makes great literature. The way ahead lies in respecting the author's intentions, giving him his due, while also understanding that modern novelistic discourse has evolved so greatly from its beginnings that the reader, too, is a moral agent every step of the way. Fiction works best when both forms of agency are in full swing. When a work of fiction is transparently successful, it brings into question our settled notions of what is lifelike and what is artifice, calling attention to the necessary stylistic choices that have gone into creating this uncertainty. Understanding novelistic realism is perhaps little less than understanding reality in life; this is where fiction derives its moral purpose.

<u>EDITORS SELECT</u>

David Matlin, *It Might Do Well With Strawberries*, Marick Press, 2009. Matlin, poet, novelist, essayist, is that dangerous thing, a writer's writer, which usually means only discerning readers come to his pages—or to the pages of the *NDR*, where his fiction and nonfiction has appeared (and part of this volume, too.) But those that do are richly rewarded, as anyone will be who is lucky enough to discover his work. *In Might Do Well With Strawberries* is full of prophetic insight and the rough knowledge of living with mind and heart wide open in our benighted new century. This volume is a year's journal that is not just a captivating diurnal record, but one transformed into a profound literary meditation that will endure.

Lily Hoang, *Changing*, Fairy Tale Review Press, 2008. Hoang's second book (her first, *Parabola*, won Chiasmus Press's First Book Award) is, in Joyelle McSweeny's words, "an impossible thing, a dream object." Don't start at the beginning, but turn to the "Letter of Introduction and Instructions," page 133, where Hoang, a ND MFA and *NDR* contributor, writes, "Dear Reader, I am not a teller of Fates & if you are here to find your Fate, you will be sorely disappointed. I am a translator. I am a storyteller....This is simply a new translation of the I Ching, or Book of Changes..." Of course, it is not "simply" anything, but a volume of enchantment and recollection, of growing up and romance. A delicate and playful excursion with lovely prose and captivating revelations.

Susan D. Blum, *My Word!: Plagiarism and College Culture,* Cornell University Press, 2009. A professor of anthropology here at ND, Susan Blum's book is larger than its subject, the plague of plagiarism that has been, in its swine-y way, muddling through universities everywhere. It is wide-ranging cultural criticism, as well as an anthropological case study (a local one, at that.) Her research is right at the outer edge, the student body of the internet, Facebook, generation, cutting and pasting its way through academia. How these students have absorbed the new technology as their birthright, rather than as a skill-set to be acquired, separates them from us (those who teach them) in critical ways Blum's book makes clear. It's the performance self versus the authentic self and, in that battle, authorship only takes a ringside seat. A fascinating and illuminating study.

Kathleen Rooney, *Live Nude Girl: My Life as an Object*, University of Arkansas Press, 2008. A memoir, one by a post-feminist-era writer (see her contributions in this issue of *NDR*) that invokes many older feminist concerns and preoccupations of the 1970s. The woman as object captured by the gaze of men (though, in this telling, a few women groups are sketching, too.) Rooney, overall, portrays herself as A Model with a Heart of Gold, a romantic stereotype of that other oldest profession—though modeling may be an even more ancient one (see cave drawings, etc.) Nonetheless, Rooney's is a most wholesome account and that is because she keeps coming up to the edge of a darker subject, but never falls over, even during private photo sessions by solo amateur male photographers who have her act out on various sets (i.e., beds). All the necessary subjects are here: narcissism, vanity, power, potency, erotic exchange, insecurity and entitlement. In many respects, this is a work book and not to be confused with the confessional accounts of a number of older generation feminists. It's one from the inside out, not the outside in.

Jarda Cervenka, *Fausto's Afternoon: Stories of the World*, Whistling Shade Press, 2008. *NDR* contributor and Richard Sullivan award winner (*Revenge of Underwater Man*), Cervenka's new book of short stories is more than a delight, it's a continuing revelation: Transnational tales of our world in crisis by an author who fills each exotic place with exuberance and illumination. Cervenka is a compassionate man of the world and readers get to view more of its remote and damaged locales in this volume than anyone could wish for. Another memorable collection.

Tom Coyne, *A Course Called Ireland*, Gotham, 2009. Any golf book that begins with epigraphs from Joyce ("Think you're escaping and run into yourself") and Paddy from Westport ("It's no simple business being mad") has a fine self-awareness. *A Course Called Ireland* may be the first postmodern sporting tour of Ireland, and Tom Coyne's the man to write it. A "wannabe Irishman" and fine novelist (*A Gentleman's Game*), Coyne, a graduate of ND's MFA program, walked the courses that ring the coastline of Ireland in search of the perfect game, landscape, and ancestry, and hoisted a few pints along the way. He manages to tell the tale with wry good cheer, a heavy dose of irony, and a decidedly unsentimental view of contemporary Ireland (and Irish-Americans). A very funny and charming book, even for—perhaps especially for—those allergic to golf.

Three books from Notre Dame Press. Luisa A. Igloria, *Juan Luna's Revolver*, 2009. This is the new Ernest Sandeen Poetry Prize volume. Igloria's formally impressive poems deal with Filipino history and art in the context of the present global diaspora. Ranging from the sonnet

sequence "Postcards from the White City" to the stepped-down triadic lines of the title poem, Igloria's poems hide, as Sabina Murray says, "a bristling wall of spears behind their gorgeous scrims." Jude Nutter, *I Wish I Had a Heart Like Yours, Walt Whitman*, 2009. Nutter's last book, *The Curator of Silence*, won the Sandeen Prize in 2007. Like that book, the new one is dark and frightening with its revisitings of public and private history and the places the two intersect. Nutter grew up just after World War II in a house outside Bergen-Belsen where her father worked for the British army. It had housed an overflow of 869 people from the camp next door. Poems about the house repeat throughout the book, and they all begin with the same run first run of lines. "We all grow up among the dead," she writes. Reading these powerful poems, one must get used to living with the ghosts of these dead and submitting to their presence among us. Kevin Hart, *Young Rain*, 2009. *NDR* contributor Hart writes erotic poems, poems of a religious imagination (including prayers), and poems of ordinary quotidian experience. His work has long been praised by the likes of Harold Bloom and John Koethe. Charles Simic calls him "an absolutely original and indispensable poet."
Five books by Parlor Press. This relatively new series of "Free Verse Editions" from West Lafayette's independent press is one of the good things happening in Indiana. Coming into its own with the latest run of titles, all of the books listed here deserve the attention of separate reviews, and we hope to find reviewers for at least one or two in our next issue. All published this year, the books are: Miguel Hernandez, *The Prison Poems*, translated by Michael Smith; Yermiyahu Ahron Taub, *What the Stillness Illuminated: Poems in English, Yiddish, and Hebrew*; Carolyn Guinzio, *Quarry*; Jennie Neighbors; *Between the Twilight and the Sky*; Boyer Rickel, *Remanence.*

Another series we should have noticed here before is from Parallel Press at the University of Wisconsin-Madison Libraries. They have issued about sixty chapbooks in the last several years, the most recent of which are Jan Chronister's *Target Practice* and John Lehman's *Acting Lessons*. The chapbooks are well designed and printed. The quality of work is unusually high for such a series. They run to about forty pages each. See the web site at parallelpress.library.wisc.edu.

Three prize-winners. Dennis Hinrichesen, *Kurosawa's Dog*. Field Poetry Series, 2009. *NDR* contributor Dennis Hinrichsen was awarded the Field Poetry Prize of 2008. The book has some of the same tough-minded qualities in its grappling with grief and death as Jude Nutter's volume listed above. Though the poems are mostly abut the death of the poet's father, the elegiac context of mourning is both wide and deep. The death, like the life of the man, does not occur in isolation from the world and history. Along with these poems, there are others drawing on a rich range of sources, from Catullus, Sappho, Dante and Rimbaud through the fiilms of Andrei Tarkovsky, including "Tarkovsky's Horse" which appeared in *NDR* #27. Marie Etienne, *King of A Hundred Horsemen*, translated from the French by Marilyn Hacker. FSG, 2008. Selected by Robert Hass for the Robert Fagles Translation Prize (and subsequently also winner of the PEN translation prize for 2009), Etienne's novel-in-verse reminds one a bit of Lyn Hejinian's *Oxota: A Short Russian Novel.* Etienne's work is well known in France but not, alas, in this country. Like Hejinian's book, the compositional unit is a kind of "prose-sonnet". There are ten of these sonnets in each quasi-narrative section, and a hundred of them altogether. *King of a Hundred Horsemen* will be properly reviewed by Catherine Perry in our next issue. Barbara Maloutas, *The Whole Marie.* Ahsahta Press, 2009. Chosen by C.D. Wright as winner of the 2008 Sawtooth Prize, Maloutas's poems are described in the judge's citation as inhabiting "a lively, indeterminate, variously voiced and Gertrude-Steinian continuous present." The Marie in question, says Wright, "has a personality" which is "artifactual and wondrous."

Janet Holmes, *The Ms Of My Kin.* Shearsman, 2009. Former Sandeen Prize winner (*The Green Tuxedo*, 1999), Janet Holmes's last book, *F2F*, made use of text-messaging conventions to tell a myth-haunted story of two lovers. The present book uses the technique of "erasure" to isolate various words and phrases from the poems Emily Dickinson wrote in 1861 and 1862, the first years of the Civil War. The title itself demonstrates the method, leaving behind twelve letters from *The Poems of Emily Dickinson.* What is left of Dickinson's poems of the Civil War tell a contemporary story of the wars in Afghanistan and Iraq. As Tom Raworth says of the book, "War is war and its words already written."

The latest Oxford paperbacks in "Greek Tragedy in New Translations" include Volume IV of *The Complete Euripides*, with translations by two *NDR* contributors. Brian Swann is translator, with Peter

Burian, of *Phoenician Women*, and Reginald Gibbons, with Charles Segal, is translator of *Baccchae*. Also new in paperback is the translation, by Alan Shapiro, general co-editor of the series, of *Trojan Women*. The whole idea behind the Oxford program is that "only translators who write poetry themselves can properly re-create[the Greek tragedies] and go beyond the literal meaning of the Greek in order to evoke the poetry of the originals." Though it is sometimes dangerous to encourage and celebrate "going beyond the literal meaning," most of the work commissioned for these translations is very impressive

Henry Weinfield, *The Music of Thought in the Poetry of George Oppen and William Bronk*. University of Iowa, 2009. *NDR* advisory editor Weinfield believes that George Oppen and William Bronk are the best among the generation of poets that emerged out of the Second World War. In spite of their obvious differences, the two poets are seen both as "extraordinary thinkers in poetry [who] have something original to say and for whom thought really matters [and] at the same time poets for whom thought acquires the resonance of music, poets whose best work is sensual and intellectual at the same time." There are not many who would choose these two poets as the best of their generation, but Weinfield makes a strong case for them in this engaging and well-written study.

CONTRIBUTORS

Michael Anania's most recent books are *Heat Lines* and *In Natural Light.* He received the Charles Angoff Prize for Poetry in 2008. He lives in Austin, Texas and on Lake Michigan. **Alison Armstrong** teaches Literature and Writing at School of Visual Arts in Manhattan. Her publications include *The Joyce of Cooking*; a volume of textual scholarship in *The Manuscripts of W.B. Yeats* series; reviews in *Irish Literary Supplement* and *American Arts Quarterly*; as well as short fiction. "Ismene" is the first in a projected series of one-act plays—monologues by "forgotten characters." **Robert Bense**'s book of poems, *Readings in Ordinary Time*, was recently published. **David Black** is an award-winning screenwriter, novelist, journalist, and television producer. He has published ten books, including the novels *Like Father* and *An Impossible Life*, and nonfiction works, such as *The King of Fifth Avenue* and *The Plague Years.* He lives in New York City. **Jackson Bliss** was the 2007 Sparks Prize winner, awarded by ND's MFA Creative Writing Program. He is now a Ph.D. student in Literature and Creative Writing at the University of Southern California. He has work published or forthcoming in the *Kenyon Review, Connecticut Review, African American Review, Stand Magazine (UK), South Loop Review, Writers Post-Journal, Ink Collective, Pittsburgh Quarterly, 3:am Magazine, Word Riot,* and *Fringe Magazine,* among others. **Andrea Brady** was born in Philadelphia, and has lived in the UK since 1996, where she teaches at Queen Mary University of London. She is the director of the Archive of the Now, and co-publisher of Barque Press. Her publications include *Vacation of a Lifetime*, *Embrace*, and the hypertext verse essay *Wildfire*. **Beverley Bie Brahic** lives in Paris and Stanford. A poet and translator, her poems have appeared in *Poetry, The TLS, The Southern Review,* and in *Against Gravity*. Her most recent translations are Hélène Cixous's *Hyperdream,* and *Unfinished Ode to Mud,* a selection of Francis Ponge's prose poems. **Mark Brazaitis** is the author of three books of fiction, including *The River of Lost Voices: Stories from Guatemala*, winner of the 1998 Iowa Short Fiction Award. His latest book, *The Other Language*, won the ABZ Poetry Prize. He directs the creative writing program at West Virginia University. **Renée E. D'Aoust** has numerous publications to her credit, including, most recently, an essay in the anthology *Reading Dance,* edited by Robert Gottlieb. **Paul Scott Derrick** is associate professor of American literature at the University of Valencia in Spain. He has published two collections of critical essays in English and has co-authored a number of bilingual, critical editions of works by Ralph Waldo Emerson, Emily Dickinson and Sarah Orne Jewett.

He is also co-editor of *Modernism Revisited: Transgressing Boundaries and Strategies of Renewal in American Poetry.* **Joe Francis Doerr** lives in Austin where he teaches English at St. Edward's University. He is the author of two books of poetry: *Order of the Ordinary* and *Tocayo.* He is the editor of the forthcoming *Salt Companion to John Matthias.* **James Doyle**'s latest book is *Bending Under the Yellow Police Tapes.* He has poems coming out in *Poet Lore, Natural Bridge, Illuminations, Roanoke Review,* and *The Carolina Quarterly.* He lives in Fort Collins, Colorado. **Kevin Ducey**'s book is *Rhinoceros.* He lives in Madison, Wisconsin. **Robert Estep** lives and works in Houston. His most recently completed project is *The Unbearable Dream Of Harar,* which deals with Arthur Rimbaud's life in the Horn of Africa. A book of poems, *Sueno(s) For Alejandra,* is forthcoming. **Adam Benjamin Fung** currently lives and works in Chicago, exhibiting with Zolla/Lieberman Gallery. Fung's paintings can be found in various collections, ranging from the Microsoft Art Collection to the South Bend Museum of Art's Permanent Collection. **Amina Gautier**'s stories appear or are forthcoming in *Iowa Review, Kenyon Review, North American Review, Pleiades, Shenandoah, Southern Review,* and *Storyquarterly,* among other places. Additionally, her work has been anthologized in *Best African American Fiction, Notre Dame Review: The First Ten Years,* and *New Stories from the South: The Year's Best, 2008.* Her fiction has been honored with the William Richey Prize, the Jack Dyer Award, the Danahy Prize, and a grant from the Pennsylvania Council on the Arts. **Mary Gilliland** lives in Ithaca where she serves on the Board of Namgyal Monastery Institute of Buddhist Studies, the Dalai Lama's seat in North America. Recent and forthcoming poetry can be found in *AGNI, Chautauqua, Passages North, Seneca Review,* and *Stand.* **Henry Hart**'s most recent book is *Background Radiation.* He is currently working on a critical biography of Seamus Heaney. **Kevin Hart** is Edwin B. Kyle Professor of Christian Studies, and incoming Chairman of the Department of Religious Studies at the University of Virginia. His most recent volume of poetry is *Young Rain.* **Margaret B. Ingraham** is the recipient of an Academy of American Poets award and the 2006 Sam Ragan Prize. Her second chapbook, *Proper Words for Birds,* was published this year and *This Holy Alphabet,* a collection of lyric poems based on her translation of Psalm119, is fothcoming later this year. **Mary Kalfatovic** is a writer and librarian in the Washington, D.C. area. **Bruce Lawder** lives in Switzerland with his wife. **Raúl Fernando Linares**'s most recent book of poetry is *Minotaur to Germinate.* **Jill McDonough**'s poems have appeared in *The Threepenny Review, The New Republic,* and *Slate.* The recipient of fellowships from the NEA, the Fine Arts Work Center, Stanford's Stegner

Program and the Cullman Center for Scholars and Writers, she has taught incarcerated college students through Boston University since 1999. Her first book of poems is *Habeas Corpus*. **James McKenzie** is professor emeritus of English at the University of North Dakota. He lives in Saint Paul, Minnesota. **Kevin O'Connor** teaches at Phillips Academy in Andover, Massachusetts and has recently published poems in *Fulcrum*, *The Recorder*, and *Alhambra Poetry Calendar 2009*. He is an editor of *One on a Side: An Evening with Seamus Heaney and Robert Frost*. A graduate of Notre Dame, **Michael Patrick O'Connor** was a highly regarded scholar of the Old Testament and an accomplished poet as well. At the time of his death, at age 57 in 2007, he was chair of the Department of Semitics at the Catholic University of America. *Field Notes: The Selected Poems of Michael Patrick O'Connor*, will be published this year. **Allan Peterson**'s latest book, *All the Lavish in Common* won the 2005 Juniper Prize. Recent print and online appearances include: *Gulf Coast*, *Northwest Review*, *Ourorboros*. Work is forthcoming in *Shenandoah*, and *Denver Quarterly*. Recent prizes include the 2009 Dos Cosas Award, the American Poet Prize, and the 3rd Boom Chapbook Prize. **Jay Rogoff**'s most recent book of poems is *The Long Fault*. His book of poems concerning dance, *The Code of Terpsichore*, is forthcoming in 2011. He has new work in *Field, Literary Imagination, The Southern Review,* and *The Hopkins Review*, where he also serves as dance critic. **Kathleen Rooney** is the author of the nonfiction books *Live Nude Girl: My Life as an Object* and *Reading with Oprah: the Book Club that Changed America*. Her first poetry collection, *Oneiromance (an epithalamion)* won the Gatewood Prize. With Elisa Gabbert, she is the author of *That Tiny Insane Voluptuousness*, and with Abby Beckel, she is a founding editor of Rose Metal Press. **Jane Satterfield** is the recipient of a 2007 National Endowment for the Arts Fellowship in Literature and the author of two poetry collections: *Assignation at Vanishing Point* and *Shepherdess with an Automatic*. Her new book, *Daughters of Empire: A Memoir of a Year in Britain and Beyond*, will be published this year. **Anis Shivani**'s short fiction collection, *Anatolia and Other Stories*, is being published later this year. A novel, *Intrusion*, is nearing completion. New work appears in *Georgia Review, Threepenny Review, Michigan Quarterly Review, North American Review, Harvard Review*, and elsewhere. **Mike Smith** has published three chapbooks, including *Anagrams of America*, which is permanently archived at *Mudlark: Electronic Journal of Poetry and Poetics*, and has been nominated for the Pushcart Prize four times. He has had poems appear in the *Carolina Quarterly, Gulf Stream, The Iowa Review,* and *The North American Review*. His first full-length collection, *How to Make a Mummy*, was published last year. **Bruce Snider** is the author of *The Year We Studied Women*. He lives in San Francisco. **Brian Swann** has published a number of books in various genres and fields. His latest, *Born in the Blood: On Translating Native American Literature*, is forthcoming. **Charles Tisdale** received his B.A. in English from Sewanee and his Ph.D. from Princeton University. He has, over the years, published poetry in about fifty different magazines, including a sestina in the *Notre Dame Review* last year.

SUSTAINERS

Anonymous [Four]

Nancy & Warren Bryant

Tony & Jessyka D'Souza

Gary & Elizabeth Gutchess

John F. Hayward

Samuel Hazo

Tim Kilroy

Richard Landry

Steve Lazar

Carol A. Losi

Jessica Maich

Vincent J. O'Brien

Kevin T. O'Connor

Daniel O'Donnell

Beth Haverkamp Powers

Mark W. Roche

In Honor of Ernest Sandeen

John Sitter

In Honor of James Whitehead

Kenneth L. Woodword

Sustainers are lifetime subscribers to the *Notre Dame Review.* You can become a sustainer by making a one-time donation of $250 or more. (See subscription information enclosed.)

Field Notes:

The Selected Poems of Michael Patrick O'Connor

In person Michael Patrick O'Connor was expansive, demonstrative, even theatrical, and his intellect was equally broad, wide-ranging and voracious, but it had, as well, an extraordinary grace, an ease of movement between subjects and languages that seems, as it is reflected in his poetry, at once effortless and certain. These are for the most part poems that begin in reflection, then move, as though it were the most natural thing imaginable, into their own realms of poetic speculation. O'Connor's sources lie in the patience of the later Auden, the linguistic acuity of early Matthias, and the unwavering faith in the sentence of middle Ashbery. There is a voice preserved here, a highly evolved poetic voice, worth cherishing.

— Michael Anania

✦

Although best known as a dedicated teacher and ground-breaking scholar of the Old Testament, Michael Patrick O'Connor was also a gifted poet. After his death at age 57, a group of his family, friends and colleagues joined to sponsor the publication of *Field Notes: The Selected Poems of Michael Patrick O'Connor.* The book commemorates his life and his poetic achievement, drawing from two decades of creative work. Across a broad range of themes and poetic forms, readers will get news of the world both real and imagined, and through that, a renewed sense of the faithful poet in our time.

$22 Cloth / $15 Paper • 99 pages • ISBN 978-0-9824151-1-5 / ISBN 978-0-9824151-0-8

Patsons Press
790 Stewart Drive
Sunnyvale, CA 94085
408-732-0911
info@patsons.com